Havana X

Havana X

A NOVEL

by Shelly Gross

ARBOR HOUSE New York

*To ROBERT LUDLUM without whose
encouragement and demonstration of the true
meaning of friendship this book
would not have been written.*

SHG

Chapter One

February Sixth—Midnight

It was a night meant for invaders. No man contemplating murder could ask for better camouflage. The northern rim of the Caribbean was like a poorly illuminated theatrical set. A crescent, waning moon fought a losing battle with ponderous clouds blocking its view of the developing drama below. At the surface, mist, thick as surgeon's gauze, challenged vision. All was silence but for rushing wind and an occasional foghorn moaning its loneliness. Nothing could be more insistent than an oncoming tropical storm at sea. Nothing was born so hastily or died, fulfilled, so suddenly.

For Ramon Santiago, stormy weather bore neither fright nor fascination. It was merely another fact to be dealt with in a life of turbulence and struggle. He had first gone to sea in a leaky, wind-driven fishing skiff when he was not quite twelve. And when the wind was stilled, he had rowed shoulder to shoulder with men twice his age until the blisters filled with blood and the muscles in his scrawny arms and back begged for mercy. He had watched in awe as his Uncle Miguel had

1

been washed into a saline grave by mountainous waves that lashed their craft. He had prayed silently to the Holy Mother as voracious sharks had ripped Miguel from limb to limb. And later, as a merchant sailor, he'd tasted salt tinged with the spice of death as typhoons had wrecked his ship off the coast of Zanzibar. Now, at seventy-three, he was an earthen jug emptied of fear and the imagination that feeds it.

He peered through the heavy mist in search of land swells that would confirm his judgment. A check of his primitive compass assured him that he had not guided the tiny, barnacle-laden craft astray. He had sailed these waters too many times to make that mistake. It was like leaving his small home in Miami on Sunday morning and walking to church. The boy beside him showed no sign of doubt either. He, too, a water rat by birth, had sailed here too often even to think in terms of being lost. Soon, certainly, they would see the shore.

"Hey, old man, you want café?" he whispered, holding up a thermos. Ramon nodded, took the bottle, drank deeply, swishing the hot liquid around in his mouth a few times before swallowing, then, pointing to the silent man seated astern, he asked, "You give him?"

"He says 'no,'" answered the youth, Tito Gonzalez. "He says he drink when he hits the beach."

The man crouching at the rear of the tiny, weather-beaten fishing boat showed little interest in the coffee or the conversation. Like a mysterious visitor from another planet, he looked only to the sea. Like the beacon of a lighthouse, his head swiveled from port to starboard, over the bow, then back to the stern, searching, seeking, peering into nothingness.

He was dressed in a wet suit, his head covered by a close-fitting rubber helmet, his cheeks greased and glistening in the shrouded spill of moonlight. Strapped to his neck were goggles and a snorkel, which he hoped not to use. At his waist there was a leather scabbard from which the rubber-bound handle of an eight-inch hunting knife stuck out its blackened nose. This, too, he hoped not to use in combat. But, after all, he realized, there was a limit even to hope.

Then, with no explanation, the clouds moved on as if bored with the sights below. The sliver of moon pushed to the surface of the sky and the choppy waters subsided. Even the moaning wind was stilled. God tipped his ear earthward but all was quiet.

"*Aqui.*" Ramon pointed as he flattened the fly-specked chart against the forward gunwale. And then he traced a line from the southern tip of Florida, first southerly, then sharply westward, as his gnarled finger caressed the Province of Pinar del Río on the northwestern tip of Cuba. His goal, a small, quiet inlet near the city of La Esperanza.

There was a moment of intense anticipation. The world was ruled by an eerie silence. And the three men aboard the little fishing craft *El Libelula, The Dragon Fly,* knew that their journey was nearing its end.

The curtain of mist parted and there was land and trees and tropic foliage not five hundred yards ahead. The sea sucked in its breath and only the lapping of the water against the paint-scarred bulkheads of the boat broke the silence. Even the water bugs skipped on muted skis.

Santiago cut the motors and the little boat, riding the crest of barely visible waves and drawn by the magnet of the shoreline, inched imperceptibly forward. Now the five hundred yards had become four-fifty, now four, now three-fifty. The tension grew, time stood still.

Finally Ramon Santiago found what he was seeking, the tiny lip bent inward that housed the mouth of the inlet. He swiveled astern, where the man in the wet suit had risen and was hovering at the port quarter, ready to mount the gunwale and slip into the sea.

Ramon and Gonzalez pointed in unison.

"*Alla!*" Your target.

Without a word, the man swung over the side and was gone in a splash of phosphorescent spray.

"Buena suerte!" whispered Gonzalez, and made the sign of the cross. But the frogman was on his way, silently stroking the three hundred yards to shore. And Santiago was too busy for idle words; he had swung the boat sharply to starboard and, completing a one-hundred-eighty-degree arc, was now heading for deeper waters, engines at flank speed. There was danger here, and Miami, with all its foreignness, meant safety. There he would deliver a simple message: "Martin ashore," and collect his one thousand dollars.

A mile inland, at a camouflaged command post, Rafael Garcia was dozing over a book on introductory navigation. It was too late to feel sorry for himself. It was his luck to draw the dog watch the very night his girl Rosa has given him the news that her parents, watch dogs that they were, were to be away for the weekend visiting her cousins in Camagüey. Even her pain in the ass of a brother was out for the night and the house and bedroom were theirs. And he, God take the cursed coast guard, had drawn the duty. Even the damn radio was a bore with its blaring reggae crap. Well, to hell with it all, he'd sleep it through.

And then there was a buzz like a bee calling him to attention. It was repeated, this time louder. He slammed the book shut and turned up the light as the action indicator on the sound-detection monitor lighted up a blazing red. Santiago, in his haste to move to safer waters, had erred in revving those ancient motors at such a speed. Rafael Garcia might be unhappy, but he knew the meaning of this buzzing bee.

Picking up the intercom, he called his officer of the day.

"Hey, lieutenant. The damn Yankees are at it again. We'd better search the beaches."

Chapter Two

January Second

More arrogant than the lead car in a politician's funeral cortege, the sleek black custom Cadillac limousine pushed its nose from the curb, leaving little doubt that it would give ground to nothing on wheels. Even in this elegant island of stately mansions, the gleaming, steel-ribbed behemoth would tolerate no competition. At the wheel, dressed in a form-fitting gray uniform. Armando Velez barely nodded his head in response to the greetings of other neighborhood domestics. To be a chauffeur was not a great honor perhaps, but to be this man's driver, that was something yet again.

In the rear seat, dressed in a black mohair suit, his face hidden behind the morning edition of the *Wall Street Journal* delivered by messenger each morning to his home, sat a lean, tall, prematurely gray-haired gentleman, the very model of self-confidence, success, power. His name was John Lawrence Martin III.

"*Buenos dias*, Señor Martin. And happy New Year."

5

"Morning, Mandy. Thank you. To you and your family too."

"The *oficina,* yes?"

"Yes, on the double, please."

There was respect but little affection between the two. Even after a decade it was the most functional of relationships. But though little conversation passed between the two men during the ten years since Armando Velez emigrated to Miami and accepted employment with the Martin family, he was not blind. Despite the formality with which he greeted the man who controlled his life, he could tell that all was not so well in Martin's Garden of Eden. Which was a bad omen for the new year.

Pressing the intercom button, Armando asked, "I stop for the *Times* of New York, *si?*"

Annoyed by the needless interruption, Martin snapped back, "Yes. Just like every day for the past ten years."

"Sorry, boss."

Armando guided the car across the Arthur Godfrey Causeway, enjoying the pristine beauty of the bay waters, the islands dotted with palm-rimmed mansions. No matter how annoyed the boss was, he insisted on taking this, the longer route, to work so that he could enjoy the ritual of breathing in the elegance of Miami's stately skyline. Sometimes Armando wondered what it must be like in Havana today. Secretly he vowed that one day he would go back, maybe only for a visit. His old Uncle Angel still worked with his hands in the fields around the capital city and he would see him one day before he died. Oh yes, he remembered the way he had been mistreated when he tried to leave. How he had waited two full years before finally getting word that he had been granted an exit visa. But Cuba had been home for the Velez clan since the eighteenth century and no cigar-chomping bearded dictator, or so he appeared to Armando, could silence the call of the land. Yes, one day he would go back, if only for a visit.

The *Journal* brought Martin written proof of a story he already knew too well. A four-point drop-off in United Ventures, Ltd. stock; fourteen points in nine trading days and still dropping. A feature article on area conglomerates made the unpleasant prediction that the trouble, even in well-managed companies, was just beginning. Investors, so the article said, wanted to know that they were putting their money into the hands of specialists in one field or another. They were losing faith in corporate barracuda that swallowed down any edible morsel that swam their way with little feeling or understanding for the marketing problems of the new acquisition. Besides, the article reasoned, no man—or no company, for that matter—could be right all of the time. So some of the companies swallowed, it would seem, would have to go sour, depressing earnings and holding down the price of the stock. Conglomerates, the article concluded, were swimming against the stream of specialization that characterized American life. And then the article went on to list the recent financial history of five typical southern Florida-based conglomerates, and there was his company, United Ventures, Ltd., leading all the rest with the worst of the recent financial reverses.

Yet, when Martin thought back to the condition of the company when he first took over as president and compared it to where it had soared, yes, and even to where it was today, he could not help but feel a twinge of pride. He well remembered that day when old man Randall had called him and literally demanded a meeting. Charles Webster Randall, a Boston Brahmin, ninth generation in America, had called him, John Lawrence Martin III (né Juan Martinez III), and demanded an immediate meeting. That had been ten years ago. He was only thirty-two years old at the time and had made the trip from Cuba only seven years before that. He remembered every nuance of that first meeting as if it had happened yesterday. It all boiled down to one goal: Randall wanted him to be president of United Ventures, Ltd., and he himself

7

would move into semiretirement as chairman of the board. No demands he made, no matter how outrageous, discouraged the old man, not even his insistence that if he were to accept the position he must move the corporate headquarters to Miami.

"Miami?" the old man had repeated incredulously. "What in the blazes for? Jews, oranges and marlin. What else do they have down there? New York, Philadelphia, Boston— that's where high finance is centered and that's where growth companies should be located."

But Martin had held his ground. And in the end the old man came around, and he didn't come around very often. Straight as a ramrod, a low-eighties golfer even today at seventy-two, Charles Webster Randall was accustomed to having others compromise to meet his terms. In this case, however, he was completely taken over by this young Cuban aristocrat from the very first time he had met him on vacation in Acapulco. It was blue-blooded Harold Caldwell who had arranged the introduction. But C. W. Randall took nothing on somebody else's say-so. He had learned through his own investigation of the man's extraordinary financial successes, and every profile he had drawn painted Martin in ever more brilliant tones. An old-fashioned Bostonian, perhaps, but not too old-fashioned to recognize the need for young blood to give the company injections of vitality, Randall decided he had found the man he wanted . . . Martin could picture the old man's choleric rage when he read this morning's *Journal* and saw United Ventures stuttering on the financial skids. There would be calls from Maine, all right. He might as well anticipate them.

They were in Miami proper now. Early morning traffic was clogging the highways but Armando thought better of his usual end-run tactics. Slower and steadier today. That made more sense in the face of the boss's obvious foul humor. They hit Biscayne Boulevard just in time to get stranded behind a

8

three-car wrinkled-fender melee. There was much shouting and blaring of horns sounding contrapuntally behind the screeching of police sirens. Armando spotted the boss shifting his weight irascibly in the back seat. He tried one of his skirting movements. No use.

Finally, they were free to move again and the trip southward to Flagler was uneventful. There, at long last, was company headquarters, twelve floors of iridescent glass and steel shining like a brilliant obelisk in the morning sun. Armando pulled to the curb, literally hopped from the front seat, and dashing around to the side of the car, opened the back door before John Martin even had time to collect his papers.

"Orders, boss?"

"Just hang around. I may need the car in a couple of hours. And you'd better get out that rag and rub a little. It looks kind of dull to me."

"Sure, boss."

And Martin was off without a smile. Hardly acknowledging the doorman's morning salute, he headed for his own executive express elevator. He had the foresight to insist that he alone have the services of this elevator after being trapped down on the lobby floor one day for more than ten minutes waiting to reach his office. He also had insisted that the timing mechanism be speeded up so there was none of the usual delay while the doors reluctantly slid together. He once had timed the entire procedure—from the car to the lobby to the elevator to the twelfth floor to his outer office to his inner office to the desk and into the chair with hot coffee in his hand, exactly fourteen seconds.

Sarah Jenkins, spelled biblically with a final "h," was chosen by Martin as his executive secretary after a six-month trial in the typing pool: she was efficient at her work, she kept her mouth shut, she was so unattractive that no one could ever accuse Martin of having her as a mistress. And since sex was not important to Sarah, she could be trusted to be his ally as he manipulated his intricate social—sexual—calendar.

She followed him now through the reception area, past her own enclosure, then closed the door of his office behind her. She placed a cup of steaming coffee before him and got to the point. "Stormy weather, Mr. Martin." It was always "Mr. Martin."

"Such as, Sarah?"

"Such as Charles W. Randall. He's read the *Journal* and he's hopping mad. He knows you get here promptly at nine but he's been on the phone three times since eight-thirty."

"That's one squall. What else?"

"A Miss Myra Rubin has been calling. I mentioned that to you last week. She keeps insisting that you know her and must see her. She refuses to state her business."

"Stall her at least two more times, then if she continues we'll have to see her."

Miss Jenkins raised an eyebrow. Usually, Martin could duck and dodge forever if the spirit moved him. "We could say 'no' to her, you know," she added, somewhat tentatively.

"I know."

"Just a suggestion on a pressured day."

"What else?"

"Mr. Margolis has been here twice and on the phone as well."

"And what does my good friend Herschel want?"

"Simple. He wants your job, he wants the presidency. But he says he has to see you at once. Very, very top priority."

"Let him in as soon as we clear a few calls. Anything else?"

"Your private line has been busy busy."

"I'll handle that. Thank you, Sarah. Please get me CWR. He's in Maine, right?"

"Yes. At the estate. I'll get him and tell Mr. Margolis you'll see him in fifteen minutes." And she was gone, the door closed discreetly behind her and the double doors slid together behind it.

The private line was jangling again. He hesitated, then picked up resignedly. "Hello, darling."

"How many darlings do you have? How did you know it was me?"

"I knew, Billie, because you are the only one besides my wife who has this number. And she never gets up before noon."

"Well, at least I share the number with good company."

"You do, darling. Miss Jenkins tells me you've been calling. Anything wrong?"

"Darling, why must something be wrong for me to call you? Can't I just call to say I miss you . . . terribly?"

"You can. But that's a strange message from you at nine o'clock in the morning. You're a night person."

"Darling, let's stop quibbling. I called because I need you. Desperately. I haven't seen you in three whole days. You *must* drop by at five today." And with a touch of mystery, "I've got a special surprise for you."

"Billie, this is a terrible day for me. I really can't promise, much as I'd love it."

"You always tell me it's a matter of priorities. You find time to do the things you want to do—"

"Now why wouldn't I want to see you? The greatest body in America. A face like an angel." The super-salesman at work. "And we won't even mention, or belabor, the greatest little box God ever gave woman."

She started to giggle. He had her now.

"But, honey, I still want to see you tonight."

"I'll try my best." He heard Miss Jenkins signaling that CWR was on the line. "Darling, I really have to run now. They're holding a very important long-distance call for me. I'll call you at four. Bye." He clicked off before she mounted another protest.

11

The squawk box carried Jenkins' relay. "Mr. Martin, I have Mr. Randall. He's been holding for about thirty seconds."

"Right. I have it . . . Hello, CW. I hear you've been calling me. Not about that ridiculous piece in the *Journal*, I trust."

"You know darn well that's exactly why I'm calling. Shall I wait until we're in Chapter Eleven before contacting you?"

"CW, I don't object to anyone being disturbed when he's maligned, but the fact is that that whole article is as full of crap as a Christmas turkey." He never went too far in using profanity with Randall. There was something about those Boston genes that paralyzed the four-letter word in mid-flight.

"I'm not concerned with what that half-baked writer thinks about the future of conglomerates in this country. What I am concerned about is the chart that shows us the number-one foul-up in the whole region."

"Again, all bull crap. We intentionally wrote off five million dollars worth of deadweight in the third quarter. You agreed to that yourself. Our year-end figures are going to snap back so hard it will make their silly heads spin. Sales are up ten percent over same quarter last year." He conveniently failed to mention that costs were up seventeen percent.

"Margolis tells me the manufacturing division is down nearly sixty percent." It was a ploy. Randall knew that the very mention of the name Margolis was enough to throw him off balance.

"Margolis is a sales and promotional genius. That's why we hired him." Ploy for ploy. Margolis is put down indirectly by saying what he knows—and implying what he doesn't know.

"Well, I don't share your confidence in the future. But you've got the helm and you'd better watch out for the reefs and the icebergs, there are a hell of a lot of them in sight. I'll be down in Miami week after next. We'll talk *at length*."

"Great, CW. We'll spend a lot of time together. Let me

1 2

know when to expect you. Good-by, sir." The "sir" served up an unavoidable smidgeon of butt kissing.

Before he could settle back to think on the call, the private line rang again. This time it was his wife, Margaret. It was rare indeed, as he'd said, that Margaret rose before noon and rarer still that she buzzed him at the office. She informed him that Ginny, their sixteen-year-old debutante daughter, was unexpectedly coming home from school to spend a few days between exams and was bringing one James Westerly Mc-Bride, heir to the McBride copper fortune, and coincidentally her latest love. Ginny, as he knew, made few demands but had requested that he be home from the office an hour early so that he could meet Jim and get to know him a little.

"You're the third one I've said this to in the last twenty minutes, Margaret, but this is one terrible hell of a day for me. I just got off the phone with CW and he's charging like a rhino in heat. I can't promise I'll be home earlier than usual, James Whatshisname McBride notwithstanding."

"That's the usual help I get from you in raising our children—"

"Oh, balls, Margaret. Our children are older than we are."

"And I can do without the profanity too. Save it for your girl friends!" She hung up.

Now there was Herschel Margolis to face. He was pawing the turf, waiting in the reception room. When he entered, Martin decided against inviting him to sit down, though he had too much gall to need such an invitation. He came in, deposited himself in a chair in front of Martin and blurted out, "And what in the hell are we going to do about this . . . unfortunate publicity?"

Martin had been an outstanding athlete, a collegiate boxing champion at college in Havana, and light heavyweight champion of his division in Vietnam where, as an officer, he needed special permission to participate. Perhaps because he had nothing to prove, he seldom was tempted to use his fists. But Margolis was an exception. He had a face that asked for a punch. His personality matched his appearance. How he would have loved to punch him out, but instead he asked calmly, "And why is that your concern?"

"I'm in charge of sales, sales promotion, and, incidentally, of all publicity for this company. That's why it's my concern."

"Then don't recommend that I do interviews with cunts like Mavis Turner who spit a little poison at us in the *Journal* today. If you hadn't had such a hard-on for a big publicity break this might never have happened—"

"So now it's my fault that our figures are off."

"Yours. Mine. Every one of us at United Ventures. And we're going to do something about it to improve the picture, except for those of us who are too busy making telephone calls to New England . . ."

"Mr. Randall directed me to keep him abreast of all late developments. I don't like the implication that I'm some sort of stoolie—"

"If the shoe fits, Herschel . . . Meanwhile, I've got a mountain of work here and I'm sure you do too. Why not head back to your office and let's see if we can't shove it up Miss Mavis Turner's keister. If she has one."

Margolis rose. There was a mumbled good-by and he left. Further skirmishes were clearly building. Building to a showdown.

It was one of those days, and it grew steadily worse as the hours ticked slowly by. By four o'clock, Martin had a blazing headache, a whole new batch of financial results that were worse than the ones printed in the *Journal* and still no resolution of the wife-mistress dilemma. He opted, finally, for the safer way. He called Billie Lane and told her that surprise or no, there was no chance for that afternoon. He called Marty Perlish, his handball partner, and told him that he'd have to find another player. He told Miss Jenkins that he was leaving for home earlier than scheduled and had her order up a dozen long-stemmed roses as a peace offering for Margaret.

Just as he was beginning to feel a slight easing of tension, the phone rang again. It was Myra Rubin.

"It's the third time," Miss Jenkins advised.

"Tell her to come in Wednesday. I'll see her at ten o'clock."

Then he was out of the office, and fourteen seconds later, Armando at the helm, he was speeding toward Miami Beach.

Chapter Three

January Fourth

Tad Duncan selected the coffee shop on the ground floor of the Seafarer Hotel as the ideal place to meet with Rocco Floriani. No one in his right mind, he reasoned, would want to stage a confidential conference in the lunch-hour rush of a beachfront hotel. It was the incongruity of the surroundings that gave it security. On the other hand, Floriani, also known as "The Fox," thought it was so offbeat as to be obvious. "Cops and robbers crap," he called it. But he figured if Duncan, an influential government agent, wanted to pick the dueling grounds, maybe he'd get first choice on weapons.

Rocco was too smart to allow himself the luxury of overconfidence. Yet after thumbing his nose at the law for more than fifty years he knew he could handle himself in any situation. A man who had never spent a single night in jail while doing everything wrong must have been doing something right.

Truthfully, he was intrigued. Duncan was new on the Miami scene. He wasn't really sure what this agent stood for or what his angle was. The family in Newark had sent word to expect him. And they were right again—he arrived on schedule. Out of Vegas there were warnings of high-level government maneuverings centered in Miami, but since The Fox was clean so far as indictable charges were concerned, why not meet the man face-on and find out what made him tick?

Duncan was there over coffee and Danish at the agreed upon table. Floriani came in about ten minutes late, eyed the coffee shop critically before entering and, having decided that ambush was about as logical here as selling Nazi armbands, he strolled in, brushed by the Cuban hostess, neatly laying five dollars in her hand as he passed, and headed for Duncan's table.

Duncan hardly reacted as he joined him. It was almost as if they were two hotel guests, unknown to each other but sharing the same table. After a few moments had gone by, Duncan turned to him, smiling, and said: "Thanks for coming. I thought you might stand me up."

"I give my word, I show."

"So I hear. Everyone says Floriani can be trusted if he gives his word."

"And how about you? You can be trusted?" There was a pause in the conversation as a waitress approached. Without looking up Floriani said, "Corned beef and pastrami and a celery tonic." And when she left, "You'd better learn to eat Jewish around here, Duncan. With coffee and Danish, well, you're still on the borderline."

"Sometimes it's safer there. You asked me if my word is good, right? I'm just a dummy sitting on Uncle Sam's knee. And his word is the law. You've heard of the law, Mr. Floriani?" The moment the words left his lips he was sorry. He could feel Floriani withdraw into a shell.

The reply came out softly, almost gently. "Sure, I heard of it. I live by it. That's why no one, no matter how hard they tried—and they tried, Mr. Duncan, believe me—has ever been able to prove one thing I did was illegal. I hope you're not going to try to prove anything. I hope that's not why you invited me to this fine restaurant."

"You know better than that, Mr. Floriani. I really came to meet you. You're a very famous man and I thought I ought to know you better. For example, I just learned that you don't take jokes too well."

"Try me on another subject, maybe I surprise you."

The two simultaneously examined each other. It was part curiosity, part preparation. They were well matched, however different. Duncan was tall, lean but broad-shouldered, fair complexioned, with sharp blue eyes that could fix the object of their attention. Floriani was wiry, slight—he stood no more than five feet six—and his complexion and black hair, now streaked with gray, pointed to his Sicilian roots. His eyes were furry brown and they, too, gripped the victim. Duncan wore clothes easily, informally, even sloppily. Floriani was meticulous, the crease in his trousers newly pressed. They were an intriguing contrast, and well matched.

Lunch had arrived now and the tension eased. As he bit into his corned beef–pastrami special, Rocco was sorry that he had taken the heat. One up, he thought, for Duncan. Now, he would take the lead as if nothing had happened.

"You're new down here, Duncan. My friends tell me you're with the intelligence. The CIA, right?"

"Intelligence people never reveal their employer, Mr. Floriani. It's bad for business. You can understand that."

Rocco smiled. "My friends also tell me you're quite a war hero. West Point, Korea, Vietnam. All kinds of medals and honors in South America, and all that. I'm impressed. I never met a real hero before."

"I'm the one who's impressed. I hear a kid can't shoot craps in any city on the east coast or in the islands either without your okay."

"Well, I get around a little. I think people like to exaggerate, don't you?"

1 8

"Hell, yes. That's how I got those medals . . . I think you and I are going to get along."

"That's good. And what are we going to be doing together to be getting along?"

"Well, I guess this is going to amuse you, Mr. Floriani—mind if I call you 'Rocco'?"

"It's all the same with me."

"Good. You call me 'Tad.' . . . Rocco, this government, whose laws you say you always obey, needs a favor. It needs your help. Surprised?"

"At my age nothing surprises me too much. But I got to admit that's a funny idea. Little me help big Uncle. What's he need, a loan?" He burst out laughing, charmed by his own sense of humor.

"No, Uncle's not hurting for money. He needs your connections, your skill."

The crowd was thinning out now and the two friendly adversaries were in a more or less deserted corner of the coffee shop. Floriani decided the fencing had gone on long enough. "Let's get to the point, Duncan. What do you want?"

"Okay. For once in your life you've got a chance to do something for this country that's been *very* good to you. And you can make one hell of a deal in the process. A lot of money. A lot of favors. And no exposure. Sound good?"

"Well, I like money, I like favors, and I like privacy. So what's the job?"

"Murder."

"I hear you right?"

"Nothing wrong with your hearing."

"That's a crime, Mr. Duncan. You can still go to the chair in some states for killing—"

"Depends on where and why."

"Like when you won all those medals in the war. Where and why. Simple."

"Mr. Floriani, there's nothing simple about you."

1 9

"Maybe not, but I need facts. Who does my dear Uncle want me to have knocked off?"

"I can't tell you everything on our first date. I can say that he is a man who would like to see this whole country knocked off. And he's not too fond of you and yours either. Believe me, it's no exaggeration to say this man is a real threat to the security of *our* country, yours and mine. You have the best of connections, we're told. We'll make it worth your while. How about it?"

"It's a big order, Mr. Duncan. I got to think about this one. And I got partners too. I got to talk to them."

"How long for your decision?"

"What's the rush? This man going somewhere?"

"There is a rush. I can't explain, but time is important. I need your word very soon."

"You want it now, it's no. You want to wait a couple of days, it might be maybe or even yes."

"Okay. I need word within the week. As soon as you know, call this number and we'll meet again."

Duncan placed his card on a five-dollar bill and got up. Floriani sat back and finished his sandwich. No need to rush about in Miami Beach's ninety-three-degree heat.

Chapter Four

January Fourth

John Martin was happy that he had listened to the advice of his secretary Sarah Jenkins when he had moved into his present executive offices.

"Silence is not only golden, Mr. Martin, it is absolutely essential for anyone who has to make as many decisions as you do every day."

"I suppose you're right, Sarah," he'd answered, "but for me . . . well, if I don't hear those bells jangling and lights flashing, I'll fall asleep. You can't make good decisions when you're snoring."

In the end, though, he'd gone along. There were only two phones in his office. One, his private line, the other an extension tied into a complicated call director on Miss Jenkins' desk. She handled the calls, seldom letting one reach Martin when avoidable. She was the goalie, he was the goal; and the puck rarely if ever got by.

As he sat with the blinds drawn that afternoon, he gave thanks for the silence and tranquillity of his hideaway. He was in a strange mood. In spite of the troubles of these past weeks, a sense of calm had come to him. Forced into a corner, he became reconciled to the knowledge that his moment of truth was approaching. He had faced other crucial decisions in his life: he recalled when his parents and he had been forced to turn their backs on a fine life in Cuba and run for their lives. True, their political connections and foresight in making overseas investments had made the move not only possible but one without financial hardship. Still, to leave one's native land was a wrench, especially when return or retreat was impossible. He also recalled Vietnam, when his conscience and his flair for derring-do had made him a decorated hero. His survival had come from his ability to face up to the challenge of injury or death, with a kind of stoic equanimity. He was also very good at what he did—killing. He was a man who performed best under pressure. Now that the pressures were rising around him, he felt the old ability to relax, to find the eye of the storm, and to plan his moves. Let Margaret—a mistake—complain about his infidelities. Let Charles Webster Randall carry on about the reversals of United Ventures. Let Billie Lane complain—he was flattered—about his too frequent absences from her bed. Let Herschel Margolis connive to capture the presidency. He'd face them one by one and he'd put each of them down.

But Myra Rubin, whom he was to see in half an hour, was quite another matter. She was his equal in too many ways to be readily handled. Of all this crazy week's unpleasant happenings, her calls had been the most unsettling.

How long ago had they first met? Of course, he realized, the date was easy to set. It was twenty-three years ago. They were both nineteen then, both brilliant students at the University of Havana. He heard her name first when a professor of European history had called her before their class to praise her midterm examination. The professor had awarded her an impossible grade—A double plus. He had gotten a simple A and it was the first time in his recollection that anyone, particularly a foreign student and a girl at that, had bested him academically. He had gone up to her after class and teased her about it. She had answered, "The future repeats the past. History fascinates me." It was that simple—to her.

After that they became close friends, and eventually lovers. She was a poor, Jewish girl from the Bronx who for some inexplicable reason had always dreamed of broadening her education by studying in the Caribbean. The University of Havana was by far the best school available to her. It was a struggle for her parents to pay her way. But Myra helped by working at a whole rainbow of part-time jobs and somehow made ends meet, though at times just barely.

When she finally accepted his repeated invitations to dine with his family in their elegant apartment at Miramar, Havana's finest suburb, she had trouble coping with the surroundings. As Minister of Finance to President Batista, his father Juan Martinez was engineer of most of the country's economic policies on both a national and an international level. Fulgencio Batista and all of the men surrounding him had mastered the technique of feathering their own nests, but to Juan Martinez it was more like a game. He was the scion of a long line of wealthy landowners and had known wealth from the day of his birth. He had been an outstanding professor of economics at the University in his earlier years, later rising to the position of university president. He had entered politics more as a challenge than a need, but once he obtained power he used it. And even in those pre-Castro days there were rumors around the University that Martinez was somehow associated with international racketeers who controlled gambling, prostitution and narcotics throughout the island.

Perhaps it was these unsavory stories that made Myra less than eager to visit the Martinez home. Once she did, however, the old man won her over immediately. He was smooth as polished steel, and as unbending. Being young and in love with his son, tough as Myra liked to consider herself, she was no match for the convincing gallantry of Juan Martinez, Senior. In those days, of course, John Lawrence Martin was Juan Martinez III, his grandfather having also borne the same impressive calling card. It was only years later in Miami that he decided his progress would be aided by ridding himself of all foreign entanglements, including his Cuban name. To Myra, though, he was always "Johnny," and she was the only one who had ever addressed him that way.

John Martin settled into the depth of his executive command chair and in the artificially created darkness thought back to 1953, the year of their first encounter. It was an historical year in more ways than one: on July 26, 1953, an unknown adventurer named Fidel Castro, an ex- and sometime scholar at the University Law School, had led an outrageously courageous attack on the Moncado Barracks. The attack—some historians would later compare it to the attack on the Bastille in the French Revolution—was a fiasco. Only three men were killed of Castro's attacking force of one hundred fifty-three; but sixty-eight were tortured, then executed by Batista, and thirty-two, including Fidel Castro, had been imprisoned on the same Isle of Pines where the Revolutionary Government would later establish its own principal political prison. From this ill-fated and somewhat ludicrous military expedition would come the name for the Cuban revolution—the Twenty-sixth of July Movement.

Life was exciting in those days. The campus was in constant turmoil and the Batista forces scarcely knew what opposition was to be treated good-humoredly and what was of real danger. In the European tradition the University had a certain autonomy, but certainly not enough to prevent an occasional visit by Batista gorillas, resulting in a few broken heads. Myra and Juan were merely on the surface of stormy waters—even had Castro been taken seriously at the time neither of them would have supported him; Juan would have considered him too disruptive and Myra would have found him not progressive enough for her left-wing tastes. At the time, Castro was not considered to have formal affiliations with Communism, and for Myra the words "Communist" and "revolution" were inseparably linked.

Myra was very much the modern woman of her time. Brought up in the Hispanic tradition that sheltered young virgins from the realities of life, Juan found this dark-browed, full-breasted Jewess mysterious and fascinating. What difference if her economic ideas of confiscatory equality were childish and contrary to his family's position? She was an exciting, passionate woman, as she demonstrated when they met for their encounters in the small apartment she maintained on the edge of the campus. In retrospect, he realized he'd never since experienced such love-making. Myra Rubin had not so much given herself as made him a partner in an ecstatic joint venture.

He could scarcely recall what it was that finally ended their affair; one of their many economic disputes, no doubt. Myra had grown more and more sensitive to the terrible inequities of wealth in Cuba at the time. Her heart was broken by the illiteracy, disease, lack of medical care and other privations of most of the people. And when it came to pointing the finger at exploitation, she was, of course, pointing directly at Juan's family and their friends. It had to lead to an eventual break. Later, they would meet occasionally as she stayed on for graduate studies and he rose to wealth and position, first in the manufacture of light farm machinery and later in the export business. On several occasions he had sought her out and tried to revive at least the physical side of their relationship, but she had told him: "Sorry, Johnny, but it won't work. My brain sends messages to the parts of my body you enjoy most. The message reads 'off limits.' I'm sorry . . ." And she was.

His reminiscence was shattered by the sharp buzzing of the intercom. Slowly, he depressed his talk lever. "Yes, Sarah?"

"It's Miss Rubin, Mr. Martin. Shall I send her in?"

"In a few moments, yes. I want to finish what I'm doing. I'll buzz you."

He opened the draperies to let the Miami sun come blazing in, splashed some cold water on his face and recombed his silver hair in the adjoining washroom, took a deep breath and then signaled for Myra's admission.

He couldn't believe what he saw. She was an old woman. He was not actor enough to hide his shock. He took her hand, considered a comradely kiss on the cheek for a moment, thought better of it and simply invited her to have a seat while he took his place behind the desk. She smiled and there was an endless, awkward moment of silence.

Finally she spoke, looking around the room. "Well, Johnny, you're still rich."

"Still the exploiter of the masses. And how are things with you, Myra?"

She laughed. "Come on, Johnny, you see what you see. These are wrinkles and gray hair. They don't come from cocktail parties in Miramar mansions."

"Age is a matter of genes, some people age earlier than others and I've never thought it had anything to do with lifestyle—"

"That's a comfortable thought for you."

"You came to see me after all of these years to fight—just like in the old days?"

"I didn't come to fight, Johnny. But you don't blank out all the memories . . . And how are your parents doing in America?"

"My mother hasn't been totally well, but who is? My father still dabbles in business. He misses the power he had in Cuba, but he's a tough bird and he doesn't allow himself to dwell on what was. He's still quite handsome, and he still loves the ladies."

"Yes, he was the . . . what shall I say? . . . I guess the

French would call him a *boulevardier*. He was the Don Juan of Havana. I never told you but he actually propositioned me, right in your own living room."

"Did you say yes?"

"I don't kiss and tell, Johnny. But he was powerful. I damn well considered his offer."

"I'll tell him I saw you. He'll probably ask you again."

"Your father wouldn't want me today. You see what I look like after living for nearly eight years in the Cuba I dreamed about and the one you and your family ran away from?"

There was a long pause. John wanted very much to learn what she had to say about those years in between, but he realized she would choose her moment.

Finally she said, "You're entitled to know what happened and why I'm here . . . . We didn't see each other very much those last few years, but you knew, I'm sure, that Castro and his revolution were all I ever wanted from life. I remember seeing him march into Havana. It was just after New Year's day in 1959. You and your people had already gone. I thought of pictures I had seen of Christ marching to Calvary and somehow I connected this tall, gaunt, bearded man in fatigue greens to the man bearing the cross. Everyone was crazy happy. They rode trucks, farmers' pickups, tanks—whatever they could commandeer on wheels. He smiled and waved that big cigar. But somehow, he was an island of calm strength in a churning world. It was as if he was too busy planning to save their lives really to celebrate. And I fell in love with that man that day, Johnny. I decided then and there that what he was doing was to be my life."

"I had heard through friends that you joined his forces and later his government."

"I did. And I was well received. One of the few Americans who played a real role in those wonderful days . . ."

"Then what happened?"

"Maybe what happens to every dream, Johnny. I worked

2 7

for that revolution for five years and I watched it move from what it was born to be to what it became. More and more into the Russian, not the Marxist, camp. I couldn't agree. And gradually their own dictatorial ways replaced the ones they'd fought so bravely against. I felt as if I were choking. Of course, we Americans haven't been much help, either. That whole Bay of Pigs disaster almost convinced me at the time that I should denounce my American citizenship, which, fortunately, I didn't. But for the next ten years everything that was done only made those people hate us more. And I guess some of that hatred rubbed off on me as an American in their midst."

"When did you leave?"

"I tried to leave in 1973. Unfortunately for me, Castro had just cut off what were known as the 'Freedom Flights' that had started in 1965 at Varadero Beach. I tried to use my influence with some of the party workers who had been my friends for years. But it was tough for them too. I was called a *gusano*, but so were all the exiles and anyone who wanted to leave. But to be lumped along with them, to be called a 'worm' . . . well, finally they told me that if I worked in the fields and helped harvest the sugar and tobacco crop for one year they would let me go. I had never worked in anything but an office in my whole life, but I did it. The year became two, then three, and *finally* I got permission to get out. With one valise and five dollars in cash. Oh yes, they did give me a one-way ticket to Mexico City, and after I established my American citizenship the Mexicans let me fly to Miami. I've been working here as a waitress ever since . . ."

"You knew I was here?"

"Of course."

"Why didn't you call me sooner?"

"History was my major. What's dead is dead."

"But you did finally call."

"Yes. I heard your name mentioned so many times. I read

2 8

about your wealth, your society wife, your children, I even read the gossip columns about your love affairs"—she smiled—"same old Johnny. But I didn't call for a lot of reasons, and maybe vanity was the biggest one. I wanted you to remember me the way we were then, not the way I look now—"

"But you did finally call."

"Yes. Don't be impatient, I'll get to the point. I came, finally, because I'm desperate. My parents are sick and broke in New York. My brother has five children and works in a clothing factory that's about to go under. I'm in debt. I want to get out of here and back to my family. I need two thousand dollars. Will you help me?"

He hesitated. "I know this is going to sound ridiculous to you, Myra, but I really don't have it. I'm in trouble here, I'm in trouble at home. To borrow money would look bad for . . . well, you couldn't have picked a worse time to—"

She was already on her feet, walking briskly to the door, where she paused, then turned to face him. "Yes, Johnny, it does sound ridiculous." And then she was gone.

If she hadn't mentioned earlier the hotel she was living and working in, he would never have known where to reach her again.

Chapter Five

January Fifth

The posh Paddock Club at Bay Harbour Islands, just off the Miami Beach Broad Causeway at 96th Street, had started its operations with a "restricted" policy—meaning white Anglo-Saxons only—which lasted about two months and was discontinued just before bankruptcy set in. It was then that the owners were forced to accept that money had its own exclusivity and the drawbridge was lowered. For a short while those who at first had been excluded stayed away, but not for long. The club's reputation for gourmet cooking, the finest of wines and gorgeous "working girls" soon spread. The "out" place became the "in" place in a matter of months. The grateful owners made a twenty-five thousand dollar contribution to the United Jewish Appeal, a similar one to the United Catholic Charities Drive and still another to a joint campaign aiding Protestant missionaries. The Paddock Club was made. A stiff fifteen hundred dollar initiation fee and annual dues of a thousand dollars kept away the riffraff.

One of the Paddock Club's touted assets was a series of

hideaway bars where those special problems—dining with your best friend's wife, for example—could find privacy.

Juan Martinez, Sr., was a charter member of the club. He loved everything about it, including the ladies for hire who occasionally frequented the bars. It was not women, however, that drew Martinez to the Paddock this night. Greeting Gino, the maître d', he asked if his request for a private hideaway bar had been relayed to him by the office staff.

"Of course, Señor Martinez," Gino answered, bowing as though he were royalty. "Is señor expecting a little friend tonight who we can keep our eye open for?"

"Not tonight. It is a friend. And he is little. But his name is Rocco Floriani, and he should be here very soon, I should say in a half hour."

Not thirty minutes later, because Rocco Floriani believed devoutly in punctuality, he was led into the room where Martinez waited for him. It was always difficult to read Rocco's mood; he'd trained himself to be difficult to read. Nonetheless, Martinez was uneasy with what he did see. Rocco looked unhappy—which meant considerably more trouble than met the eye. Rocco didn't like evening meetings. He didn't like being seen in places like the Paddock. And especially he didn't like welchers. Until he proved otherwise, Juan Martinez was a man who hadn't met his obligations to Rocco and his friends and hadn't done so for a long time. A welcher.

He ignored Martinez's greeting, accepted only a small glass of white wine, and after a tentative sip got down to cases. "What's the latest report on your buildings?"

"Not good, I'm sorry to say. Costs still rising. The unions will not listen to reason. Delays everywhere."

"And sales?"

"Terrible. Only yesterday I read in the *Herald* where there are seventy thousand unsold condominiums in southern Florida. And they say there are another thirty thousand under construction."

3 1

"This shouldn't surprise anyone. Every dope knew we were overbuilding. It's a shame you should be the last to get the word."

"Well, Rocco, let's be reasonable. The signs were all good. When I told you about the project you didn't raise questions. You lent me the money without the slightest hesitation. And you've lent me more since."

Rocco's features tightened, his voice cut like a knife. "Listen, man, and listen good. I'm no business consultant, you understand. My friends and I lend money when we know there is a way to get it back. I always listen to the other guy's dreams, but I don't give a shit if he's on course or crazy. I lend you the money and you pay it back. You know the deal. You owe us more than a million and a half, and more if we count this month's interest. When do we get it back? You're overdue."

"Look, Rocco, I'm sixty-eight this month and I have never welched on any commitment. Let me remind you, my friend, that we did much business together in the islands and I lived up to every obligation. I put you in business in some of those islands. I made sure the legislation you needed passed. I saw that your competitors were barred. You and your friends, as you call them, made a fortune twenty times over because of me. Please—let's not forget that."

"We forget nothin'. You got paid every time. We put that money in American banks here in the States just like you asked. How in the hell did you and your wife and that son of yours make it to Miami if it wasn't for that dough and for our connections? I seem to remember a charter plane waiting for you the day that bearded prick took over. Hell, you and yours got out before Batista. We paid off our debts to you, Martinez. It's all history, ancient history, you understand? It's got nothing to do with now and here and a million and a half dollars that you borrowed. You ain't paid us a cent in fifteen months. We want our money."

"Rocco, don't you think I want to pay you your money? I've been so certain this is going to be a huge winner I was willing to pay you twenty-five percent interest *plus* a percentage of profits. All you have to do now is be patient and I assure you you'll be made well—"

"We're goddamned tired of your promises, señor. What about that son of yours? Why can't he help?"

"Juan has, I'm afraid, more than enough of his own problems. I can't ask him for a thing. Not any more than I have already. You know I didn't want to get him involved the last time. I did so only because you insisted—"

"Yeah . . . well, he was okay for a while, but he ain't cooperating now. One of my friends called him and tried to sell him some padding and paper boxes. He had the nerve to say he couldn't buy from us anymore unless we bid the job like everybody else. If I want to bid, I don't need Mr. *John Martin*."

"You have to understand that my son doesn't own that company, he's just a salaried employee, even if he is the president. There is a board chairman who expects him to do what's best for United Ventures, not what's best for his father."

"I understand plenty. When you wanted for your son to get going fast in Cuba you found a way to ask me for favors and I delivered. He made a small fortune in that export business of his. We helped him for one reason, one reason only—you, his pop. We didn't owe him a goddamned thing. And I don't remember him showing us too much thanks either. The juice I got out of his deals I could have put in my left eye."

"Juan is not the sort to forget kindnesses. He favored your suppliers whenever he possibly could, whenever I asked him. He spent many thousands of dollars with your companies, and you know how they price their goods."

"We're not out to lose money. He's got kosher receipts for every penny he spent with us. Things get slow for us, too, you know. If he wants to help his old man he's got to buy

33

some more. And you gotta find a way to come up with some cash. We're not waiting forever."

"You must give me more time. If you press me now, the whole project can go under and that's not good for either of us."

Martinez knew that the one thing he must not do was allow any outward show of fear. Floriani and his "friends" worked on one principle: squeeze a man until he showed signs of breaking, after which it was merely a question of calling the tune. Any hope for compassion, or even understanding, was foolish. It was a question of toughing it out and Martinez, despite his age, was not easily bluffed. Certainly Floriani and his people were capable of any act of cruelty that would make points. On the other hand they knew that governmental surveillance had increased considerably since the days when they ran roughshod and terrorized the entire business community. The days of bombings, extortions and union goons were not entirely forgotten, but the mob's tactics tended to be somewhat more genteel now. Still, any show of weakness was an invitation for them to exploit.

"Every time we meet you ask me to be patient and give you more time. What's in it for us?"

"I've already given you points and a high interest rate. What else do you want?"

"I want to think about that. By the way, I was talking to some guy the other day and he mentioned your son. He tells me he was a big war hero in Vietnam. Is that on the level?"

"It certainly is. He received a Presidential citation for bravery beyond the call of duty. As a matter of fact, there was some talk he might even win the Congressional Medal of Honor. I believe you know they don't give too many of those away."

"Not to guys who don't croak. What'd he do to be such a hero?"

"Juan doesn't like to talk about it in detail. I know he had commando training and he received his citation for infiltrating the enemy lines alone at night. He's a skilled linguist. He learned to speak the language there and set up listening posts and brought back intelligence reports on their next moves. Once he was trapped and singlehandedly fought his way through a whole battalion of Vietcong. That won him his citation."

"Well, shit, if he's got that much guts he can't be afraid of no board chairman. What's the guy gonna do to him, blow out his brains?"

"Fighting a war and fighting a business tycoon are two distinctly different projects."

"Look, you want more time on the loans, right? I need some dough and I need it fast. I got other problems besides yours. I ain't saying yes to you and I ain't saying no. I want to talk to your boy. I got some idea he might be able to help us. He helps us, we help you. Simple. One hand scratches the other. You tell him I'll be calling him to set up a meeting."

"I've already told you, Rocco, this is my problem, not his. He's helped all he can—"

"You'd better let me decide that." Rocco got up then, indicating the meeting was over. His brief interlude of friendliness—if one could call his interest in Martin's war history friendly—was over. He assumed the same coldness with which he had entered the room. He was not, however, without a sense of drama. Pausing, he looked straight into Martinez's face and said very slowly: "I'm going to be calling your son in a couple of days. He'd better want to meet with me. He will if he knows what's good for him, and for you too."

He turned, nodding good night, and hurried from the room. A long history of mob executions by "friends" had taught him not to linger over farewells.

Chapter Six

January Seventh

Three days after Myra Rubin had visited Martin in his offices, serious irregularities were uncovered in the accounts payable ledgers of United Ventures, Ltd. Independent accountants, conducting their annual audit, found a series of unpaid invoices hidden away in unlikely corners that totaled several hundred thousand dollars. Had they been properly entered, they would have seriously affected the profit and loss statement of the parent company. Reluctant to cause a stir unnecessarily, the junior accountants on the job informed their superiors who, again without giving warning of the discovery, joined the review team to determine if the irregularity was actual and significant. A few days of questioning low-level bookkeeping clerks were satisfactory to assure the auditors that top management had indeed attempted to disguise the true loss that would have resulted from the proper entering of these newly discovered bills.

Still avoiding a showdown with top officers, the auditors brought in additional bifocaled bloodhounds who found that there was still another serious problem—not only had these bills been hidden, but there was absolutely no record of anyone having held competitive bidding before signing the contracts that resulted in the expenditures that were being concealed. The chief auditor, Bernard Sloane, had been a college classmate of Herschel Margolis and still saw him socially on occasion. Although Margolis was essentially involved in sales and promotion and was hardly an expert on accounting procedures, it was natural for Sloane to speak to him first when his suspicions grew into unpleasant realities.

Over coffee, Bernie Sloane unburdened himself to Hersh Margolis, and had he brought news of a gold strike to a starving prospector he could not have received a more enthusiastic reception. Margolis was still smarting from his meeting with Martin. More important, once he fed this news to C. W. Randall, which he had every intention of doing, his own bid for the presidency of the company would have new impetus. Seeing Margolis's gleeful reception of the news, Sloane did feel that it had been indiscreet of him to make the disclosure before talking to the comptroller and the president of the company, and urged Margolis to keep the matter under wraps . . . It was like telling a major stockholder not to sell out when he learns that a company will go bankrupt in thirty days. By the time Sloane had met with John Martin and Ted Vernaca, the company's comptroller and vice-president of finance, Margolis had already called Randall, who in turn notified Martin that he was on his way.

"Well, John," Randall said laconically, "so this is it."

"This is what?" Martin answered with pretended innocence.

"You know damn well what I am talking about, John, so let's not play games. The one thing I won't stand for is dishonesty. And it's the last thing I'd ever expect from you. I couldn't believe my ears when Margolis—"

"Exactly. Margolis. What does the sales promotion manager know about accounting? He's so hot for this job he'd sign an affidavit that Miss Jenkins and I are lovers."

"She's probably the only woman in Miami who doesn't qualify."

The best defense was a strong offense . . . "My social life, Mr. Randall, doesn't belong to United Ventures, Ltd. I have a wife, fine children, and a record you thought important enough to justify offering me this position. Do you really think Herschel Margolis should be allowed to offset all that—?"

"You are a very smart man, John. You think you can cover this over by making Margolis the heavy in the situation. It won't work. In the first place, Margolis didn't uncover the accounting irregularities, it was Brown, Brown and Ewings, and they happen to be one of the biggest and best accounting firms in the world. In the second place, it is not Herschel Margolis who worries about your infernal skirt-chasing, it is me, C. W. Randall, chairman of the board of directors. On two separate occasions I've come to the rescue and bought you out of paternity suits and alienation of affections litigation. I've helped pacify your wife when she was ready to divorce you and held back the Board when they asked for your head. Let's leave side issues such as Margolis where they belong— as side issues. Let's deal with the facts."

"Fine. The facts are that to protect you financially I risked my reputation and told accounts payable to bury a few bills."

" 'To protect me'?" Randall repeated incredulously, " 'to protect me'? Just how do you figure that?"

"Easily. Our stock has dropped twenty-three points in the last sixteen months. If another heavy loss quarter were reported it would drop precipitously again. You are the major stockholder in this company, are you not? I felt that if I could hold those bills for a few months we could subsume them in the heavy profits I'm projecting for the next quarter and thereby ease the effect on the stockholders. Is that 'to protect you,' or not?"

"A good try, but I don't buy it. I do not believe in stock manipulation, which is precisely what your *subsuming* maneuver smacks of to me . . . not to mention that it is forbidden by the Securities and Exchange Commission."

"Okay," said Martin, "if that's your feeling we'll just let the chips fall where they will. I try to protect this company and its equity position. That's my job. Sometimes it means taking difficult positions, even chances. But of course we can let the public know when we are hurting, if that's your policy—"

"That is exactly my policy, which doesn't mean you have to run around yelling 'rotten fish' just to teach the Board a lesson . . . And, by the way, you haven't explained the lack of competitive bidding on these contracts. Was that for my protection too?"

"Since I knew I wasn't going to declare these liabilities, it was logical not to want too many people to know about them."

"How's that again?"

"It's simple. I knew that these contracts would run up heavy additional expenses for the company, which I was planning to hold in abeyance until the next fiscal period. I was concerned that if I held open bids on them everybody and his brother would know about them and it would make my job of temporarily holding them out that much tougher. So, logically, I believe, I opted for a quiet approach and went to only one supplier."

Randall took a deep breath and looked at Martin in near-admiration. He knew that the explanation was ridiculous. And Martin knew that he knew it. But he had to admit that this president of his was ingenious and had testicles. And that he liked. Despite his anger at the company's recent reversals, he had to admit to himself that he liked Martin's spunk far better than that Margolis's ass-kissing, tattletaling scramble to the top. He pulled his chair closer to the front of the desk, faced Martin and changed his tone.

"Look, John, let's put an end to this bickering. You're my man, not Margolis. But you can't screw the world and get away with it forever. I want you to play by the rules I've set down for running this company. I want you to gain back the respect of your entire staff and of your family. I want you to settle down and show the kind of talent you have inside you, which you've shown in the past. This is *our* last chance. And *yours*. Truly. Either you turn this company around, and quickly, or my investment will be down the drain, and so will you."

"CW, there is no way, and I mean no way, that I'd let you down or let this company float down the tubes. We've had a rough inning or two but that's behind us. Second quarter advance orders are already way ahead of last year. You go back to Maine and do some hunting and fishing and just bet on me like you did in the beginning. We'll make it, and in style too!"

It was, of course, what he wanted to hear. "Okay, I'll take that as a promise, John. Be sure to make good on it . . . And what do you propose I tell Margolis, with whom I've scheduled a meeting in half an hour?"

"I've never used profanity with you before, CW, but at the risk of sounding disrespectful, may I suggest that you tell him to go fuck himself?"

"You may."

Martin decided to celebrate. He really owed Billie Lane a session in the sack, but after CW's lecture, even he didn't have the nerve to indulge in an illicit matinee. Billie would, of course, carry on like a banshee when he told her that she was once again not on the schedule. But Margaret could scream too, as he was well aware. Better not to contact Billie at all. She'd, hopefully, think he'd been called out of town if she didn't hear from him. It had happened before. No news was bad news.

As Armando guided the car up the driveway of his fine home on Indian Creek Island, pride and a feeling of comfort and relief filled John Martin. It had started like a day in hell and actually was ending on a rather pleasant if distinctly unsettled note. Next time was out, clearly. He had explained away the favors he had been doing to keep his father out of hot water. He'd even overcome his need for sex and returned to the bosom of his family in time for dinner. He'd ended for the time being the threat of replacement by Herschel Margolis. He had, in short, lived to fight another day. Even Margaret had seemed pleased when he phoned and told her he was coming home for an early dinner with the children.

He swung through the door, greeted Lucille, their maid of many years, kissed Margaret on the cheek in husbandly affection, and went whistling up the stairs to his bedroom to shower and shave before dinner.

When he came down to dinner he was surprised to find the house virtually deserted. Johnny and Melinda had been sent off to dinner with friends and Lucille, having set the table, had been given the night off. Margaret seemed strangely quiet as they took their places at the table. John had a queasy feeling that all was not well in the Martin household. He tried to bury his sense of foreboding in a whirlwind of pleasantry.

"I had a terrible day today. Old CW arrived with a barrel of complaints, but before he left he was eating out of my hand. That bastard Margolis has been at it again, but I think we buried him once and for all . . . How was your day honey? Any word from Ginny and her love, James Whatshisname McBride?"

"No word from Ginny and I had a terrible day, thank you."

"What's wrong?"

"Don't you know?"

"I guess if I knew there would be no need to ask."

"Really? What's *wrong* is that I received a call from one Billie Lane. She insisted on meeting me for a drink and when I said no she told me that the meeting was for my protection. I laughed at that and she laughed back. So out of curiosity I met her. I must say your taste in women is deteriorating."

"Billie Lane is an aggressive little climber I met at a convention in Palm Beach. She doesn't mean a thing to me and she knows it—"

"Wrong. You may know it. But she thinks she is the grand passion of your middle age. And you are middle-aged, let's not forget that. She quotes you as saying, among other things, that you are forced to administer large doses of penicillin to yourself before going to bed with me for fear of catching pneumonia. She says you told her that when you get an erection with me it isn't passion, it's frozen stiff. I must say I was touched."

"Oh, balls. This is ridiculous, Margaret. You take the word of a blackmailing little hustler—"

"Yes, indeed I do. And now you take my word, because it's the last one I'm going to have on the subject—if you ever so much as see this lady, talk to her or deal with her again in any way, I am leaving you. And as I go off into the sunset, I'll pull you down with me. I spoke to my father today. He and mother are vacationing at La Costa. He's never trusted you or liked you any more than you like him. He asked me to remind you that it was his friendship with CW that got you that first job interview even though you like to think you did it entirely on your own. One more indiscretion, darling, and you've had it. There's a certain loyalty at work here that I doubt you'll understand. He'll meet with CW and see to it that you are tossed out on your fine Latin ass once and for all—"

"Good girl. At least you're not afraid to say the word." It was weak, and he knew it.

"Oh, you've taught me a lot of things, John. I can say 'ass' without flinching. Big deal. But I can't say it without thinking about you. Think it over. Is it the Billie Lanes or the boring little wife and children? And have no doubt where their loyalties lie . . . I've had my dinner, you'll find some cold salad in the kitchen. Make yourself some coffee if it doesn't remind you too much of the bad old days when you were a big shot in Cuba. I'm playing bridge at the McLeods'."

"One moment for the condemned man, please. He has a last word. The bank informs me that our joint account is overdrawn again, for the fifth time in two months. They're getting tired of it and so am I. I glanced at those department store bills upstairs and you're still going at it as if this is an annex of Fort Knox. You *promised* to ease up. I'm not as fancy as your blueblood parents, true, but I'm also not made of solid gold bullion."

"I buy what I want because that's my only real pleasure in life. If you can't support a wife in style, you're more of a failure as a husband and father than I thought you were. I'm not going to 'ease up,' as you put it. Stop buying gifts for Billie Lane and maybe you'll have a few pesos left over for your *family.*"

Three minutes later she was out the door and he was alone. Thank God. He went up to his study, locked the door and built himself a stiff drink of Scotch. It tasted like another and he found no relief until the fourth one had gone down. He turned the lights down, lit an Upmann cigar and allowed his thoughts to drift off. He measured what he was and what he might have been. All of the good fortune in his life that had seemed so important when he came home for dinner tonight suddenly had drifted off in a puff of smoke.

Here he was, forty-two years of age, the head of a company that was in deep financial trouble. And he wasn't even the head. The real power was a WASP from New England who could mash him into nothingness on a whim. He had a loveless marriage with a cold bitch of a wife who hated him. His children looked on him as a meal ticket, and would, as she had said, desert the moment he stopped laying the golden eggs.

Outside of the home his love life was meaningless. Showgirls, part-time hookers, kept women. And even these were growing more and more demanding, more and more impossible as his money problems escalated. Hell, he wasn't even as good in the sack as he used to be, so they probably cheated on him as well . . . He had to smile at the absurdity of *that* piece of irrelevant jealousy.

What was it all *about* anyway? Who needed this crazy struggle, this constant hustle after empty victories in a life that had no meaning? Certainly, in some ways he had contributed to his own predicament. But surely all the fighting, the charming, the figuring should bring something better, more satisfying, than what he'd managed.

What he needed was what most men his age wanted but never got—a new start. Just show me the way, he declared to himself romantically—what the hell, he *was* a Latin—and I'll chuck all of this and start fresh. Show me a new life with new opportunities and I'll show the world what kind of man Juan Martinez, also known as John Lawrence Martin III, really is. I won't let them put me down. In a new place, with a fresh start—even with a new name—I'll climb back up and make them all kiss my ass . . . And then he drifted off to sleep.

Chapter Seven

January Eighth

At high noon Northshore Park, just off the Seventy-ninth Street Causeway, was deserted. Mad dogs and Englishmen might venture out into the noonday sun but not the knowledgeable residents of Miami Beach. The previous night's revelers were just arising and even the perennial sun worshipers, oil-drenched like imported sardines, were just beginning to confront the blast-furnace rays of the tropic sun. It would have seemed to the casual observer that life was at a momentary standstill, but plans were being formulated, deals were being made.

Seated alone on a deserted bench charitably shaded from the fire ball above, Rocco Floriani was studying the racing columns in the morning *Herald*. His black and white vinyl-coated shoes, canary yellow slacks and boldly printed sports shirt belonged more appropriately, perhaps, to a retired condominium dweller from the north than to the ex-hitman and gambling czar of the entire area. Mafia Dons normally were expensive but understated in their attire; knowing this, The

Fox had assumed what might be described as the uniform of the day in order to be less conspicuous. It was, he reasoned, a case of more being less.

Now and again he glanced casually at his wristwatch to check the time. He was a punctual man by nature and by vocation. Smooth operations, he had learned over these many years, started on time and ended as scheduled. Too often delayed starts signified trouble. He had made it a practice to allow ten to fifteen minutes' cushion for any meeting. If there were an inexplicable delay beyond that time, he cased the area, and having satisfied himself that he was not walking into some sort of trap, moved out, and quickly. At the moment his watch informed him there were six minutes to go.

Tad Duncan was also a punctual man. As a young FBI agent in South America, he once had dallied over a second cup of coffee and missed his contact, who later was found with a cut throat on a nearby coffee plantation. He'd never forgiven himself. But Duncan had another operating principle that he considered equally inviolable. He seldom showed up first for any meeting, even though he had chosen to in his first encounter with The Fox. To do so, he believed, gave the other man the impression he was overanxious. And holding back a few minutes gave him the edge to survey the territory for possible ambush. Actually, today he had arrived five minutes before Floriani's appearance, had circled the park several times, keeping out of sight, and then headed for his man at what he considered the correct psychological moment. Floriani saw him approaching but made no move at recognition.

"Light, mister?" Duncan asked.

"Sure. Have a stick of cancer," Rocco replied, pulling a lighter from his pants pocket.

"Have one?" Duncan asked, holding out the pack.

"Why not?" He accepted a cigarette and lit up while Duncan sat down beside him. In the sweltering noon heat, they were the only two persons in the park.

"You've considered my proposition?"

"Considered. If the money's right, you've got a deal."

"I hear you're a reasonable man."

Floriani smiled. "You can't be talking about me. No use bullshitting around the bush. The price is two million—one on a handshake, the balance when the job is done."

Duncan nodded. "You're right. I wasn't talking about you." But, of course, he had expected a high tab.

"Another thing. I got a favor to ask too. That's part of the deal."

"More yet?"

"More yet. My cousin, Vito Sarina, he's just been nicked for ten years on tax evasion and extortion. I want that reversed, or no butcher job."

"Look, Mr. Floriani, I can do just so much. I'm not the Chief Justice of the United States Supreme Court. They chased Sarina for eight years. Now they've given him a fair trial and he's been convicted. What the hell can I do about that?"

"Tell you what. You like fair trials. Give this guy you want we should bury a fair trial and leave me alone, okay?"

"Okay, okay, I'll try. What more can I say?"

"Trying don't mean one shit to me. Either Vito is cut loose or we don't do business. You know what you can do and what you can't. We can stop this meetin' right now or we can go on. You name it."

"We go on. Vito is free in thirty days." Duncan had anticipated the request and cleared it with his boss before the meeting.

"Good thinking. Now when do we get the down payment?"

"Hey, wait a second. I've got a couple of questions to ask too. I think I'm entitled for two million dollars . . . After we free Vito and pay you the first million, how do I know you'll do the job?"

"You want a receipt?"

"I want to know that I'm not being taken. It's Uncle's

money and I'm damned careful how I spend it. I'm not interested in one-liners, Rocco. I want some sort of guarantee."

"The organization's word is its guarantee, Duncan, and you know it fuckin' well. The guys who break their word to my men end up under water."

"You make this sound like a cheap movie . . . honor among thieves . . ."

"My word ain't cheap, Duncan. But how about Uncle's? How do I know once we do the job you don't crack down with some kind of murder rap, seeing you know who done what?"

"Fair question. I think my outfit's word is almost as good as yours. Wouldn't you agree?"

"Hell, no, I wouldn't. This ain't the first deal we've done with you people. They'd fuck us every time if we let 'em."

"I don't know anything about past history. I live in the present and the future. You do your job, you get the money, Vito gets paroled. It's that simple. One million down when we shake on it. The balance when we read about the funeral. All I ask is to meet the man who is going to do the job. It's no deal unless I okay him. And I won't debate that."

"Before we get to who does the job, maybe you'd better say who's the target. That might have something to do with who we get to make the hit, right?"

"You've got the man picked already, don't kid me. And I think you know the target . . ."

"You know, Duncan, you're so fuckin' smart, how come you don't knock off the bearded wonder yourself?"

"I would, but I can't stand the sight of blood."

It was out in the open now. Duncan was reasonably certain from the first moment of the first conversation with Rocco that recent day at the Seafarer Hotel coffee shop that The Fox knew his proposed target without him drawing any pictures. It was obvious that underworld connections in Cuba had been deep-rooted after generations of infiltration, and that they also held tremendous hatred for the Castro regime that had shut down their lucrative operations under Batista. It was also well established that Fidel Castro was a constant thorn in the diplomatic side of the U.S. giant ninety miles north of his border. For the Central Intelligence Agency to risk the ugly publicity that would result if it were ever revealed that it had formed an assassination pact with the Mafia, as unlikely as this teaming might at first appear, there had to be a strong presumption that such an alliance would succeed. There was: logic supported the conclusion that the Mafia had a far better chance of managing the job (already previously botched by U.S. intelligence forces) than any paid agent or counter-agent. Duncan, figuring the odds rather than the p.r. aspects, chose Floriani. Floriani had his own incentive—beyond money—to eliminate Castro. Working for the U.S. Government to eliminate a common enemy—a patriotic act—was perfect. Partners. If they succeeded, the Mafia might well find its way back into the lucrative fields it had enjoyed during the Batista era, and Uncle Sam would have far smoother sailing in the Western Hemisphere.

Duncan extended his hand. "It's a deal, then?"

"It's a deal. When do I get my money?"

"When do I meet your man?"

"About two or three days. He'll call you. I got your office number. He'll say I sent him and you'll know."

"Make it fast. Time is important here. You'll get your money as soon as I meet him and can satisfy myself that he has a good chance for success."

"I don't object to that. You'll like my man. And time is important to me too. I gotta spring Vito before Columbus Day. He likes to march in the parade."

Duncan studied the little man for a moment. If politics made strange bedfellows, assassination plots make stranger marriages.

Chapter Eight

January Ninth

They met at a small bar in the Cuban section of Miami, about a half-mile from Martin's office. Martin had resisted the meeting when it was first requested but gave in to his father's urgent—and yet reluctant—request when it became apparent that the older man was deeply worried, however much he tried to downplay it, about his safety as well as his financial future. Martin had no illusions about the mob's possible cruelty if they were crossed. His father's debts were long overdue and he certainly was in no position to make any loans to his father. He also knew that there would be no way to continue buying from Mafia-tinged companies now that the auditors were on to him and the word had been passed to CW. He considered himself a man of ingenuity but this was one box that seemed escape-proof. He had no idea what Floriani expected of him but he knew before he met with him that the consequences would be distasteful.

The Fox got right to it.

"Your old man owes us a million and a half. We want it. You're gonna get it up?"

"Stones don't give blood because they have no blood to give. Threatening an old man may be your style, but it won't make anybody any richer." Might as well play it strong.

"So far, nobody's threatening anybody. They're your words but now that you mention them maybe they're a good idea."

"Let's stop muscle-flexing, Mr. Floriani, and face some facts. My dad was cooperative with you and your friends for many years. He never broke his word to you and he helped make you rich. When he borrowed the money his intentions were honorable. You know that. He can't help it if the construction business in Miami went to hell. But these things have a way of evening themselves out and you'll get your money if you'll just give him a little more time. I am in no position to help. My company is in trouble and so am I. They know all about those supplies I've been buying from your friends and I've been ordered, as they say, to shape up or ship out. Believe me, I'd help if I could."

"No kiddin'."

"What the hell kind of comment is that? You know damn well I'd help if I could. I did before, didn't I?"

"Some." Floriani paused, then drove it home. "There's a way you can help, now. You can make two million bucks pretty quick—a million and a half for us and the rest for you and your pop. And you might even be a hero at the same time. Interested?"

"I don't know what in the hell you're talking about, and of course I'm interested. I only tell you that I can't involve United Ventures and I won't involve my parents and my family any deeper than they are now—"

"Sure, sure . . . I got a new partner and he needs a job done. You can do the job."

"Who's the partner? What's the job?"

"Not so fast. I want to hear first that you'll deliver. I gotta tell you there's some risk here."

"What kind of risk?"

5 1

"You could get killed. That's what kind of risk. Or maybe you could go to the can for a lot of years."

"If you think I'm going to break the law and risk going to jail so that you can get your goddamned money . . . look, I want to help my father but it's no help to him to have his son a lawbreaker or a murderer or—"

"You go too fast. You ask the questions, answer them, argue about them, and never even give the other guy a chance to talk. What's this speech you're giving me?"

"I'm only telling you what I will do and what I won't do to help my father. There's no point in your telling me about some kind of superplot if I can't accept the honor. So let's talk straight now. Who is your partner?"

"Uncle Sam."

"Come off it."

"That's right. Uncle Sam."

Martin laughed uproariously. "Next time you'll tell me your enemy is Little Mary Sunshine. What kind of bullshit are you trying to feed me, Floriani?"

"I don't blame you for laughin'. I did too at first. Seems the boys in DC who keep their ear to the ground are at it again. They got a guy about ninety miles south of here who's still one hell of a pain in their ass. They still want him blown away and they think we have the connections to do it. Besides, if we do, or if we botch the job, they figure their skirts are clean. Even if it does leak to the papers eventually, no one will really believe it. So, believe it or not, they came to me, Rocco Floriani, and offered me a shitload of money plus some other favors to find the man to do the job, with our connections greasing the way. Now, it just so happens I've got this guy owing me a fortune who happens to have a son who was a war hero, a big deal jock athlete who knows that country like the back of his favorite broad, and no doubt hates the guy with the beard to start with. So I figured it all fit together real nice and cozy. Any more questions?"

"I've never even thought of anything like—"

52

"I found out about you, all the medals and unit citations and that kind of crap in Vietnam. You killed before and from what my boys tell me, it sounds like you maybe even enjoyed it."

"What a man does in combat, he does to save his own life. That doesn't mean he enjoys it. Besides, I was in my thirties then and I'm forty-two now. A man changes . . . I have to think about this. How would I get there? Who would help me? How long would it take?"

"My contact wants to tell you all about this himself. I promised him I'd give you about six reliable contacts who still work for us in Cuba. You want 'em, they're yours. You want to use Uncle's contacts, you use them. You got your own, better still. It'll all work out if you go along. And if you don't, my friend, I promise big trouble for you, your parents and your whole family. And that is a threat, make no mistake about it."

The two men sat back and looked at each other without either saying a word. There was little feeling exchanged between them, except a kind of mutual respect. Floriani knew he had found the right man. Martin felt that in a strange way providence was somehow favoring him once again. Here was the unpredictable opportunity to get out and start over that he had only fantasized about. If he accepted, he could clear his family's debts, have a sizable stake to finance a new start and realize that dream of "dropping out" and escaping the pressures that had made his life a nightmare. More—and not incidentally—he could even a score with the despot he believed had ruined his homeland, tortured and destroyed his friends and caused him and his parents to abandon a deservedly good life on the land that had been theirs for generations. It was out of the blue, right on target. He could not afford to appear too anxious or eager to accept. On the other hand, how could he afford to refuse?

Looking Floriani in the eye, he said, "It's worth consideration. I'll call you tomorrow with my answer."

"One day, okay," Floriani replied. "That beard has to be

shaved and you're my pick for barber . . ." He smiled, well pleased with his turn of phrase, and the conversation so far. "We're all counting on you, hero."

Ignoring the sarcasm, he said, "I'll let you know tomorrow."

He wasn't kidding anybody. He knew he would accept the job. The Fox was sure of it.

Chapter Nine

January Tenth

Martin met with Tad Duncan the next evening after a call to Floriani telling him what both men already knew: he would accept the assignment. Duncan had selected a little-known Chinese restaurant on the Beach for the rendezvous. He arranged for a table in the rear that was more or less isolated and where they could talk with security and without interruption. He assured the owner he would pay him for two of the most expensive meals on the menu if he could be certain they'd be left alone.

"You know, Mr. Chung, one from Group A and one from Group B. Group A is quiet and Group B is no bother us." Mr. Chung appreciated the point, if not the humor.

Whereas Floriani had been eager to get to the point and find his answer, Duncan's attitude was entirely different. He seemed to want the meeting to go on for a long time. The longer they talked, the more he could learn about Martin. As it turned out, the more he learned, the more he liked. Martin was content to permit Duncan to set the pace. He, too, had a good many questions and wasn't in a hurry to blurt them out.

"I hear you were quite an athlete at the University of Havana a few years ago." It was more a question than an observation.

"Years ago. That's where the emphasis should be."

"Well, I've read the record blown up on microfilm. It reads like Jack Armstrong, the all-Cuban boy."

"I was fair. Football—you call it Soccer—was my specialty. I made our Olympic team but never went because of the war. I was also a pretty fair swimmer and broke a few long-distance records that still stand, from what I can learn. Of course, I would have been just another jock in this country, though I boxed pretty well in Vietnam."

"You captained the basketball team, didn't you?"

"Almost forgot. I'm not really big enough to be a threat on the court today, but I was pretty fast and tough under the boards in those days. Don't tell me I was a baseball star. I was the original guy who couldn't hit the side of a barn with a bulldozer."

"You can't win 'em all, Mr. Martin. Incidentally, so we wouldn't be disturbed by prying waiters I took the liberty of ordering for both of us. There's enough of an assortment to satisfy almost anyone, and I see it's ready now." There was a brief pause while two waiters spread the food in front of them, then, as arranged, beat a hasty and strategic retreat. The two men served themselves in silence, and the conversation resumed.

"Did you play any ball over in Nam?" Duncan asked. He wanted to open up the Vietnam chapter in Martin's life.

"Not really. I boxed competitively. A little tennis at the officers' club. I was past thirty when I enlisted. I was made an officer pretty quickly because of training I'd had in military school as a boy. With my swimming ability, they trained me at first with commando outfits and later I worked on infiltration and guerilla tactics ashore. It was a good thing, too. In

Vietnam ninety percent of my action was spent inside enemy territory. Of course with the rapidly shifting battle lines and constant guerilla attacks it was hard to know which side of the fence you were on from one day to the next. I ate mud there for two-and-a-half years, then I was sent home for rest and rehab. Mr. Randall, he's the retired chairman of our company, felt that I'd done my part, and maybe he was right. Anyhow, the company was hurting for top executives so he used some political drag and got me released. All in all, I served thirty-nine months."

"I'd say you did your share. Especially after I read about all the citations and honors you won."

"Well, don't believe everything you read, Mr. Duncan. The military was getting a lot of black marks and they needed heroes pretty badly in those days . . . Now, if you don't mind, I have a few questions. Floriani tells me the pay for this job is two million dollars, one million up front and the balance on delivery. Right?"

"That's the price and we okayed it."

"It's not good enough. I want half of my end, that is, half of a half million, up front. I want it in the bank before I start. You can put the balance in an account I'll open in Switzerland after you've decided that I've delivered."

"Floriani asked for one million up front. Now you want an extra two hundred fifty thousand."

"Exactly. I'm not sure I'm going to be alive for the payoff. And—don't get angry, Mr. Duncan—my reading of your organization tells me that I probably will be very expendable and very dangerous when I get back. I doubt you'll really want me around. So I don't plan to give you the chance to get rid of me. I'll disappear like snow in the summer. The money you'll give me up front will already be invested, waiting for me in a city where I'll start life over again. I'll pick up the balance from Switzerland by courier. Agreed?"

Duncan nodded. "You get the two fifty up front."

"Good. How much time do I have to finish the job?"

"Eight weeks from tonight. In March the Organization of American States holds a major meeting in Lima, Peru. The conference opens on March 7 and lasts for five days. For months now the propaganda mills have been grinding out all sorts of support for the readmission of Cuba. You may recall they were expelled in 1961 because of the Communist influence in their government and their international policies. Now Castro wants back in and he wants back in bad. He's been working his tail off in one South American country after the other and it'll all come to a head at Lima. We want to keep him out of the OAS as badly as he wants in. If he happens not to be around by the time the meeting convenes, a leaderless Cuba will flop around and never know how to press its advantage, and we'll have held them off for another five years. So . . . that's why the job has to be done in eight weeks."

"I can understand the timetable more than the project, unless I'm not reading the newspapers right these days. Are you telling me that the senators, the network people, encouraged by the Administration in Washington—that it's all a phony?"

"I never said that."

"Not in so many words. But on the one hand I read about the possible reopening of tourism in Cuba, the desire to trade, the recent exchange of athletic teams . . . and meanwhile, you're trying to hire me to bump off Fidel. It doesn't exactly figure."

"Mr. Martin, if you're going to read the papers, please read everything. Are you unaware that our Cuban neighbors have infiltrated seven different African nations under the guise of sending 'advisors'? Have you heard of the Cubans in Ethiopia and Angola? Hell, they're up to their asses in Sierra Leone, Equatorial Guinea, the Congo Republic, Somalia, Tanzania, Mozambique and Guinea-Bissau. And who knows where next? It's not entirely inconsistent for the Administration to be opening up relations with Cuba on a person-to-person level, but also reacting to the realities of power in the world, no matter what the media says."

"How come that's your job? I thought things were shaken-down at the CIA so that you people were back to collecting information and handing it up to the people elected to making policy—"

Martin had, he quickly realized, discovered Duncan's boiling point. All of the warmth now drained from his face, his tone chilled and the words became clipped.

"We'd better come to terms on this quickly, Mr. Martin. The job offer is not contingent on your directing the CIA."

"Don't get sore if I ask a few questions, Mr. Duncan. It's a big order and I've got to understand my assignment—"

"You understand it. And I thought you would believe in it too. If there are ideological differences . . ."

"If by ideological you mean me being against the Castro regime, don't worry. I just want to make sure that what you are asking me to do has the government's backing. I'd feel like a damn fool risking my life and then finding out that what I was doing was against the government's plans—"

"What the government says to the press, or even does at any moment, Mr. Martin, and what its underlying goals are *may* be diametrically opposed. Besides, the Administration may or may not always be the government, and vice versa, if you get my point."

"If your point is that the CIA sometimes has to march to its own tune, I understand you. And I suppose the professionals in your agency have served a number of administrations and may have a different perspective on some of the recently adopted policies."

"You're an intelligent man, Mr. Martin." His tone warmed noticeably. "The man we select for the job will understand all this. More important, he'll dismiss transient political considerations from his thinking. Are you our man, Mr. Martin?"

"I may be. I need more information. Suppose you start by telling me what you are going to do to help me complete the job."

"Anything you want or need. We'll give you a list of at least a half-dozen strong contacts who will help you, if you want them. I understand Floriani has a similar list. Frankly, his group may be stronger than mine. If you trust our contacts, use them. If not, commit the list to memory and use it if and when."

"What about transportation to and from the country?"

"You didn't think we'd ask you to swim both ways, did you, Mr. Martin? Well, actually, we do feel you should swim in the last few hundred yards—we regularly deposit lookouts who bring us information we need; they usually land by small boats and swim a short way in—then, when the job is over, we'll give you additional papers and fly you out to Mexico City."

"Additional papers?"

"We've been preparing false identification papers for you so that you'll be ready when you need them. There is no doubt that you'll be frequently asked to identify yourself."

"And who am I?"

"Your name is Carlos Palma, a free-lance journalist working with British Reuters as a foreign correspondent in Cuba."

"Is there such a man?"

"There is a well-known writer by that name working for Reuters but he is from Barcelona, has strong right-wing convictions and would *never* come to Cuba. Although obviously the man was not told the reason, British intelligence is assisting. They've arranged a two-month vacation with pay for Mr. Palma in Capri. There'll be no conflicting by-line stories by him during that time. Reuters has no permanent setup in Havana, so there should be little risk from that source. Should you ever be questioned, just say you're on special assignment and Reuters in London will confirm. Incidentally, Palma has written a few books on international affairs, which we'll supply you so you can familiarize yourself with his work."

"And if they press me for details, what is my 'special assignment'?"

"A definitive biography of Fidel Castro. That will be your project, and that will provide a most reasonable basis for your wanting to meet Castro. Personal, one-on-one research is clearly the best for anyone writing a biography, right?"

"Yes, I suppose, but Reuters is a press service. Why would they want a full-length biography of Castro?"

"They're going to serialize it. They've made a deal with Italian and Spanish publishers who want to print it in its entirety. We'll supply you with foreign publishers' names in case you need them. But if the Cuban authorities want to check up on you, there's a hundred-to-one chance they'll at least start with Reuters and we're completely covered there."

"What if my being a well-known journalist doesn't fit the circumstances at some time?"

"Good question. We've given you an alternate identity as Carlos Palma, itinerant field worker and part-time construction hand from Santiago de Cuba. Sometimes one wants to change one's identity but keep the same name. So you'll have duplicate papers to cover that situation. Of course if you want to change identities completely, we're supplying a number of different sets of papers all with different names and varied jobs or professions. Use them as you need them. Your code name is The Barber. The project will be known as Operation Shaving Mug. We like to think we have a sense of humor."

"I'm sure. Well . . . it sounds like a hairy job"—he didn't smile, nor did Duncan. "And suppose I need you, how do we communicate?"

"In Havana, on Calle Twelve, not far from the Cemetery de Colón, there's a small office of the Anglo-Swiss Trading Com-

6 1

pany, a corporation with offices in London and Lausanne dealing in international exchange. Nothing major is ever attempted through these offices. We just sort of hold it there as insurance in case it's ever necessary to infiltrate. In the meantime they collect information for us. When you go there, let the word out that Pepe sent you and that you bear tidings from his old Aunt Cintia from San Pedro. Whoever is there will relay messages for you and help when you're in a bind. But I'd avoid using those facilities for anything but a message drop, if at all possible. We never know when our operating centers are being observed."

"Will I be seeing you?"

"I have easy access to Havana, Mr. Martin. I'm known by a different identity there so don't be surprised if I show up."

"I don't like being tailed, Mr. Duncan," Martin said. "My thought was whether I could see you if I needed you, not the reverse."

"You were in the service, Martin. There are such things as channels of authority. You'd better let me decide whether I need a Cuban vacation." His tone had grown cold once again.

"What you do in Cuba is your business, Mr. Duncan. But it's my life that's involved here and I think I should decide whether I work solo or head up a team."

"There's no team involved. I have reasons for coming to Cuba now and again. I've perfected a way of moving in and out without causing suspicion. I have no plans for being there when you're there . . . but I may be. So let's move on, keeping in mind that if your government didn't trust you to do this job, you and I wouldn't be sitting here now."

They talked on for several hours. They were to meet the next morning. Duncan would have all the papers necessary for Martin, the money he insisted on in advance, weapons, several vials of poison and full instructions about his landing site and where he would find supplies waiting for him. Martin in turn said he would head for Philadelphia, a city he knew well from having taken graduate work in economics at the Wharton School of the University of Pennsylvania. There he would make his plans and get himself into top physical condition. Although he had kept his body trim with squash and tennis and exercises since returning from Vietnam, the basically sedentary life he'd led was beginning to have its effect. There were telltale bulges, and flabbiness was beginning to threaten. His wind wasn't what it once had been. He would punish himself with endless miles of road work. He would climb, jump, run, torture his lungs, his muscles. He would stop smoking, give up drinking. He would work at this round the clock for four weeks, and then he would be ready to return to Miami and to the island where his target waited.

"My God," Duncan complained, "that will only give you four weeks to do the job—"

"Plenty of time," Martin said. "I mean to do this job. I *want* to do this job."

The two men clasped hands and found each other's eyes.

"I think I believe that," Duncan said. And the meeting was over.

Chapter Ten

January Eleventh

He packed a small bag and left for work the next morning, telling Margaret that he would not be home for dinner and planned to work late to catch up on reports that required his immediate attention. He left the office after checking his mail, telling Sarah that he could not be reached for the rest of the day. Duncan was waiting for him at the airport, as prearranged, and was ready to deliver all of the items promised. He examined them carefully but avoided counting the money, which was enclosed in several sealed manila envelopes. He then returned all except the currency for safekeeping by Duncan until he returned to Miami from Philadelphia. Before departing, he changed his mind and accepted one small pistol and holster, in case of an unexpected emergency. Duncan supplied an unlisted telephone number where he could be reached during Martin's initial absence.

A noon flight brought him to Philadelphia by mid-afternoon. He had taken the precaution of using an assumed name and of stowing the pistol and holster in his flight bag, which was checked on through in order to avoid metal-detection devices at the passenger check-in line. The manila envelopes containing two hundred fifty thousand dollars in large bills were nestled in his inner jacket pockets, which he patted at safe intervals during the flight. He elected to travel tourist class to avoid any embarrassing and unplanned meetings with any of his rich friends.

Arriving in the Quaker City on schedule, he reclaimed his bag and caught a cab for West Philadelphia, directing the driver to a hotel he had once visited during a University of Pennsylvania alumni outing. He selected a moderately priced room, informing the clerk that he would probably stay at least a month while he took refresher courses at the Wharton School, where he'd gotten his graduate degree. Since most of the hotel residents were in one way or another connected with university activities, his explanation was readily accepted. He paid for his first week's room rent in advance, resisting the temptation to use credit cards, his basic currency for so many years. Even though there was little chance for anyone's discovery of his whereabouts, he elected to use his true name, "Juan Martinez III" to avoid that freak coincidence whereby someone he knew might for some reason examine the hotel register. Again, as a precaution, he avoided using the hotel vaults for the treasured manila envelopes lest some red-tape requirement of the hotel called for an inventory of valuables. The room assigned him was adequate—a double bed, desk, easy chair, reading lamp and the ubiquitous Gideon Bible. And, of course, there was the color television set, the traveling salesman's mistress.

He took a short walk around the campus and was delighted with what he found. The University had been spending its "annual giving" dollars well; there were new buildings, highly attractive, planted walks and a general feeling of growth and energy wherever he strolled. The students were warm and friendly even though he was hardly in the uniform of the day;

now he was in the land of denim and sweatshirts. No matter. He would buy such casual clothing to blend in with his surroundings. One of his favorite joints from campus days was still there and still thriving—Smokey Joe's, where generations of Pennsylvanians had tasted their first brews. He went in, ordered a beer and watched from a side table as a group of undergraduates came in. A bright-eyed, large-breasted girl sitting alone at a nearby table offered him an inviting smile and he was tempted to start up a conversation until he realized that he might be flirting with a girl not much older than his daughter, Ginny. It was his first and only thought of home the entire day.

Returning to his hotel for dinner, he was delighted with the quality of the food. His waiter explained that a gourmet chef had just arrived from Los Angeles and taken a position at the hotel to be near his daughter, a student at the college. The entire dinner cost him less than nine dollars, about fifty percent of its cost in any other major city first-class restaurant. Actually, there was no need for economizing. He was loaded with Uncle's money.

He read himself to sleep with the daily papers and awoke refreshed for the tasks ahead. Having secured a vault in a nearby bank, he deposited his money, first counting it carefully. He kept only enough on his person to get him through the next few days. Next, he visited the university's gymnasium office and with little trouble registered for a graduate's visiting privileges, being assigned a locker and instructions on hours when he could use all of the gym's facilities. At a campus haberdashery he bought his uniforms—blue jeans, sweatshirts, sneakers, T-shirts, the works. He also purchased shorts, supporters, sweatsuits, bathing trunks and terrycloth robe. At a neighborhood bookshop he picked up a guide to organic foods, and though he didn't plan to be a faddist, he knew that during the next few weeks, the calorie-laden poisons of the middle-aged were to be taboo.

He began his reconditioning regimen that afternoon. He

6 6

started with a half-mile on the indoor track and gradually increased his distance each day until he could lope five miles without breathing too heavily and end with a lung-bursting quarter-mile sprint. He would rest briefly, then join one of the many pick-up basketball games that were always on hand. An hour of running from one end of the court to the other, chasing some young squirt half his age was no mean feat, but he accomplished it more easily every day. A half-hour work-out with weights and pulleys followed and, finally, his specialty, a long, long swim in the university pool. Here, he was pleased to find that he had not lost his skill and since he had never been a heavy smoker his breath didn't fail him. He had always done better at the longer distances and had never competed in the short sprints. Now he practiced both, punishing his body with unbelievable demands and increasing his goals steadily each day. One day he was even approached by one of the coaches who asked if he had ever competed in collegiate events. He assured him that he was never that good and swam only for his own enjoyment. The coach seemed a bit dubious as he clocked him slipping smoothly through the water for lap after endless lap. But since he was far too old for a team prospect, he was dismissed as some aged jock who most assuredly would be pulled from the pool one day suffering from a severe coronary. After that day, he nodded to the coach, avoiding any further conversations, as he did with everyone else he met.

He limited his intake to organic foods, green vegetables and heavy protein supplements. He was pleased to see his slight paunch disappear, his muscles grow firmer and his weight drop to a point where he was no heavier than in his competitive college days. By the middle of the second week he grew increasingly bored but would not permit himself the luxury of relaxation. The miles he ran and the water he crossed, he figured, might one day save his life. Boredom was a small price.

He decided to grow a beard. For one, it might give him additional anonymity when he reached his destination—after all, many Cuban males, in obvious imitation of their leader, had forsaken shaving the day El Comandante was ensconced in Havana. In addition, he wanted to do all he could to vary his appearance since it was quite possible that he might meet up with people he'd once known. Since he was blessed—or cursed—with a luxuriant, heavy beard, he could see his new cover taking form in a matter of days. As he could have forecast, it came in silver streaked, reminding him of the silver fox stoles that his mother had worn in the old days.

Some faces, he decided, seem naturally shaped for hirsute adornment. Others, once bearded, seem improperly decorated. Picture, for example, the Smith Brothers of cough-drop fame or Abe Lincoln without beards. They cry out for them. A boyish Charles A. Lindbergh or a gnomelike Mickey Rooney would look strange indeed if bearded. John Martin found his new face hair perfectly suited to his look and his personality. He avoided barbering it too neatly. It was rough hewn and masculine, adding years and changing his entire appearance.

On weekends when gymnasium hours were limited he visited the school library and soaked up anything he could find about modern Cuba. Much of the material, though, was outdated and much was familiar to him, but he read hungrily, feeling that he might just learn some fact that could unexpectedly come in handy. Because of his fluency with Spanish, he went through South American and Mexican journals and found frequent reports about the land of his birth, the land he would soon revisit. One helpful librarian suggested that he try the main public library on Philadelphia's famous Parkway, which was patterned after Paris's Champs-Elysées. There he found much more up-to-date information about modern Cuban activities, including governmental crises, cultural happenings and construction developments.

He bought the Miami papers at the railroad terminal for

news of home. Sure enough, he found a report of his own disappearance and smiled when he read of himself as "that well-known, handsome young millionaire." He considered sending a note home without return address to assure his family that he was still alive, but this was quickly discarded. They would just have to adapt to his absence. Somehow he doubted they would have much trouble. He did hope that Herschel Margolis was not already ensconced in the United Ventures presidency. If he were, poor Sarah would be looking for a new job. No, he decided, old CW had too much taste to make that executive blunder.

He was concerned about his parents. Although he did not see them regularly, he was accustomed to calling his mother at least once a week. His father and he met whenever business matters called for their getting together. He'd planted a seed before he left by calling them the night he had met with Duncan and casually mentioning that he was planning a business trip that might well keep him out of the Miami area for a number of weeks. No doubt Margaret would phone them when she became aware that he was absent without leave. Either his father would be able to put two and two together, or he would find some way to get word to him later. He could *not* risk contacting him now.

In the middle of the third week he located a phone booth and tracked down Myra Rubin in Miami Beach. She had mentioned that she worked in the coffee shop of the Sunburst Hotel, but there turned out to be three hotels by that name in the greater Miami area. When he finally got the right one, they were reluctant to call her to the phone; casual employees weren't usually given the courtesy of receiving personal calls during working hours. He was persistent, and on the third call, having convinced the restaurant manager that this was a matter of extreme urgency, they brought her to the phone. She was frightened that there had been a death in her family, but as soon as she heard his voice, coldness replaced panic.

"What do you want?"

"It's very important. I must see you."

"I can't get off work."

"You have to. I have that money for you. And you don't have to give it back. It's a gift, not a loan."

"That's what I expected to hear three weeks ago in your office instead of a stall. Where do you want to see me?"

"I'm not in Miami. I'm where I went to graduate school. You remember where?"

"I can't come there, I'll lose my job."

"Lose it. I'll make it up to you. I'll pay all of your expenses. Take a six o'clock flight tonight. I'll wait for you at the airport. Where the luggage is stacked. Bring clothes enough to stay a few days. You have to do this for me. And no one, I mean no one, is to know where I am."

"What am I going to do, take an ad in the Miami *Herald*? . . . Okay, okay, I'll be there tonight."

"Good. Bring heavy clothes. It's cold."

He asked the desk to hold another room for his sister, who would be arriving that evening for a couple of days.

It would have been far more convenient to rent a car, but that would have required identification. Instead he took a public vehicle to Center City and from one of the larger hotels he boarded an airport limousine. He had an hour to kill before the plane's arrival so he busied himself reading the evening papers, then headed out to the gate where Myra's flight would terminate. She arrived exactly as scheduled and seemed pleased to see him, though obviously surprised at the change in his appearance and mystified about the reason for her flight.

"Welcome to Quaker City," he said warmly.

"I'll bet there isn't a Quaker in sight. They tell me they make the Arabs, the Jews and the Orientals look like bad businessmen, not to mention the Turks and the Persians. They're probably all in Africa trading with the natives."

He laughed easily, kissed her a fraternal peck on the cheek.

He ordered a cab after they had picked up her luggage, a badly worn flight bag that he seemed to remember from their days in Havana, and directed the driver to their hotel. They rode along almost silently, she sensing that what they had to discuss was not for the cabby's ears.

"You hungry?"

"No, thanks. They stuffed us on the plane, the usual dreck. All calories and starches, but I ate it just the same. After all, with my figure, who's going to know the difference?"

"Stop putting yourself down, Myra. You used to do that in college and I didn't like it then."

After she had checked in and had had a few minutes to wash up, he joined her in her room. He had remembered that she was a Scotch drinker and had put a bottle on the night table.

"Johnny, you really shouldn't waste Pinch Bottle on the likes of me. I used to roll in the hay with you for a swig of bad rum."

"I know," he said lightly, "but like old wine, you're worth more now—more mellow."

There was no point in stalling any further. He sat down and gave her the picture. He had to. Without her, it couldn't work. He had to trust her. He was sure he could. He explained that she would be the only private person who would know why he would be absent and where he was going. As such, he needed her promise of complete silence even if it meant risking his life, or possibly hers. He told her about his father's problems, his involvement with underworld characters, his construction misadventures in Miami, and the pressures brought on him to help the old man. He went into detail about the unpleasant relationship that had existed these many years between him and Margaret, and in doing so he tried to make it clear that he was as much to blame as was she. He made no effort to hide his infidelities, and his problems with an ego that seemed to demand a constant diet of beautiful women. He told her about the problems at United

71

Ventures, Ltd., and how thin the ice was that he'd been skating on the day she visited him and asked for help.

Myra made little comment, interrupting only occasionally with such remarks as, "So, Johnny, you've been a bad boy. What else is new?"

Finally he got to the meetings with Floriani, whose name he withheld from her, and the eventual rendezvous with Duncan, whom he described as a big deal with the CIA. He did not withhold their names out of mistrust, but for her protection in the unlikely event that she might somehow end up in the wrong hands. That was hardly a probability, but the fewer hard facts she had, the safer for all concerned. And then he told her the part she'd already guessed, what it was that they had asked him to do. He ended by telling her that an advance payment made it possible for him to give her the two thousand dollars she needed so badly and offered to give her more if there was a further need.

"They picked a good man to do the job, Johnny, and there is need to do the job, I'm very sorry to say. I've always hated bloodshed, you know that, but once in a while I think back to the suffering of my people under Hitler. You begin to wonder how many millions of innocent people might have lived if someone had had the courage to kill him when he was first giving those crazy speeches in the beer halls around Munich. Fidel has given up purging people recently, but if they refuse to obey his whim he'll be back at the tortures and the sudden "political" imprisonments, don't you worry. But the main thing you haven't told me yet is how *I* can help."

"I need two things. One is easy. I need one person in the States I can trust and can contact if there's ever a need. The second, and this is more important, I need contacts in Cuba I can turn to for help. I'll try my best not to compromise them, but no one man can do this job alone. I must have people willing to hide me, if necessary, who can give me clothing, money, whatever, at least for a short time. I think you might know such people."

"I do. And they *will* risk themselves. They're already doing it and *they* need help. For example, there is a good friend of mine in Guane. Her name is Alicia Ortiz. Her husband opposed Castro and was found dead . . . no prosecution, naturally."

"Tell me about her."

The rest of the night was spent in detailed rundowns on a number of Myra's Cuban friends who, she was sure, would help him. He questioned her extensively about each one, took notes that he would later memorize and destroy. They talked until four o'clock in the morning and planned another session the following evening after he had completed his physical workouts, which he couldn't afford to interrupt.

The following night was a copy of the first, except that after a few drinks of Scotch, which he steadfastly denied himself, hints of their old, forgotten relationship returned. Finally, they were in each other's arms and undressed for bed. But even if they both had been younger, there was no way to recapture the magic quality of those nights in Havana they'd shared nearly twenty years ago. Now she was ashamed of her body, he was troubled by his motives, and together they could manage only the most mechanical sort of union. Fortunately neither could find the words to express their disappointment. They fell asleep side by side, like two old friends seeking, needing, warmth and companionship.

The next morning he waited for the bank to open, withdrew three thousand dollars from his vault and forced her to accept it. "A little extra, just in case," he said. She smiled, kissed him and insisted that he already was late for his daily schedule and said she would go to the airport alone.

Less than two weeks later he was a solitary figure, clad in a wet suit, swimming from Ramon Santiago's boat toward a quiet inlet near the city of Puerto Esperanza, Province of Pinar del Río, on the northwestern tip of Cuba.

7 3

Chapter Eleven

February Sixth—One A.M.

Even at night, the waters of the Caribbean were crystal clear like those of an artesian well. The moon, having escaped from its bed of clouds, spilled light on a gently rolling sea and uncovered the Cuban coastline with its jagged limestone crust jutting unevenly into the sapphire waters that surrounded it. Stroking powerfully and smoothly, the man in the wet suit moved toward the inlet at La Esperanza, causing little disturbance to the silence that surrounded him. In a matter of minutes he was close to the shore and sensed the waters growing shallow underneath him. He could stand now but elected to switch to a breaststroke rather than rise and risk being sighted from the low hills that framed the inlet. Finally he could no longer swim and he stood and moved swiftly ashore. Avoiding slippery rocks and boulders that blocked his way, he climbed to a small hillock about fifteen feet above the sea and paused there to take inventory.

Martin remembered the area with amazing clarity. Here, as a boy, he had frequently swum and fished, never, of course, imagining that some day he would return as . . . what? An invader of his own country? Looking to the east he watched the twinkling lights of small villages beckoning toward the stronger illumination of Havana, where eventually he would have to perform his task. Suddenly the silence was broken by the barking of a large dog. He scrambled farther inland, burying himself in the deep undergrowth that covered the land scarcely one hundred yards from shore. The first chill of fear went through him, along with a rush of adrenaline, pumping blood more rapidly and raising its pressure. He breathed deeply to regain control.

There was quiet for a few moments and then again the dog's barking. He had images of bloodhounds and vicious guard dogs. Again he sucked in his breath. He warned himself he was overreacting, his keyed-up imagination overworking. He had yet to face the important dangers that surely lay ahead. Rising carefully on his elbows, he peered toward the beach below, which was still within his clear vision, and found comfort in what he saw—a peasant walking his shaggy pet in the cool of the early morning hours, the dog frolicking in the shallow water, sniffing a few empty shells on the beach as he circled his master in ever-widening patterns.

A slight breeze stirred the palm trees above and behind him, which was a blessing . . . the winds were from the sea masking his scent from the beaches. The peasant whistled for his pet and the dog dutifully returned to be leashed. Now they retraced their steps, finding the path that led them to the beach and returning to the road that circled above. The swimmer waited another few minutes and then, convinced that he was safe for the present, rose and moved inland, avoiding paths and open spaces.

He reached the edge of the heavy vegetation and spotted the road. Keeping to the edge of the road, where he felt protected, he moved several hundred feet to the left and found the small woodland he was seeking. He reentered the covered area and began his search, not wanting to risk the use of the flashlight that was strapped to his thigh. Working methodically, he crisscrossed the ground like a farmer seeding newly turned earth. And then he found his sign—an innocent-looking axe handle lying on a tattered burlap sack.

Now he worked more quickly. Five yards to the left and three yards toward the sea was an area covered with a rusty piece of tin. He moved the metal aside and found a loose accumulation of earth beneath it. Kneeling and using his hands, he shoveled the dirt away and finally, as promised, half-buried in the ground, was an old sea chest. He swung the lid open, resenting the noise of the rusty hinges. Neatly stacked inside the chest was the clothing change.

Now he peeled off his wet suit and proceeded to change identities. There was a pair of coarse chino pants, a faded openneck shirt and a floppy straw hat. Mud-encrusted, sturdy leather choes completed the outfit. He smiled at the precision accuracy of the planning—the clothing fitted him perfectly, he was as comfortable in his new garb as a *campesino,* a peasant, of the mountains. There was also an old wallet with a supply of money to supplement what he'd brought along in his money belt. He found, carefully wrapped in foil, a few pieces of fruit, which he stuffed into his pockets. And there was a message: the single word "present." He understood its significance. There had been rumors that his target might be leaving the island for a few weeks, but apparently that would not be the case. Which would, of course, simplify his task.

Nearby he sighted an abandoned pineapple grove going to seed. The chest, not heavy, was lugged to the grove and broken into pieces that were concealed in the heavy underbrush. Next he used his knife to cut up the wet suit into tiny pieces, which he scattered about in the dense thicket. He was ready to move on—

Loud voices, the revving of motors, the sky punctuated by moving beams of light originating from the beaches below. No doubt of it—a search party. Somehow his arrival had not gone unnoticed, despite the careful preparations. Did the peasant with the dog see him, after all? Or, worse, had the men who'd commissioned him decided to abort the mission—which meant he was, to put it mildly, expendable? *Had he been set up?*

He rushed back to the small road that had brought him to the woodland, turned eastward and ran down the road's shoulder full-out. No point in saving his stamina for any final kick in this race. It was all a home stretch. The noises from the beach grew fainter as he ran, but still he challenged his body and ran even harder. He fought for breath, the pain was a knife, his overworked lungs screaming for relief. He could not allow himself the luxury of slowing down. A quarter mile, another quarter and still another and then, in the distance, he spotted a wooded area that seemed to offer some protection if he could reach it. There were no voices now, but he would not look up to see if the searchlights were darkened. He only knew he was nearing the small forest, and just as his breath gave out he reached the woodland and collapsed into its womb, wrenching his left ankle as he fell headlong into a nest of brambles. He grabbed for the gun strapped to his chest— an empty gesture . . . his enemy was a heavy vine wrapped around his foot. He pulled it free and winced from the effort. Lying on his back, gulping huge draughts of air to refill his lungs, he twisted the foot in all directions, then sat up to test the ankle. It was a sprain, but fortunately a mild one. It shouldn't bother him too much by morning. He loosened his boot to provide breathing space for the natural swelling that would soon come. He stood and moved quickly again, deeper into the woodland. Again he fell, reinjuring the same ankle and adding bramble scratches on his face and hands. He picked himself up slowly and moved inland once again.

The insect world wasted no time in discovering its newest banquet, descending now on and around his face, hair and neck. He had to find a place to spend the rest of the night and decided, considering his ankle, that it would have to be where he was. He located a small, easy-to-climb palm tree, swung from one of the lower branches to test its strength, and having satisfied himself that it would hold his weight, swung his body in an arc until his feet had found a higher limb. Pushing himself forward until he straddled the limb, he moved carefully, slowly, until he found a nest at the crotch formed by the limb and the tree's trunk. He settled in and waited for the sun to rise, calculating that full daylight was at most about four hours away. There would be no sleep tonight, but the sun would bring more meaning than just a new day . . . It would mean he had survived.

Chapter Twelve

February Sixth—Morning

Martin got down from the tree as the first rays of the sun peeked over the horizon, and gingerly tested his left ankle. He was grateful to discover that the pain was gone. He squeezed the flesh, and though there was a minor amount of swelling there should be no serious problem. He jumped up and down a few times, turned it to right and left, all with good results.

He wished there were water to wash in and drink but that could wait. He remembered the fruit in his pocket, removed a large orange, peeled it and gorged himself on the luscious pulp, sucking the tangy juice to relieve his thirst. There was a slightly squashed and unripened banana and this, too, he swallowed.

He squatted, examined a small map he carried in a leather pouch attached to his money belt, and calculated his present position as one mile east and a few hundred yards south of the outskirts of La Esperanza. To the west and slightly north was the city of San Antonio de los Baños, population approximately twenty-three thousand. He figured the distance was just under ninety kilometers. With luck he could get there by noon. He'd taken care not to write down the names of any of his intended contacts. Only a fool would record such information.

The sun had risen fully now and its piercing heat was already evaporating the morning dew. He treaded cautiously to avoid any more tripping accidents and headed toward the road, where the noise of motors in the distance informed him that others were also awake. He kneeled at the edge of the small forest that had hidden him and peered in both directions. Apparently there was no search being conducted and as the first few trucks passed by he was confident that, for the moment at least, he was safe.

Traffic increased now and the line of farmers' trucks grew longer, most filled with pineapples and tobacco, a few with plantains and bananas. An ancient pickup truck chugged along, wheezing as though with emphysema. Almost on cue it rattled past his hiding place, slowed down, and staggered to a halt by the side of the road. It seemed the perfect opportunity. He moved onto the road and followed to the spot where the old vehicle was parked. There the cursing farmer, having lifted the hood, was gazing at the mysteries within.

"*Buenos días, señor.*"

"*Buenos?*" the farmer questioned. "And what is so good about a morning that begins with the truck going dead?"

"Perhaps I can help?" Palma—it was the moment to completely assume the new identity, including the name—asked. He had already moved the farmer aside, rolling up his sleeves and testing here and there under the hood. Luck was with him for the trouble was really easily cured. "Here"—he pointed—"here's your trouble. The distributor cap. It worked its way loose and caused a short. You have a wrench or pliers?"

"I'll get them," the farmer answered, obviously relieved.

8 0

He produced the tools and in a matter of minutes Palma had the cap back in place, the wires reattached. "Go start her up," he said. The ancient vehicle coughed and chugged, then, belching black smoke, ran again.

"I thank you, my friend," the farmer said. "I'm heading for Güines, can I give you a lift?"

"Fine," said Palma. "I won't go all the way with you, but part of the trip anyhow." He had thought of mentioning his specific destination, but decided against it. No sense giving out information that later might be recalled on interrogation. He knew the terrain well enough to realize that anyone driving from La Esperanza to Güines must go through San Antonio de los Baños, so at the proper moment he'd just say good-by and take off. Perhaps the old man would not even remember where he had let him off.

Despite the intense heat, which had already seized the island, the trip was pleasant and, more important, uneventful. The farmer explained that he was heading for an independent farmers' market held at Güines three times a week. There, by barter and cash sale, a man could gain an edge on the ever-rising cost of living. A limited amount of individual enterprise was permitted even on the larger state-owned farms, and smaller farms, limited in size to one hundred sixty acres, were still operated in many cases by private landowners. This fellow was just such an individual entrepreneur and he watched for every opportunity to market his crop of pineapples for the highest profit. With many mouths to feed and taxes always climbing, he found himself on the road almost every week. Palma was happy for a chance to try out his conversational Spanish. Apparently he had not lost his touch, because the farmer chatted amiably and asked no embarrassing questions.

It was a long, slow trip to San Antonio de los Baños but he was a dry desk blotter absorbing information, impressions . . . it had been seventeen years since he had fled this country as a young well-born millionaire at twenty-five. Despite his hatred for the man who had made his exile a necessity, despite his often-stated hope that the Revolution would some day fail, despite the tingling nerve endings resulting from his role as invader and would-be assassin, it was good to be home again. The countryside seemed little changed and yet things were somehow different. He decided that it was a new feeling of determination in the faces of those he saw walking the roads and riding by in newer, if not new, vehicles.

"Life is sometimes hard these days," he said, breaking the long silence.

"Not like the old days," the farmer answered. "Now we have food. The doctor comes when we need him. I have seven children and all go to school. Fidel says it will be better still in five more years."

"He should know," the rider commented, hoping his sarcasm didn't come through.

"El Comandante usually does. He tells us we must work hard for the better life. We do and life improves. True?"

"Positively, he is the best man."

This was a strange time to reexamine his motives for taking on this assignment. Was it possible that his feelings were completely biased because of his own financial interests? Could this man really be Cuba's savior and could he be completely twisted in considering him a true enemy of the people? Be careful . . . he had no room for such doubt, he needed total dedication to get through the days ahead. What about the political prisoners? . . . no trials . . . thousands of decent people, many his friends, who without cause or justification were still in political prisons at La Cabena or the Isle of Pines? What about the nuns who were stripped nude in the cloisters on phony grounds of harboring secrets against the state? No, this man, he reassured himself, *was* a proper target . . .

They stopped at a relatively modern gasoline station, and

he offered to pay for some of the fuel. At first the driver refused, but with insistence he got the man to accept a few pesos. It was his first expenditure—but money should not be a problem if his prearranged channel stayed open. He bought two soft drinks and handed one to the driver, who protested weakly, "But you are my guest." And then their trip resumed.

"I am Teodoro Escobar," the old man said. "How do you call yourself?"

He realized that this would be the very first time he would hear himself speak the assumed name although during the pressure-packed weeks of preparation he had often repeated it to accustom himself to the sound of the words, the feel of them . . . "Carlos Palma."

"Ah, I knew a lot of Palmas in my youth. You have a cousin named Ruben?"

"No cousins who are men. Only girls, I'm afraid."

"I knew a Josefina Palma once." He took one hand off the steering wheel and made an arc to indicate big breasts. "Ah, *beldad!*"

"I knew a cow once who was bigger," Palma said, and with that he turned away further questioning.

They approached a road sign now announcing four kilometers to San Antonio, and Palma decided that now was the opportune time to make his move.

"I think I'll get off here," he said suddenly. "I have friends who live just a kilometer or two back in the woods and I am going to surprise them. Take your time and pull over here, please."

The driver did, they shook hands, exchanged thanks and the old vehicle wheezed off as Palma took to the shoulder of the road to find some shade from the punishing heat of the afternoon sun and headed for San Antonio de los Baños.

With a population of approximately twenty-three thousand, San Antonio de los Baños was large enough to offer some reasonable degree of anonymity, small enough to make contact with his underground connection. It would also call for great caution. Despite his good luck so far this morning, Martin wasn't yet convinced that government authorities had abandoned their search for the man who had landed at La Esperanza. He had to believe that his arrival was responsible for the noisy search, the searchlights and the concomitant excitement on the beaches . . .

Life was bustling in the small marketplace in the center of San Antonio. Shops were filled with buyers and the ubiquitous peddlers with their open carts were apparently doing a thriving business. School children on their way home from their studies were running about, joyful over escaping the discipline of their schoolmasters. It indeed seemed to Martin a newly energized Cuba, with traditions of siesta being ignored. He moved about nonchalantly, eager to find the municipal building and determined to ask for guidance only when absolutely essential. The end of the work day was still two hours off and time was on his side.

In the Bureau of Health, Rolando Duran was busy completing a report on the provincial incidence of malnutrition. Early indications were favorable and despite lack of meat, diseases relating to protein deficiency were rare. These statistics would please the chief in Havana and support Duran's claims often made in country-wide medical conferences, and his own bureaucratic progress would now be accelerated.

Duran was annoyed when his clerk informed him that he was wanted on the telephone. A Señor Palma insisted upon being put through. The report would have to wait.

"Duran here. Who is this?"

"Palma. Carlos Palma."

"I don't recall your name. What is your business?"

"I have news of new laboratory equipment. And, incidentally, I bring greetings from Pepe. He says you are old friends."

There was a pause. The name "Pepe" had its prearranged meaning for Duran but it also brought warning that he must not react too quickly.

"And how is his dear old aunt?"

"Cintia is quite well, thank you. She, too, asks to be remembered to you."

The code name and verification were in order. One last check could not hurt. The costs for error were too high.

"And where is she living now?"

"Still at San Pedro."

All seemed secure. "I am really quite busy now finalizing a very important survey. I cannot see you in my office today."

"I am only in town for a short time. Perhaps after work we could meet for a drink?"

"Fine. There is a little tavern—El Fragua—at four-thirty. We can chat about your laboratory equipment there."

"That will be good. I saw that tavern down the street as I came from the marketplace. I drink only white wine and I'm sure they have the best. Good-by."

At precisely four-thirty Rolando Duran strolled into El Fragua, casting his eye from table to table in a rapid sweep. Most of the early customers were government workers he easily recognized. Toward the rear of the room, at a table that commanded a clear view of the entire premises, sat a roughly garbed peasant sipping a glass of white wine. Their eyes met and identification was made. Duran approached Palma and extended his hand. It was warmly grasped.

"It's kind of you to meet with me on such short notice. Pepe told me that I could depend on you for a good hearing. My equipment is the best and it is manufactured in Mexico, from which it can be easily shipped."

"We are always in need of new equipment. I'm happy Pepe sent you to me. How long can you stay in town?"

"Three days, perhaps four. I know I told you on the phone that I was just passing through, but you will forgive an old salesman. We all lie a little just to make a sale."

Both men laughed. Duran ordered a beer and Martin re-filled his own glass from a bottle that sat on the table.

"And where will you stay? There is no hotel active in this city. There was one once, but now it's a clinic . . . We have more injections than tourists."

"That may be a problem. You are my only friend in San Antonio de los Baños."

"No problem. I live alone and there's a wide couch in my living room. I'm a bachelor and usually don't cook, but we will find a way to keep you from starving."

"You are very kind, but I ate while waiting for you to finish work. Frankly, what I really could use is some sleep. Let's say that my quarters last night were less than first class. The view was fine, understand. So much so I stayed up all night just watching."

"I understand. Drink up then and we'll go along to my home. It's small but adequate."

Martin didn't realize the extent of his own weariness. Nervous energy had stimulated him to a point where he'd forgotten that nearly forty-eight hours had passed since he had closed his eyes. The moment he lay down he drifted off and neither dreams nor anticipation of what lay ahead disturbed him. He awoke at two in the morning and found a note from Duran.

"I am in the bedroom. Please wake me but do not disturb the lights." Only a small table lamp illuminated the premises. Walking into the bedroom as he had been directed, he shook his host lightly and Duran was immediately awake. They moved back into the parlor and by his hushed tones Duran let him know the need for security.

"They know you are on the island . . . Actually they don't know it is *you*, but there were definite reports of a landing at La Esperanza. A signal was received on the sound-detection equipment, and a local told the police that his dog barked and acted strangely, especially when he returned to the road above the beaches."

"How can you know all this?" Palma asked, almost suspiciously.

"It's a story that we hear many, many times. It was in this evening's governmental news reports and I went out and bought the evening paper while you slept. Here, see for yourself."

It was a featured story. "MORE SPY LANDINGS" was the headline.

> "Coast Guard authorities at La Esperanza report receiving signals of new illicit landings on our northwestern coast. According to Captain Juan Metilos there can be little question that one or more spies, undoubtedly sent by the CIA, landed there last night. A man walking a dog in the early morning hours gave reports of his animal acting strangely and barking loudly as he walked above the beaches. A thorough search was unsuccessful, but the intruder or intruders will be found, as they always are."

"They waste no time spreading the word."

"True. You must understand that these people think Fidel is their savior. They are totally loyal. The government realizes this and by spreading the word of any landings—real or imagined—they make allies of the whole peasant population in their actions against spies and intruders. But some of us . . . well, El Comandante and his people *have* done some good things, but we know about the bad that far outweigh them which is why we work to overthrow him."

"Well, this newspaper story can cause me trouble—"

"It can, true. You must be doubly cautious. Tomorrow there will be government troops asking questions in every town and city. I assume you have identification."

"Of course."

". . . How do you plan to get close to him?"

Martin hadn't forgotten his basic training. No matter how

8 7

helpful a stranger might be, no matter how open he was, you looked on him with a reserve of healthy mistrust and you lived to tell the tale. The moment had come to apply the brakes.

"Truthfully, my plans haven't yet reached that level. I have confidence there is a way and I will find it."

He couldn't be sure whether Rolando Duran was offended or not, but there was no alternative for him. Duran at least got the point and would ask no more such direct questions. Instead he raised a problem. Having completed his report on malnutrition he was to take it to Havana the next day to discuss it with his superiors. It was only about twenty-five kilometers, an easy bus ride, but Palma would have to fend for himself. He could, of course, remain in the house. Except that would not bring him any closer to his objective. If he needed time to gather information, Duran made it clear that it was safe for him to use his home as temporary headquarters. The decision, of course, was his. On the other hand, if he decided to move to Havana, it would be best that they travel alone and not risk open association.

Martin elected to stay behind for at least twenty-four hours. In making this decision he was troubled by one particular doubt: when they had met in the tavern Duran had offered to be his host for three or four days and had made no mention of any upcoming trip to Havana. Was it just something he had forgotten, or overlooked? Unlikely. Had he thought that Palma could safely look out for himself? It all could be very innocuous, but the inconsistency was noted, and it bothered him.

"You make your trip to Havana. I know this country. I had a girl friend who lived in this town once and my uncle's father-in-law was the postmaster. So go ahead. I'll be here when you get back. Maybe you can bring me some late word on our friend's whereabouts. I have a message to deliver to him, and I want him to get it soon."

Duran left for Havana early the next morning. An hour later Martin was on the street reliving his memories and making his plans. He was happy with his ability to mix and mingle with the populace and if anyone thought of him as a stranger there were no overt stares or comments. At noon he went into a small restaurant off the town square and ordered a meal of bread, beans and cold fish. He was served by a voluptuous waitress who, peering beneath the peasant costume, discerned a damn good-looking man who gave her ideas. On his part, Martin considered her a fine prospect for some quick relief.

"What's your name?" she asked.

"Christopher Columbus. Who are you, Joan of Arc?"

"My name is Rosita. Do I look like a saint?"

"Rosita, you look so hot you make me think of fire and that's why I thought of burning at the stake. My stake." In Spanish it sounded less ridiculous. Not much, though.

"You're a pretty fresh fellow. How do you know how hot I am, or maybe how cold?"

"Rosita, I am no fool. When I see a *woman,* I *know* how she is." His line was now so corny it sickened even him. But Rosita smiled, blushed just enough to be attractive. She would be finished with her work by two-thirty or three o'clock and then she would meet him in the small park just south of the marketplace. The rest of her day was his.

They met as arranged and chatted for an hour in the cool shade of a grove of palm trees that linked the park. He spotted the soldiers before she did but knew he could not afford to make or suggest any sudden departures. A small platoon, moving informally, entered the park and after brief consultation divided into teams of two and approached everyone who was seated inside the park. Since not to comment on them would be unnatural, Carlos referred to their arrival first.

"Ah, I see we have company. Probably looking for women to bed down with too. Well, they can't have mine!"

"That decision isn't yours . . . my God, you're conceited. And I am not yours either, yet. They are looking for spies, American spies. Don't you often see this in your town too?"

Although she hadn't yet asked him about his hometown and reason for visiting San Antonio, he decided the best answer was, "Of course. And they will find them, just as they always do. The local paper is right."

A few minutes later there were two soldiers standing beside their bench, requesting identification. Apparently they knew Rosita Florez; their examination of her papers was perfunctory. Their questions for Palma were, he thought, a bit more critical.

"Papers, please. Name?"

"Carlos Palma."

"Business in San Antonio de los Baños?"

"Sales. Medical equipment."

"Home?"

"Santiago de Cuba."

"Current mayor of that city?"

"Ramón de Jesús."

"Population?"

"About three hundred thousand."

"You enjoy the park Almeda de Paula?"

"That, my friend, is in Havana, not Santiago."

Apparently satisfied with Palma's replies, the soldier returned his papers to him, grunted thanks and moved on. Martin was instantly grateful for his homework on the city he was claiming as residence. Of course as a boy he'd visited there many, many times, but he'd taken the precaution to read up on current events there in pamphlets and news sources he'd obtained through Duncan.

"Not much sense of humor? Right?"

"No. A soldier's job isn't much fun these days. When they come into the bar they act much different. They flirt and laugh and raise hell. But once they are back on the street they are like little boys playing grown up. Always with the frowns

9 0

and the questions. Sometimes I think I will tell them I am working for the underground just to see how they react. I think they will run in fear."

"Better not try it. You might be surprised . . . Say, how about tonight, what will we do and where do we go?"

"And what did you have in mind?"

"That, too. But first, where do we eat and drink?"

Rosita told him, much to his surprise, that she had the use of a friend's car and suggested that they could have a great evening in Havana. Tomorrow would be a late day for her to report to work and she really was available tonight. It was an earlier visit to the capital than he'd wanted, but it might seem strange to refuse her offer, so he accepted.

He returned to Duran's home, borrowed shirt and slacks and enjoyed a quick shower. He'd worried at first about his credibility as a salesman in farmer's clothes, and then reminded himself that clothes definitely didn't make the man in Castro's Cuba—after all, El Comandante himself still affected the common soldier's garb in the most formal settings. Thirty minutes later he'd rejoined Rosita at the marketplace, where, true to her word, she was waiting for him in her friend's car. And in less than an hour they were circling the city via the Malecon, Havana's famous "string of pearls." For Martin, it was an emotional experience. He had not traveled these roads, seen these sights, for more than seventeen years. Even Rosita sensed that he was somehow moved.

"What's wrong, *caro*, you lose your tongue?"

"No. Just thinking."

"About what?"

"You. You and me. And our beautiful Havana."

"You are a poet. I think I shall beware of you. I don't trust myself with poets."

"Las mujures siempre se salen con la suya."

"Yes," she answered, "women do always get their own way, but poets have ways of changing their minds."

Later that evening, much to Rosita's delight, he agreed to

take her to the Moscow Restaurant, which she had described as the grandest club in town. There they dined on filet mignon, a Mexican import, tough but tasty, and washed down their food with a surprisingly delicate Beaujolais. A tangy, sharp imported Camembert was a delightful dessert. The tab for dinner alone came to more than seventy dollars in American money, and there was a charge for dancing and drinks later in the evening as well. Rosita was in heaven and kept questioning Carlos about whether he was spending himself into bankruptcy. He laughed and reassured her. At one point, though, Martin thought he recognized an old friend from his university days. He couldn't recall the man's name but recognized him as a fellow with whom he had played soccer. The man was seated on the other side of the dance floor so that they could not see each other that well, but at one point their eyes did meet, held for an instant, and moved on. It made him nervous, but he had anticipated such incidents and felt confident that his own physical changes in the seventeen years had provided their own brand of camouflage—his silver hair alone was effective disguise, not to mention his beard.

They drove back to San Antonio early in the morning, Rosita so blissful he felt he could have stopped the car and taken her by the side of the road. When they reached her small house he assumed he would be invited in and was surprised when she resisted. He finally extracted the explanation—yes, she wanted him too but was reluctant to keep him with her all night . . . she was still enough of a Catholic and product of her past to be uneasy and to worry about gossipy neighborhood tongues.

"You can't stay all night if I let you in."

"That's fine, I'll leave soon . . . but not too soon."

"But where will you stay? You didn't say where you are staying."

"I'm visiting an old friend right here in town."

"Do I know him?"

"Perhaps. He's with the Bureau of Health. Rolando Duran."

They were already inside the house and Rosita was busy drawing the blinds covering all but a few of the windows. He could not be sure but he thought he noted some reaction to the name. But all she said was, "Yes, I know him," and then he took her quickly in his arms and they exchanged a long, passionate embrace. His hands played across her body. She gasped for breath as he took off her clothing, lifted and carried her into the bedroom. He wasted no time as he mounted her, entered her and pumping furiously brought them both to climax. They lay wrapped in each other's arms for about fifteen silent minutes. Then he started again, and again it was consummated in primitive haste.

Later, as they dressed and Rosita put a pot of coffee on the range, she took his hand and looking closely at him, said, "*Caro*, I do not trust your friend."

"Oh . . . Rolando? Why not? He's always been a good man—"

"No. He is, how do you say it, a climber. One day he is on one side, the next day on the other. They tell me that he was strong for Fulgencio until Fidel became El Jefe. Then he was a political prisoner for a little while and came out like a trumpet for Fidel. Some people say he is a government spy, an agent who pretends he does not like Fidel but secretly works for him. Some also say that he has been known to disappear for months at a time and no one can explain his absences. No, I do not trust him."

"Maybe he's just a free spirit who travels—"

"No, Carlos, it is more than that. Last year he came back from one of his trips and he brought a young man with him who acted very strangely. Soon after, soldiers came and took him away. I heard one man say, 'Duran is the bait in the trap.' Do not trust him, *caro*."

Palma returned to Duran's home only long enough to

gather his few belongings. Whether or not there was real substance to Rosita's fears, or to his own queasiness over Duran's sudden decision to travel to Havana, he couldn't, of course, be certain. But he obviously couldn't afford the risk. He hiked out of town, again rejecting his need for sleep, and headed south toward Güira de Melena. Another night with Rosita Florez would have been delightful. But he had work to do.

Chapter Thirteen

February Eighth

It was well past midnight, roads and highways were deserted. Occasional passenger cars passed him but he resisted the temptation to seek a ride, fearing that a lone hiker at this hour might arouse suspicion. He had noted police and army vehicles on security patrols and since he was unable to identify them until they were alongside him, he would take to the underbush when distant headlights signaled an oncoming car. After hiking about three miles he came to a small woodland not unlike the one he had spent his first night ashore in. Having helped himself to an old blanket from Duran's house, he entered the woods, spread it in a well-shielded clearing and lay down to rest. After the sumptuous meal, the wine and the love-making, he was soon fast asleep.

He was awakened by the distant barking of a dog and found the sun well above the horizon and the temperature already rising sharply even in the shaded glen where he had camped for the night. A small stream nearby gave him the opportunity to wash and afterward he returned to the road and waited for a ride. It was only about twenty kilometers from San Antonio to Güira de Melena but there was no point in wearing himself out in the tropical heat.

He had considered the notion of leaving some sort of note or explanation at Duran's house but had decided against it. He had no proof that Rolando Duran was any sort of counter-agent, but Rosita Florez's warning had been enough to act on—or against. Besides, he still was suspicious of Duran's seemingly abrupt need to leave and go to Havana, and in any case there was no point in taking needless risk. He planned to call Duran at work one day soon and simply say that he had received unexpected orders to move on. He regretted that Duran knew what he looked like. If he were really a Castro agent, he was in serious trouble. There was always the chance, though, that Duran was working against the government and the seemingly pro-Castro acts that disturbed Rosita might have been to cover his tracks. Of course, he'd never revealed his assignment to Duran.

He hailed an open truck bearing a cargo of sugarcane, which came chugging down the highway. The driver was a humorless farmer in his mid-forties with a Fu Manchu mustache and dark slits of eyes that drilled through him.

"I'm heading for Güira de Melena. You're going that far?"

"*Si*. That far and beyond. Jump on. I'll carry you."

Palma's worry over Duran intensified his distrust of his companion, who just happened to come along . . . They rode silently for about five minutes before the driver spoke.

"My name is Adolfo Maso. Yours?"

"Carlos Palma."

"I live in Matanzas. And you?"

"Santiago de Cuba. Near there." He was carefully vague.

"What's your job? Farmer? Laborer?"

"A little of each. I take jobs where I find them. I harvest the sugar. Just like you. Sometimes I find work in the building trades but I'm no artisan, no real skill."

They drove on for a few more silent minutes but Adolfo Maso wasn't content. Perhaps he, too, had his suspicions. Perhaps innocent ones.

"What brings you to this area?"

"I've friends and relatives here. I work near here sometimes on the farms."

There was something about this laconic hitchhiker that interested Maso. The very fact that he was shifting about for a job caused suspicion. With sugar-harvesting time coming on, virtually any able-bodied adult could find employment. The one thing that the regime had provided was plenty of work. How well he remembered the old days before El Comandante when a man had to travel miles to find a day's labor, and then at pitiful wages. How often he'd seen his children cry themselves to sleep from hunger. That was all changed now under Fidel. Life was still brutal at times, true, but at least there was food for everyone and work if one was not lazy. This fellow was lazy, or maybe he was hiding something . . . Adolfo had always considered himself a good judge of character. There was something about this man's alert manner, his polished speech, that didn't quite fit his claim of a laborer picking up casual jobs. He decided to press for further details.

"You know, I am surprised. There are plenty of active farms operated by the state in the area of Santiago. Why travel so many kilometers west to find a job when you could have one easily at home?"

"You sound like my mother-in-law. She thinks I dodge work too. Calls me lazy . . ." He hoped this would satisfy, and for a moment considered getting off and looking for another ride, but that, of course, would have been much too obvious. He decided he'd best tough it out and try to divert the man.

"Well, I'm not your wife's mother, but when a man in Cuba today—especially at harvest time—travels so far for a job, well, it is a little unusual, no?"

"Yes, I guess so. The truth is I didn't tell you all of the facts . . ."

"Oh?"

"It's a little personal but I don't mind telling you, you seem like a trustworthy fellow. My father-in-law is the supervisor of several state-operated sugar plantations around Santiago. My wife and I have been fighting and she caught me having an affair with a young girl who helps with our children. She went to her father, he had me fired, and I had to move out. So I came here hoping friends could find me work on a temporary basis. Then, when it all blows over, I'll go back to my woman and we'll make up. It's happened once before like that."

"Ah, I understand."

But he didn't. Adolfo Maso was suspicious by nature. Working four years as a guard of political prisoners on the Isle of Pines had sharpened his mistrust of his fellow human beings. He'd joined the Revolutionary forces just before they triumphed over Batista and his reward had been the political plum of a uniformed job guarding prisoners. He couldn't cope with the authority of the job and soon started showing sadistic tendencies. From the earliest days, Castro announced that the sole purpose of political interment was the rehabilitation of the prisoner and the conversion of his family to Revolutionary precepts. Any cruel or sadistic treatment of those in custody was denounced by the top authorities. But national policy and local administration were often widely separated, and Adolfo's reputation soon brought him into open conflict with his superiors. After repeated warnings he was fired and returned to his home, where he resumed his life as a farmer. At first he was bitter but after years he had mellowed and felt that perhaps he had betrayed El Jefe and therefore redoubled his loyalties in order to justify his original failure. In his own mind he operated as an unofficial guardian of the national regime and was constantly mistrustful of strangers. Martin's thumb had flagged down a dangerous, even paranoid enemy.

Maso concocted a simple scheme to test his doubts about his passenger. He'd engage him in easy conversation about local happenings and test just how well informed he was.

"Santiago is a good city for sports. I love to go there to watch the football, that Munoz fellow is as good as Pelé."

"Well, Pelé is the best in the world . . ." He didn't know who the hell Munoz was.

Actually, there was no Munoz and Santiago had not had a decent soccer team in ten years. Maso thought Palma was being shrewdly evasive. He was right.

"How do you feel about the recent elections?"

"A long time coming, right?"

"Yes. But now we're ready for self-government. Not before. Do you agree?"

"Well, it does take a lot of years to develop mature judgment. I agree with Fidel on that."

Now, Maso's nose truly began to twitch. His chance guest was saying the right things but he was definitely avoiding specifics, such as that anybody over sixteen could now vote. He waited another few minutes.

"I see you agree with most things our leader says . . . Do you think it's fair to suppress the voodoo cults? After all, these people are all good Cubans and if they want to believe in the dark arts, why should the government persecute them?"

"The government must decide what's good for all of the people. I'm not an expert on all these complicated matters . . ."

Again, the stranger was proper but evasive, or at least strangely uninformed. El Comandante had given the same freedoms as any other religious group to the voodoo cultists even though their teachings were against socialism. Maso also recalled hearing the government radio blaring news of new spy landings in this general area, and there was that story of the peasant walking his dog the other night and suspecting trouble near La Esperanza. Could this just possibly be an infiltrator riding alongside him? Maso, feeling very important and excited, would check.

"I will have to stop for gas. This old pirate drinks it up like a cat lapping fresh milk. There is a service station over there, we won't be long." And he steered the truck onto the station grounds.

Martin's general uneasiness had grown during the last few minutes. He more than suspected that he was being interrogated for good reason. Nor was he sure that his answers hadn't been too vague. Even though Maso quickly shut off the ignition so that he could not get an immediate reading, he had noticed earlier that the truck had a full gas tank and there was no way it could have used up so much fuel in so short a drive.

A hurried and whispered conversation between Maso and the station attendant was rather obvious in its meaning. This man might be inept, but he was distinctly dangerous. Of course, it was possible that Maso was only explaining why he had stopped for gasoline when his truck had a full tank. The attendant, certainly no actor, stole a glance at Martin as he stepped from the truck, which told the whole story. He would have to move, and quickly.

"I need a toilet. You have a clean one here?" he asked the gas-station man.

"*Si*. Here, I carry the key. It is in the back around that way," he said, pointing.

Martin took the key and headed for the rest room. He continued walking, however, circled the small building and watched the two men from the other side. They soon separated, the attendant moving into his little shacklike office, and Maso heading for a phone booth that sat precariously on the front edge of the property. Assuring himself that the attendant was engaged in other matters, Martin reached into his shirt and removed the six-inch, razor-sharp stiletto he carried

1 0 0

in a body sheath. Walking almost on tiptoes, he approached the booth from the blind side and as he drew near could hear Maso negotiating with the long-distance operator for a line to Santiago de Cuba. He heard him mention in a near-whisper the words "identification bureau" and "prefecture of police."

He swiftly drew up beside Maso, pressed the knife against his ribs. "Ring off." Maso's eyes brushed the weapon. He obeyed. "Get in the truck and drive east." He kept the dagger pressed to Maso's side. Maso had used a dagger on enough prisoners to respect its power—and his sadism was not matched by his courage. He returned to the truck and took the wheel. Since the rear window of the truck's cab was missing, it was an easy job for Martin to keep the dagger pressed against his neck as he climbed on the sugarcane cargo and quickly slipped into the passenger's seat. On his sharp command, Maso started the vehicle and drove off, his attention divided between the traffic ahead and the dagger now pressed to his ribs.

"Keep your eye on traffic," Martin ordered.

Moments later the attendant came running from his shanty, realizing that the truck had left and that he had been bilked out of payment for three gallons of gas. He shouted down the road after them, then realized it was futile. He decided that he had really been taken, that the driver's story about the dangerous spy he had picked up was probably just a trick to cheat him out of his money. No use to call the police. They would laugh at him. He would simply have to watch for that truck again and see that he got his money. Shrugging philosophically, he returned to the station to take care of an impatient customer. It was the result Martin hoped for, but of course couldn't be sure of.

Now he spotted a deserted stretch of road and ordered Maso to pull over. Pressing the dagger against his neck, he ordered him out and forced him to take off his shoes and socks. The shoes were tossed away and the socks used for binding the man's wrists behind him. After which Martin took over the wheel and continued eastward.

They drove on in virtual silence for nearly three hours. Maso was smart enough not to protest or to engage this man in any conversation that might antagonize him. Once he offered some suggestion about the road they were taking but Martin simply told him to keep quiet and that he knew exactly where he was heading. As he reached higher ground near Fomento, he found an old hiking path that led into the hills nearly two thousand feet above sea level. There was no other vehicular traffic moving in either direction. Finding a spot that was completely desolate, he ordered Maso from the truck and headed him higher into the hills, which were now crowned with heavier vegetation.

He knew what he must do. He had disliked this fellow from the moment he had met him. The man was his enemy and he could not afford to let him escape. But he wanted him quiet and unsuspecting; the uninformed victim was the easiest to handle.

"I'm going to tie you here. Your friends will find you before you starve, unfortunately." He removed Maso's belt and bound his body, face inward, around a young, sturdy sapling. Maso grimaced but didn't resist. Apparently he was relieved that this was to be his worst fate; he had had visions of beatings, torture, even death—which would have been his way if the roles were reversed.

"*Adiós*, man," Martin said quietly, "and next time you should be a better host." He never knew if Maso had fashioned a reply. With one strong movement he plunged the knife deep into the man's back, rupturing the left lung and the heart with the same stroke. A gush of forced air and billows of deep, red blood gushed from the victim's mouth. He fell forward against the tree. Death was almost instantaneous. As he pulled the knife free, Martin realized that it had been seven years since he'd killed a man in combat in the very same fashion. Strangely, he had felt more compassion then; he'd had no chance to build up any personal animosity against that specific enemy.

He waited a few minutes, smoking a cigarette to calm himself. Next, he loosened the belt that held the body to the tree. Lowering the man's pants and undershorts was now a simple process with the belt already removed. He pulled the body by the legs into a nearby clump of thorny bushes and stamped on the ground repeatedly, to give the suggestion of a struggle. He slashed both pockets and removed what money he found. He also removed driver's license and all identification papers to make the job of the police, if and when they found him, even more difficult. Then, turning the body face downward, he slashed the man between the buttocks, cutting into the anus to create the impression of homosexual assault. He wiped the dagger blade clean, kicked grass and twigs and branches over the body, then hurried to the truck. Completing a U-turn, he headed back toward Güira, with a strange new feeling of commitment to the job ahead. Now there could be no reassessment, no hesitation, no retreat.

He figured he had at least twenty-four hours before the man who thought he was heading to the sugar market would be missed. Forty-eight hours, if he was lucky. He would play it safe, heading for Güira de Melena and searching out his next contact. He would have preferred a custom limousine to carry him back, but the open truck loaded with cane would have to do. And he was still alive and on target.

Chapter Fourteen

February Eighth—Late Afternoon

Contrary to his expectations, Martin felt little remorse over the killing. Maso had been a disagreeable lout from the moment he'd picked him up. More important, he represented the enemy and what he had done, Martin rationalized, he had done to preserve his own life. There could be no question that Maso had every intention of turning him in to the authorities, which would have meant not only the end of his mission, but probably of his life as well.

The sun was completing its arc of the heavens as his watch told him it was late afternoon. There was no way to reach Güira de Melena before dark. He had no fear of driving the highways at night. Actually, the darkness offered some protection. He felt that at best the disappearance of Maso would be discovered within twelve to twenty-four hours. Perhaps he would not be reported as missing for as long as two days. Even so, since he had been heading in the direction of Güira when he stopped to give Martin a lift, the chances were that he had friends in that area who might recognize the truck and wonder why a stranger was at the wheel. No, it was not wise to arrive in Güira at night and face the problem of finding housing in a strange city.

He turned northward and traveled about ten miles until he reached one of Cuba's main arteries, the Carretera Central, which at this hour was flooded with traffic. Turning left, he headed west. A road sign informed him that he must travel at least two hundred and fifty kilometers to reach his goal, the village of Guane on the southwestern tip of the island. He could not push this old steamer too fast, forty miles per hour at best, and that meant he would not reach his destination until at least one or two in the morning. He had better call ahead and make sure that he was expected.

He stopped for gas and asked for a phone. There was a dilapidated phone booth at the rear of the station affording privacy. All of the numbers he needed had long since been committed to memory.

"This is Alicia Ortiz speaking. May I help you?"

"My name is Carlos Palma. I am Myra Rubin's friend."

"I know no Myra Rubin."

"She asked me to remember her to you. She sends word of her deep grief over the passing of Jorge. I am her friend, and yours."

There was a pause as the listener considered whether recognition was safe. "And where was she born, this Myra Rubin?"

"She came from New York City, from the Bronx, and studied with me at the University of Havana long before our beloved leader attacked the Barracks of Moncado and started the revolution that has saved our people."

"True. And how does this Myra Rubin know me?"

"When you were first doing your practice teaching at Santiago de Cuba she was part of a governmental commission studying reorganization of farm cooperatives. A mutual friend,

Jaime Sanchez, who was a co-worker with your husband, introduced you."

If this were a government ploy, certainly this man Palma had his facts well in order. If the government were trying to trick her, certainly they had gone to a tremendous amount of trouble to research her background. She finally decided to take the risk, even though she knew that as the widow of Jorge Ortiz she would never be entirely safe from suspicion and harassment.

"Yes . . . I remember Myra . . . And why do you call?"

"I am coming to your village tonight. I am driving a truck with sugarcane, which I intend to deliver first thing tomorrow. I need a place to sleep tonight, and some advice as well."

"Do you know the area?"

"Not well. How will I find your home?"

"As you come in the main street, we have renamed it 'Twenty-sixth Street,' you will see a small market and then a church and a school on either side of a large playground. Travel another half-kilometer and you will come to a water fountain. Turn right here about a hundred meters and you will see a row of houses. Mine is the last one, on the right, yellow stucco with white curtains and a large wrought-iron gate in front of the garden. I will keep the light on and wait for you. Can you remember the directions?"

"Yes. It should be between one and two o'clock."

"*Buenas noches.* I will see you then."

About two kilometers before reaching town there was a wide arc in the road, then a short bridge crossing over a deep gorge. The land below seemed wild and undeveloped, and as he crossed the bridge he realized the foolishness of driving the stolen truck into a deserted village at one o'clock in the morning. He stopped, circled back and parked by the side of the road, carefully dousing the headlights. As a further precaution, he removed the license tags. When he was convinced that he was completely alone with no possible witnesses coming down the road, he released the emergency brake, started the truck rolling, and mounting the ancient running board on the driver's side, steered the vehicle toward the gorge. At the very last moment he jumped to safety and watched the old crate hurtle to its final grave, bouncing noisily several hundred feet until it rested at the bottom of the gorge. With no fire or explosion, the sleeping countryside was undisturbed by the muffled crash. He hiked the final distance into town and even the neighborhood dogs showed little interest in him as he walked to the water fountain, turned right and approached the home of Alicia Ortiz, where he found the light burning as promised.

She was so incredibly beautiful that he actually gasped when she opened the door to admit him. John Martin had been noted for his appreciation of magnificent women. Even his wife Margaret, increasingly cold and unbending in their years together, was a beautiful blonde with delicate features and gray eyes, reminding one of the finest watercolor painted on Dresden china. His latest companion, Billie Lane, had been a runner-up Miss Universe, stood five feet ten in her bare feet, measured forty-one at the bust, with a twenty-four inch waist, and though her face hardly gave off character, she had been cover girl on a score of magazines. So beautiful women were no new experience for him. But as he stood there in the half-light of early morning he was mesmerized by this woman's appearance. Even on a mission such as this a man's juices didn't stop.

"Please enter, señor. Welcome to Guane."

He followed her into the living room. The house was small but tasteful. Whereas most of the Cuban homes he had seen had large open windows with little or no treatment such as draperies or curtains, hers were decorated with the finest imported lace that also shielded her from the eyes of her neighbors. A small but lovely blue Oriental rug warmed the cold white marble of the floor. Wicker easy chairs and sofas, cushioned in sapphire blue, gave a feeling of tropical living but avoided the bulkiness that would have given the small house a feeling of being overcrowded. Reproductions of Impressionist masters graced the walls, and a small but elegant crystal chandelier beckoned from the dining area that adjoined.

But Alicia Ortiz herself was the jewel that commanded attention in this delightful setting. She stood about five feet seven, extremely tall for her Spanish background and generation. Her hair was jet black, pulled to the side with a jeweled comb, and left to hang down below the small of her back. Her body was well shaped. Her skin was creamy white and a long aquiline nose formed a ridge between two of the blackest, deepest-welled eyes he'd ever seen. Martin thought of a Jewish girl friend he'd traveled with for a short time in Miami Beach who also was beautiful and whom he'd nicknamed "Queen Isabella." She didn't compare to Queen Ortiz. He felt like a damn schoolboy, staring at her. She smiled, motioning for him to take a chair and excusing herself, finally, to pour them both a cooling drink.

"I'm sorry to break in on you this way. Myra assured me that you were a friend who would help me—"

"I'm happy to do my part. I had word to expect you."

"I thought you might not remember her, on the basis of our phone conversation . . ."

"She was my best friend for years. But one can't be too careful these days. You can stay as long as is necessary. There is a small room that I use for guests in the back of the house."

"Aren't you worried about your neighbors? What will we tell them?"

"We'll explain to the old lady who lives next door that you are a man I met in Mexico City while on vacation. We plan to marry one day as soon as you can find work and settle your affairs in that country."

"I'm a pretty lucky fellow. I not only have found a place to sleep but a beautiful bride as well." When she didn't answer, he went on, "Myra tells me that you're a schoolteacher here in Guane."

"Yes, I teach elementary grades in the village school. During the days, you will be on your own while I am at work, but I usually get home about three in the afternoon. The less you move about the town, the better. You look exhausted. Why not turn in now and we can make our plans tomorrow when classes end?"

He slept soundly and did not even hear her leave for work. Getting up about ten o'clock, he helped himself to breakfast as she'd directed and, selecting a book from her small but ample library, spent the midday reading and organizing his thoughts for what was ahead. She returned at three and at her suggestion they went for a walk so that her neighbors would catch their first glimpses of him. The gossip mills would start churning right away and then they would feed their story of the Mexico City rendezvous to the old lady next door, who would serve as the town crier. It was a lovely, balmy day and the easing sun was just warm enough for comfort. They met only one neighbor on their walk, an old fellow who operated a roadside vegetable stand. As agreed between them, she called Martin "Gilberto," a name he was to use during his stay in her home. This would be her affectionate name for him, but if asked for official identification he would still call himself "Carlos Palma." It was another precautionary red herring to help in shielding his true identity.

Back home once again, she asked directly, "And how can I be of help to you?"

"My aim is to somehow make contact with someone in the upper echelons of the national government. Official sources in the States have given me a list of contacts, but frankly I don't trust them and will use them only if necessary . . . Is there any way you can get me introduced to some bigshots in Havana, so that I'd be in a better position to observe my . . . subject?"

She looked at him. "I have one idea. But let's talk about it later. I really have to do some shopping if we're to have dinner."

"Can't we dine out? I'd like to reciprocate."

"Not yet. There will be time. Walk with me to the market. And, incidentally, Carlos, you'd better show a little more affection in public or nobody will believe that we're planning to be married one day soon."

"*That* will be a pleasure."

They strolled to the marketplace arm in arm and were aware of the stir they were making among the gossip-hungry people of Guane. Even in the cast-off clothing that had belonged to her husband, this Palma was a very striking man. The silver beard was full and luxuriant now and his Moorish profile suggested the dignity of a Spanish nobleman. It was in all senses a pleasant stroll and both Martin and Alicia soon became aware that the attraction between them was transcending that of coconspirators. Given half a chance . . .

After they had done their marketing Alicia suggested they leave their bundles at the butcher's and continue their walk in the late afternoon sun. They had been walking for perhaps twenty minutes when suddenly the sleepy torpor of the market area was galvanized into action. Several army vehicles rolled into town, followed by the blaring siren of the police chief's new command car, the toy he paraded in full action whenever the opportunity presented itself. About three minutes later a tow truck drove into town, pulling behind it the battered remains of the Maso truck that Martin had propelled over the embankment the night before. He realized that he had not told Alicia about this and wondered if he should have. Best, he thought, to keep silent for now and continue their stroll.

Soon more soldiers appeared and jumped from their trucks in near-military maneuver. In effect they cordoned off the area and the townspeople in the market area were seined like fish in a net. The commanding officer in charge of the company faced the townspeople and called them to attention by a large bullhorn.

"Comrades, a loyal citizen has been found brutally murdered about two hundred fifty kilometers to the east. His truck was found at noon crashed over the hill in the gorge that lies just outside your city. Does anyone here know of any reason to suspect anyone else of this murder? Remember that El Comandante tells us that our first loyalty is to our national community, more than to our friends, to our neighbors, even to our family. Speak now, or be silent, providing you are certain you are not withholding information."

He looked from face to face, pausing just long enough to peer at each. All were silent. Alicia already suspected the person responsible but she peered back at the military man as if she were in school disciplining one of her errant pupils. Martin faced the officer, their eyes met briefly, and then the soldier moved on to the man standing next to him. The facial inquisition took about five minutes—the silence was deafening. Finally the officer tired of the game and once again addressed the crowd: "Please remain near or in your homes tonight in case we should want to question you individually."

The crowd scattered and Alicia and Martin moved casually back to the Ortiz home.

"Do you want to tell me?"

"Yes . . ."—what real choice did he have since she obviously suspected?—"He was my chauffeur and tried to turn me in. I had no alternative. I saw no point in telling you—"

"If you want me to help I think it best you tell me *everything*. I might have been able to save my late husband's life if he hadn't been so intent on *protecting* me."

"Yes . . . well, what's happened has to change our plans. No doubt they'll come back tonight or tomorrow and start asking questions."

"What plans can we change if we haven't made any?"

"First, let's drop this idea of my being a Mexican lover. I have papers that indicate I live in Santiago de Cuba. We'd better stick to that story. And we'd better move more quickly too. I can't stay here long. Sooner or later someone in this town will connect my arrival with the discovery of the wrecked truck."

"I agree. I've been thinking of what you said about meeting someone close to the central government and I've an idea. His name is Manuel Pérez. He's a political prisoner on the Isle of Pines—he has been for seven years. Every year they tell him he can come back to his family that lives in the rehabilitation center in Miramar just outside of Havana. Then they come and get him on some crazy pretext and he's a prisoner again."

"Pérez is a famous name in Cuba. Is he related to Ramiro Pérez?"

"Exactly. He is the nephew of Ramiro Pérez. As you no doubt know, Ramiro was long ago promoted from the governing council to the eleven-man politburo. Fidel remembers his friends. The old man was one of the first to join him back in the mountains in the Sierra Maestra days. He fought well and with great courage. Even though he's old now and hardly an asset to the young government, he still has the title of Field Marshal and Minister of Defense. It's his power that has kept his nephew alive."

"Is he still a believer?"

"He has no choice. But he's too religious really to embrace Communism. It's the thing to do, so he goes along. But his nephew is very different and very bitter. He was a teacher too, and was charged with speaking antirevolutionary doctrines to his pupils—imagine, the fourth grade! I visited him last year and he told me that he had decided to play along now, it's the only way. So he pretends to be completely won over to the Fidel government and all of its policies. I suggest we visit him as soon as possible, maybe Saturday, the day after next. He can reach his uncle and perhaps get you a job of some kind with the government. The uncle is still very loyal to Fidel, true, but he does feel guilty about all that has happened to the nephew he loves, and I suspect he will help a friend of his . . ."

That night they dined by candlelight and held their breath when they heard soldiers' voices in the streets. But no one disturbed them and in their latest escape a new bond seemed formed. He kissed her first while she was washing the dishes, not exactly the most romantic setting, but the act transcended. He kissed her again, deeply. She hardly protested, but did say, "You don't have to pay for my assistance."

He smiled. She was flattering him, as though he were doing *her* a favor.

They moved to her bedroom and quickly were lying side by side. She was modest but he insisted that they keep a small lamp burning. She had not had sex for more than two years, since her husband had been taken from her. Since then she had been, as she explained to numerous suitors, dead inside. But she was alive again now, and almost too passionate for Martin to handle. They were a bit mad together, writhing and moaning and screaming *sotto voce* until out of breath and panting they clung to each other in a full, mutual release. How many times, Martin thought, had he made love? Five thousand times, perhaps? But certainly *never* like this.

They made love three more times during the next few hours and finally, exhausted, fell asleep as the first light announced the rising sun. When she showered and dressed for school, he was still sound asleep.

That night they made plans to leave for the Isle of Pines early the next morning. It would be a difficult trip, she told him. Security surrounding the prison was extremely tight and Martin, despite his silver hair and frosted beard, might still be recognized by some old friend . . . But it was a risk he had to take.

1 1 3

As they were about to bed down for the night there was a knock on the door and they opened it to find a police officer standing at the entrance. He needed no search warrant to demand admittance. Once inside he asked to see their identification papers. Although Martin was not afraid to show his papers—they had passed police scrutiny before—he was concerned that they were apparently being singled out for attention. If the police had been engaged in a house-by-house security check he felt certain that word would have reached them by this time by a phone call from a well-meaning neighbor of Alicia's. Apparently the police, on order from the military, were mainly interested in *this* household. He thought briefly of his gun, dispatching the officer and—but immediately scrapped the thought as unwise and extremely dangerous. Instead, while riffling through his wallet to find his papers, he expressed what he hoped sounded like innocent curiosity.

"And why are we so honored by this inspection?"

"You will know in due course. Your papers, please."

He handed them over and watched as the officer examined them carefully.

"You are from Santiago de Cuba?"

"Yes."

"You are an itinerant worker."

"Yes."

"Señor Palma do you know anything about the wrecked truck and the murder of Señor Adolfo Maso?"

"No, sir. I was in the market today and had I known anything I certainly wouldn't have withheld the information from the authorities."

The officer walked to the window and determined that there was no one near eavesdropping on their conversation. He returned the papers to Martin, smiled and said, "I bring you greetings from Rolando Duran. He asked me to warn you that you are being watched and are already under suspicion.

He says to be very careful and do not linger in Guane too many days. Contact him at the Bureau of Health if you need help." The policeman smiled again, said good evening and was gone.

Martin was tempted to press for details, mainly about how Duran had been able to trace him so quickly and connect him with the Maso murder. To do so, though, would show some fear of being under Duran's surveillance so he decided against it. It was all far from reassuring, and his suspicions about Duran's being a double agent were if anything heightened.

Once he was certain that the police officer—or whatever he was—had left the premises, Martin asked Alicia, "Do you know about this Rolando Duran?"

"Rolando Duran. The name sounds very familiar. Tell me more about him." She restrained herself from pointing out that this was the second time he had withheld information from her.

"He lives and works in San Antonio de los Baños. He's with the local health bureau. I was given his name by contacts in the States and told he could be relied on for assistance. But I began to have my doubts and I took off in the middle of the night, without any explanation."

"Duran. Yes . . . my late husband knew him and at first thought that he was friendly to us. But there were some who found him otherwise. One cell of our underground was ambushed and all of its records destroyed not long after he joined it for a secret meeting. My husband never discussed things with me too specifically because I wasn't active in the counterrevolution, just sympathetic to its goals, and he wanted to protect me. But I did hear word that several of them were tortured and some even put to death after contact with Señor Duran. One could, I suppose, claim coincidence, but—"

"It's too late to worry about him now but I wish I'd followed my instincts and left the official contacts alone . . ."

They made love again that night, despite their mutual concern over Duran—his message and what he might be. Love, in their case, for the moment conquered . . . drugged . . . all. She was like a bottle of the finest champagne, he thought, uncorked after years of confinement. It was his pleasure and good fortune to joyfully imbibe.

Chapter Fifteen

February Tenth

Silence was more than a virtue for Felipe Quevedo, it was a credo. All things efficient were performed in silence. Quiet, for Felipe, meant careful, and only those who took great caution in performing their daily tasks could possibly succeed. The heavy oaken doors leading to the executive offices of the Ministry of the Interior, the controlling agency for all of Cuba's intelligence and security apparatus, swung on noiseless hinges. The carpet, deep piled and luxurious, absorbed all footfalls. Throughout the suite there were prominent signs ordering SILENCIO!

Quevedo had a foreign visitor this morning. They were closeted together behind the bulletproof metal doors on which were written in large print, "Office of the Minister, Felipe Quevedo." The thickness of the doors and the height of the print were two of the few privileges of rank that Quevedo exercised. Like Fidel, to whom he demonstrated total loyalty, Felipe was a man of Spartan tastes. Even the car he drove was a medium-size Mercedes-Benz, chosen more for its speed and maneuverability than for its ostentation. He usually drove himself, disdaining the services of a chauffeur to which, he reminded himself, he was certainly entitled. "When El Jefe stops smoking cigars that spill ashes all over his battle fatigues and starts using a cigarette holder like a dandy dressed in a cutaway, that's when I'll get a chauffeur and a limousine," he once joked. It was unusual for Quevedo to demonstrate any humor. He had no time for jokes. What spare time he managed to find for himself was spent with his head deeply buried in Marxist literature. Quevedo proudly considered himself a philosophical and theoretical Communist as well as a two hundred percent loyal Cuban. Perhaps there were those who would question his basic motivations, but in his own mind his position was quite clear: His was a loyalty of the highest order, a devotion to national duty both pure and unchallengeable.

Quevedo's visitor this morning was no stranger to his staff. Señor Carmen Raymondo was a frequent visitor, though his missions were never taken lightly. Although Raymondo did not exercise the same authority in the Mexican government that Quevedo held in Cuba, he was nonetheless highly regarded and represented the top echelon of Mexican intelligence. The message he brought Quevedo this morning was disturbing. It related to still another assassination attempt on the life of Fidel Castro.

"And what else is new?" asked Quevedo. "We receive news of such plots every week."

"I'm aware of that," Raymondo answered, "but this one is particularly serious and is already launched."

"Sometimes there are four such attempts going on at the same time. Fidel jokes that he really isn't worth all the trouble."

Raymondo took exception; it seemed that his trip from Mexico City was being taken too lightly. "Well, of course, if you're not interested in the information—"

"Don't be foolish, of course we're interested." Quevedo was all business now. "As a matter of fact, only yesterday one of our counter-agents sent word that we've got another visitor buzzing about our country. But, please, señor, tell me your information."

"We have been contacted by the Mafia, who brought us word from their Miami family. They say they were contacted by the CIA—now, I know that may be difficult to believe—and they say that together they have found a man who will soon come here, or who is here already, to kill our president . . ."

"It's not so hard to believe, my friend. They've used this connection before." Despite his adversary position, Quevedo had reluctantly come to admire the work of the CIA. Their determination, their outrageous, almost childish tactics were at times an exercise in futility, but they were creative, daring and never seemed to be diverted from their goals, regardless of the politics of this or that administration. He had studied as much of their activity as he possibly could over the many years and had even adopted some of their operating methods for his own department. He also had little doubt that some day they, too, could learn from him . . . "Yes," he said, "Mafia–CIA marriages have occurred before."

"That I know. But with all of the adverse publicity in the American press, one would think they had stopped. Apparently not. At any rate, as much as we tried, they would give us no further details. They want to sell their double cross and the price is high. They want one million dollars, or rather the equivalent of one million dollars deposited to one of their accounts in London. For this, they promise full information. They offer to supply the name of the man, his description, his history, and whatever else they know to help you identify him. I suppose it *could* be a triple cross and they could give you nothing worthwhile once they have their money, but that, my friend, is a decision you must make."

119

Quevedo remained silent for a long moment. His sharp, intelligent features seemed to grow more intense, his eyes more penetrating as he considered his decision. He felt himself between some severely conflicting emotions. He had joined the Castro movement in 1961, two years after Fidel Castro had marched triumphantly into Havana and taken control of the country. Because, in a sense, he had been two years late, he tried to overcompensate with service so dedicated that even those who had been in the Sierre Maestra with Fidel at the birth of the Revolution would consider him a charter member. From his earliest days in the government, he had felt great hatred toward the racketeers who had helped support Batista and bled the country white for their own purposes. It was their trade in narcotics, prostitution, gambling and extortion that had kept his people under foot and benefited foreign powers who wanted Cuba to remain a near-feudal state. Now he was being asked, in a sense, to do business with these same murderers he so bitterly hated. It was not an easy decision. And for more reasons than the involvement of the Mafia . . . Sometimes he felt like a cart drawn by oxen in opposing directions, threatening to tear him apart.

He would need a day or so to think this through. Rather than indicate his own indecision, he told Raymondo he needed some time to make the proper explanations to the Ministry of Finance which must give him, without too many facts, a million dollars in cash. Nonetheless, he told his Mexican counterpart to get word to his country and then to the Mafia that Cuba was most appreciative and almost certainly would make the deal. As he put it with impeccable rhetoric, "Castro's life must not be snuffed out by Yankee imperialism."

They met forty-eight hours later and Quevedo told Señor Raymondo that the money was now available to him. But he could not, he said, go along with all the terms laid down by the Mafia. This was a matter of such gravity, he explained, that he and he alone must handle it personally and privately. There were questions he had to ask the underworld informer to which only he must know the answers. He suggested a meeting on neutral ground. He mentioned Paris as an agreeable rendezvous point. He wanted to know in advance the name of the courier with whom he would meet so that he could check him out and be certain that he was not being duped by some fortune hunter. This courier must be someone high in the underworld hierarchy and not some lowly *capo* with limited first-hand knowledge and authority. If the information seemed authentic, he would have the money on his person and deliver it immediately at the end of the meeting. Raymondo agreed to discuss his terms with the contacts in Mexico and would get back to him in a matter of days.

The next evening when Rolando Duran returned from work he found Quevedo waiting for him in his home. Quevedo was wearing a white medical technician's jacket and had puttied his nose and elongated his sideburns. His hair was frosted gray and he wore heavy tortoiseshell glasses so that his appearance was completely changed. Duran was accustomed to Quevedo's addiction to disguises—the man would have done well on the stage—and recognized him the moment he said hello.

"Well, this is a pleasant surprise. Can I pour you a drink?"

"Something cold. Lemonade or pineapple juice will be fine. My time is limited."

"In a moment," Duran said, heading for the kitchen and returning promptly with the drinks. "I had forgotten that you drink nothing alcoholic."

"I think more clearly . . . I hear you have news of another invader—"

"Just a rumor, Mr. Minister, nothing more definite than that at present."

"You are supposed to have more specific news. Hernandez

says you told him you saw a man the other day who made you very suspicious. I understand that you were paid well for that lead. I hope it is not just an expensive rumor."

"Mr. Minister, perhaps 'rumor' is a bad word. Yes, I did see a man who looked very suspicious to me when I was in Havana the other day to discuss my latest medical survey on malnutrition. We chatted in a restaurant and he asked me questions about our leader that seemed strange to me. I took special note of his appearance but he would not tell me his name or where he was from or why he was here in this part of the island. He claimed to live in the east, somewhere near Santiago de Cuba, I believe. I felt it my duty to report this to Señor Hernandez of your staff and told him I would watch for this fellow whenever I go to Havana. You see, I'm there every week. I also gave Señor Hernandez a description of this fellow just in case he should come to your attention by some coincidence."

"I think you are holding out on me, Duran."

"No, I assure you such is not the case."

"I truly hope not. For your sake as well as mine," he said, rising and speaking with emphasis. "Keep in touch with us and report back when you see this man again. You can count on us for further payments when you do."

"Of course. You have always been most generous." Duran saw Quevedo to the door with considerable ceremony, but it was obvious that there was small love lost between the two. Quevedo considered informers a necessary adjunct to the work in which he was engaged, but he hated them and himself for the necessity of dealing with them.

Señor Raymondo returned from his brief round trip to Mexico City with word that Quevedo's terms had been accepted. Since the payment was to be in cash, they would accept American dollars or Swiss francs but were not interested in pesos or English pounds. They awaited instructions for their representative, who, they assured Quevedo, would be a top man in their international organization.

"Good," Quevedo said. "I will meet with them in Paris at the Georges Cinq hotel on Monday afternoon. I will register under the name of Pablo Padilla. I will expect their man to be alone, as I will be. Have him ring my suite when he arrives . . . And Señor Raymondo, I want to tell you how grateful Cuba is to her sister republic. Mexico has always been a friend. Perhaps some day we can show our gratitude."

Raymondo rose, smiling, walked over to Quevedo's desk, opened his humidor and grabbed a fistful of prewar H. Up-mann cigars. "You already have begun." They grasped hands warmly and strolled out of the office arm in arm.

Chapter Sixteen

February Eleventh

The ferry from the mainland to the Isle of Pines was always crowded, particularly on Saturday mornings when friends and relatives paid their weekly visits to their loved ones interned in the political prison. Despite the anticipated gloom of seeing a husband, a lover or a father who was not free to return home, there was usually a near-festive air on the little vessel. The visitors considered it their duty to cheer up their less fortunate hosts behind electrified wire fences, so they prepared themselves by singing, telling jokes and generally psyching themselves into a false euphoric mood.

Though the ferry was operated by military personnel under the supervision of the Ministry of Prisons, normal security measures were relatively lax. Certainly there was no fear that anyone would threaten to commandeer the little vessel. Even if they succeeded in doing so, where would they head and how would they escape the coast guard patrols that circled the island? As for security at the prison, when there were numerous visitors on the Isle of Pines, security precautions tightened like steel bands.

Something, Alicia felt, was not quite normal aboard the ferry today. She looked at the poor, mountain peasants and farmers absorbed in their own thoughts, but none seemed especially agitated. She studied the faces of the crew and it seemed to her that they were more intense than usual, more devoted to their duties. When one of the peasants carelessly lighted a cigarette in an area where smoking was prohibited, an officer slapped his hand, knocking the cigarette to the deck, snuffed it out by grinding it under his heel and without an indication of the slightest humor asked, while pointing to a "No Smoking" sign, "Do you want us to read you the signs out loud? Maybe if your brother had learned to obey the law, you wouldn't have to visit him today." The peasant was so startled by the violence of the rebuke that he didn't take time to explain that he wasn't visiting the prison but merely seeking work on a small construction job nearby.

Alicia took Martin by the sleeve and led him aft, where there was a small opening on the fantail.

"I think something is wrong. Too many security men. Too much tension."

"It's your nerves. I see nothing here to frighten us. Anyhow, if you're right, the worst thing we can do is to react. Let's not give them reason to be suspicious of us. Private conferences are a bad idea."

He moved sharply from her side and headed for the port side of the ferry, where a few seats were still unoccupied. There he took out the morning papers and started to read. Alicia took his lead and moved forward, finding an open bench about two yards from where he was reading.

As if on signal, suddenly the security men aboard rose and started a systematic check of the passengers. Since many were unlettered people, the questioning went slowly. Finally it was Alicia's turn. A particularly unpleasant-looking man with a thick handlebar mustache, a huge paunch and piggish eyes approached her and demanded to see her papers. Trying to be plausibly nonchalant, she reached into her purse and removed her wallet, offering the whole packet for the man to examine.

"I'm not interested in your family pictures, just let me have the identification."

Alicia did.

"And why are you on board?"

"To visit someone at the prison."

"Who?"

"Manuel Pérez. He is a former colleague of mine. We are both teachers. He was a friend of my late husband. I try to visit him every couple of months."

"How long has he been here?"

"Seven years. He has three to go to complete his reindoctrination."

"Ten years!" The questioner whistled. "Must be a pretty stubborn fellow."

"Perhaps"—Alicia smiled sweetly—"but I think now he is learning his lesson."

Returning her wallet and identification cards, the guard adopted a friendlier tone. "Some of us learn slowly. *Buenos días.*"

Observing them while pretending to be absorbed in his newspaper, Martin reminded himself that he was not armed. He'd left his pistol in Alicia's house, in case he were searched at the jail. Now he wished he had it with him as he anticipated another examination of his faked identification papers.

With a side shuffle, the security man moved in front of him, asked to see his papers. He smiled and reached for them just as there were sudden, astonished shouts of "El Comandante," "El Jefe," "Viva Fidel!" The mustached guard joined his comrades at the rail, ignoring his own previous order to Martin, who with the rest now looked across the water and was dumbfounded to see a sleek white fishing yacht pull abreast of the ferry, not eight yards off the port bow. Its flag bore five bright stars—and there could be little doubt that this was Castro's own pleasure craft. And at the rail, waving and shouting, stood Fidel himself. He was dressed in the usual green fatigues, smoking a stovepipe-length cigar that he waved in the air like a Roman candle. It was obvious that he was in a relaxed, expansive mood. Reaching down, he picked up a pair of paddle-footed flippers, jamming the cigar into his mouth, and waved the footgear up and down to portray a duck pushing through the water. Skin diving and snorkeling had been Castro's favorite form of recreation since childhood and he was never happier than when, armed with a spear or underwater camera, he plunged deep into the sea, challenging his own leather lungs while exploring hidden treasures. It was said that he performed prodigious feats while swimming, far outdistancing his closest competitors. Asked to explain his actions he was once quoted as replying, "On land we are all equal. In the ocean depths, we separate the men from the boys."

Suddenly Alicia found herself almost smiling. At least one mystery was solved. What she had mistaken for security measures directed against Palma were apparently only steps taken to protect the Premier while on his fishing and swimming vacation off the Isle of Pines, one of his well-known favorite haunts. She smiled at Carlos. He was also relieved that the interrogation was avoided as the obese security agent with a nod told him to pocket his identification papers. The danger seemed to have passed as Castro's yacht pulled sharply ahead of the slow-moving ferry.

Martin felt emotions beyond relief at the realization that his target had been within twenty-four feet. It was difficult to get a clear picture of Fidel with the peasants jumping and whistling and the boats apart so rapidly, but he could tell that with the exception of being noticeably heavier, Castro seemed fit and healthy, unchanged, at least externally, by the pressures of the last several years. With all of his luxuries and efforts at physical fitness, Martin wished that he had changed so little since that day in 1959 when he last heard Castro speak in public. It was then he had decided that either the Martinez family make its escape and make it immediately, or surely all of their property would be confiscated and they imprisoned. They'd fled within the week, their resettlement aided by the deposits with foreign banks that his father had been accumulating for years.

The thought also occurred to Martin that Fidel Castro was either a man of great courage or a man with small instinct for self-preservation. Certainly he was no fool and was aware that there had been and continued to be many plots against his life. Yet there he had been, standing and waving, an open target for any assassin. Castro had been questioned on this subject many times by reporters, and he had answered that he had great confidence in the people charged with protecting him, whom he often described as being very efficient, very effective. He also said, Martin had read, that there were fewer mentally disturbed people in Cuba than in the United States because Cubans under Castro lived lives with less frustration and had more freedom of will. In the States everybody was trying to pressure everybody else into doing this or that. So, Castro pointed out, he had no fear of fanatics, such as had killed President Kennedy and his brother.

Presumably, Martin thought, this attitude should make his job easier. I may not be a lunatic or a fanatic, he thought, but we'll soon see how efficient his security people are . . .

They landed at Isle of Pines a short time later, and it was only a brief walk to the outer confines of the prison. A group of guards, each working from a sentry booth, checked everybody in and carefully examined his or her identification. All were asked to sign a dated time register, were fingerprinted, and asked to name the prisoner they'd come to visit. They were informed that visiting hours ended precisely at 4:00 P.M. They were then admitted to a large waiting room from which they were paged when the individual they had come to see had been summoned and was waiting for them in an equally large room lined with long wooden benches and tables. Although they underwent little observation, there was an obvious effort to make the visiting a community activity; there were few places where one could find and enjoy real privacy. Alicia and Martin had just sat down when they were paged, checked again by another guard, and directed to the inner chamber where Manuel Pérez was waiting for them. He was obviously puzzled when they approached. He had never seen or heard of Carlos Palma before. Nevertheless, he greeted him warmly as a friend of Alicia.

"You remember our old friend, Carlos Palma," Alicia said immediately.

"I do, of course. And how is your dear mother?"

"Well, perfectly well," Palma ad-libbed.

After an hour spent in meaningless pleasantries, Manuel invited his visitors to join him in a stroll around the prison grounds. There was a ball field and a parade ground where they would not be likely to be overheard.

"And who are you, Señor Palma, and to what do I owe this visit?" Manuel asked the moment they were alone.

"Let me explain," Alicia replied. "Carlos is an old friend of Myra Rubin. You remember Myra."

"Of course. We were very good friends. I saw her often in the years she was waiting for permission to leave."

"She and I knew each other from the earliest days at the University," Martin explained. "I had not seen her in years, until very recently. She agreed to help me on my mission. Which is why I contacted Alicia. And that's why we're here today."

"What kind of mission?"

129

"There is a spear fisherman with a thick beard . . ."

"Fishing for a fisherman?"

"More like hunting . . ."

"And how can I help, here, a prisoner myself?"

They were walking around the ball field, at a safe distance from any other group.

"We aren't sure of that. Alicia here says that you have many contacts in the government, men who are at high levels and could perhaps get me into a job or a situation where I might find my subject more available."

"My Uncle Ramiro."

"Yes," put in Alicia, "and we understand why you might be reluctant to contact him. You can ask him just so many favors and it is quite understandable that you might want to save him for something later—"

"No, if by 'something later' you mean me, you are wrong, Alicia. I would have used him years ago if he were in a position to help me. Our name works against us, unfortunately. A Pérez for a Pérez is not politically expedient. The question here is rather how much we can afford to tell him. Don't forget that he has been a Castro man since the day the Revolution started in the mountains. I must think about it . . . let's move back to the building. Rain is coming."

And in true tropical fashion the sky had suddenly become blackened with clouds. They had just reached the safety of cover when the ground was swept by torrents of rain . . .

Alicia shook her luxuriant hair and rain splattered both her companions. All three of them laughed like friends at a picnic without a serious thought on their minds, but if one had studied their faces closely it would have been obvious that Manuel was excited by the challenge of Palma's request for help. If he could find a way to be of assistance, he thought, it would at least help pay for all of these years of confinement. What sweet retribution if after seven long years behind bars he were able to have a hand in the tyrant's downfall . . . Cer-

1 3 0

tainly there were others like himself, and many of them free beyond these prison walls, but they must be approached with the highest degree of delicacy. The Premier, or rather, "The First Secretary of the Party," as he now chose to be called, might speak for endless hours of the tremendous and total victory of the Revolution, but there were enemies, their number growing each day, who understood that power corrupts, especially the absolute power of Fidel—

His thoughts were interrupted by the blaring of a bugle and the entrance of a group of men in fatigues. Then, over the loudspeaker came the words, "Brothers of the Revolution, we are honored by the visit of El Comandante!"

Martin could hardly believe his eyes, but there Castro stood, laughing and joking with the prisoners and their families. He seemed completely at ease, completely without fear of personal danger. Martin couldn't help admiring his courage. But this was all part of Fidel's expected routine—the sudden unannounced visit, mingling with the very crowds where his enemies might be. It was as if he challenged his own fate. From the very first days of the Revolution, from the time he was captured in the Moncada Barracks raid, an inexplicable series of coincidences had spared Fidel Castro, as if history meant him to play his role regardless. He was tall and muscular, standing well over six foot two, his shoulders broad and his posture erect. But his courage was not a product of physical prowess. It came rather from his conviction that he was meant to serve his part in the national drama. His most fanatic enemies were at times stymied by the man's stubborn belief in himself. Strangely enough, his face revealed none of this determination. At age fifty, white hair was sprinkled through his beard and sideburns. Liquid, almost romantic brown eyes danced with humor in a face that was too soft to belong to a man of such power.

The tension was now almost unbearable as Fidel singled them out and approached Alicia. Castro had always had an eye for beauty. He virtually ignored Martin, though he brushed by him in going to Alicia.

"I hope that a beautiful lady like you is not being deprived of your man's companionship by political necessities," he said.

"No, El Comandante, my husband has been dead for several years. We are merely visiting one of his old friends."

"Losing your man at such an early age is difficult. I trust that you were not offended by my question. It was merely a poor attempt at humor."

"I was not offended in the least," she answered.

Then, turning toward Martin and examining him, almost with jealousy, Castro added, "Well, at least you are in the company of a handsome man and if he is not blind he will show you the attention you deserve. Again he stared at Martin, smiled and turned to face another family group.

Here, next to him, stood the man he had traveled a thousand miles to kill. Of course to do anything now would be suicidal, not to mention have slight chance of success. There would be another opportunity. Fidel Castro hadn't seen the last of him. He clasped Alicia's hand because he could see her literally begin to shake. They both looked at Manuel Pérez, whose face showed exactly nothing.

All three remained silent as Castro and his party left the premises as suddenly as they had arrived, like the squall that had washed the parade grounds and then as quickly disappeared. The leader had vanished, but his visit somehow made the mission seem all the more possible. There was still an hour or two until the visiting period ended, but it had all been said and it was time for them to leave. They clasped hands warmly, and Manuel assured them once again that they could count on him if only he could find a way. The approach to Uncle Ramiro must be swift, he realized, but at the same time subtle. If Palma's mission were spelled out too specifically there was the ever-present danger of the message being intercepted. Though Ramiro Pérez was a man of great courage, age might have had its effect. Perhaps he had chosen to live out his days in peace, avoiding all contact with counter-revolutionary activity. Manuel doubted this was the case but the risk was there. He had ways of contacting his uncle but he would not reveal them even to Alicia and Palma . . . the danger to those involved was too great. He would simply have to find a way to communicate with Uncle Ramiro and would think of nothing else until their next visit. They agreed to return the following Saturday, visiting hours being restricted to the weekends.

Chapter Seventeen

February Thirteenth

Faced with a precious week to kill, Martin chose to put the time to best advantage. The trip from Guane to Havana, approximately one hundred and seventy-five miles, was three hours by bus. Each morning at seven he boarded a modern air-conditioned public conveyance and headed for the capital city. He was back with Alicia each night after the sun had set. Aside from the importance of his trips, the fact that he left so early in the morning and came back after dark screened him from the view of gossipy neighbors. Those who came to know him simply accepted his presence as Alicia Ortiz's lover. After all, they asked each other, wasn't it natural and healthy that a beautiful woman, deprived of her husband's affection in the prime of her life, should hunger for a man's attention?

At Havana, he purchased a small peddler's tray, a supply of trinkets and costume jewelry, and posted himself beneath the royal palms outside the capitol building. Whenever the opportunity presented itself, he engaged the various government workers who became his customers in idle conversation, manipulating the talk, whenever possible, to the subject of Castro. He followed the same practice as he moved easily down the Avenida del Puerto, past the Ministry of Education, the National Museum and the headquarters of the Department of Public Works. At all times he was cautious, making certain to praise Fidel and laud his regime. If any of the persons he questioned made the slightest derogatory remark about El Jefe, he was prompt to defend the leader in the most vociferous terms. From these conversations he pieced together at least a partial picture of the life-style of the man he sought to eliminate.

For example, he learned that Castro spent as much time in the mountains where his revolution had started as in Havana. He spoke of the City as his office but called the mountains his home. Whenever he found the time, as in last week's fishing trip, he left the City and sought the peace of country living. And yet he could be boisterous and demonstrative and was generally very gregarious.

In Havana, he lived modestly in a small house on the city's outskirts. He rose early, usually by six in the morning, and was already on his way to work an hour later after having devoured a huge breakfast, a batch of overnight dispatches, and the morning editions of several papers flown to him from around the world. His routine was erratic. At one time he would work in offices in the Municipal Palace, at another in the Presidential Palace, and at still other times he would go directly to the Ministry where he would meet with leaders in various departments. At times he chose to stay home and work in his own crowded living quarters, where he would write all of the famous four-hour speeches he considered essential for communication with Cuba's ten million citizens. But wherever he worked, he would remain for a relatively long time. His normal workday was twenty hours, and he had been known to skip two or even three meals in a row if he was deeply involved with a particular project. True, much that Martin heard merely reconfirmed information he already knew from readings and a thorough written briefing supplied by the CIA, but who could deny the value of a first-hand update . . . ?

Martin posted himself outside the Presidential Palace three days in a row and finally was rewarded. Castro arrived there at noon, having spent the morning working on economic problems in other offices. Martin noted with pleasant surprise that the First Secretary was never too cautious about his security, which he had concluded the week before in the surprise meeting at the prison on the Isle of Pines. There were, of course, secret service men assigned to protect Castro, but he seemed to humor them more than use them. At several sightings that day, as Castro came and went for meals and meetings, he skipped ahead of them and they rushed after him rather than being in the van of his party, as they obviously would have preferred. Again, Castro seemed to thumb his nose at potential enemies, as though confident that his destiny would protect him.

There was an unfortunate coincidence that occurred on Martin's last day in the city before his planned return to the Isle of Pines. Although he normally avoided military men when peddling his wares, he'd grown a bit cocky after five successive days of uninterrupted vigilance. Spotting a soldier sitting alone on a wooden bench near the Capitol, he approached him and offered to sell him a trinket at a reduced price. The moment he faced the man, he realized that they had met before. To his surprise, the soldier called him by name. It was the very same fellow who had invaded Alicia's home the week before, bringing greetings from Rolando Duran.

"Señor Palma," the soldier said, "what a pleasant surprise. We meet again."

"Is it?" Martin asked in annoyance.

"Is it what?"

"Is it a surprise? It seems to me more like I'm being followed. This meeting is no coincidence."

"Señor Palma," the soldier said, "I assure you that I have not been following you. I have better things to do with my time. If you think I am being a nuisance, just call Señor Duran. He is here today visiting his boss in the Bureau of Health. I am sure he will be happy to meet with you. Perhaps he can even bring you news from the north."

"I see no need to call him. Or for you to follow me, either. In fact I advise you against it."

"As you wish," and the soldier rose and walked off in the opposite direction.

Why did Duran insist on having him followed? Was he really a strong CIA reference, or the double agent that Martin suspected? He would have to watch him with great care. Or perhaps there was a better plan. . . .

Dumping the tray of trinkets in a nearby trash receptacle—this was to be his last day of peddling—he left the governmental area and boarded a bus on the Malecon heading west. Getting off at Calle Twelve, he walked the few short blocks to the Cemetery de Colón and there began his search for the Anglo-Swiss Trading Company—the front Duncan had told him about. He found the building without any trouble. It was a compact yellow stucco building, two stories high with a handsome brass plate just to the right of the main entrance identifying its business. He looked around to see if the building was being watched; all was quiet in the area. Finally he walked up the three marble steps that fronted the entrance, tried the door and found it locked. There was a large wrought-iron knocker that sounded like a cannon when it banged against the iron plate it hung from. There was no answer. He knocked again, this time trying to make less noise but failing in the attempt. Obviously there was light inside the building and there was no reason for the office to be closed. He listened carefully and thought he heard a shuffling sound, as if someone were moving to another position to gain a better view. Now the door opened a crack and he heard a formal voice say, "Can we help you? State your business."

He answered in English. "Pepe sent me. Aunt Cintia is ill." The door opened immediately. He was greeted by a tall, angular man with thinning blond hair and a British accent straight from Bond Street. "By all means, dear chap, please enter."

The man, who later identified himself in Colonel Blimp fashion as Reginald Hawkins, was pleasant but not overly hospitable. It was apparent that he wanted more information before offering any.

"Have you come to inquire about some imports?"

"No. I've already told you that Pepe sent me."

"Why, yes indeed. So you did. But you have yet to state the purpose of your visit. Is there a certain type of merchandise we can supply?"

"Sir—I didn't catch your name."

"Hawkins. Reginald Hawkins."

"Mine is Palma. Carlos Palma. The name means nothing to you?"

"Why, just so. How terribly stupid of me. I should have known immediately. You are exactly as Tom Devereaux described you to me. Do sit down. I was just making tea. And, of course, you can have it iced if that is your preference."

"Devereaux? Tom Devereaux? I don't know anyone by that name."

"Really? But he did tell me to expect a call from you. Perhaps you've forgotten. Or could it be that you know him as Tyrone Davis?"

"I'm afraid not."

"Theodore Delaney?"

"This is beginning to sound like a quiz show."

Hawkins laughed uproariously, far more than the small joke deserved. "American television . . . just so, just so . . . it's

138

probably called 'What's My Name?' or something of the sort
. . . Wait, I'll have one last go at it. Consider the *initials*."

"T.D. Tad Duncan. Yes . . . well, he told me to contact
you if there were a problem or if I wanted to send any messages up north."

"You see? I knew I'd win that fridge after all! No, actually,
our friend uses all sorts of different names in his work and
sometimes I just forget which one applies. But he always
holds to the same initials, T.D. I personally don't think that is
a very good idea, but he insists on it. He says then he doesn't
have to change the monograms on his pajamas or his attaché
case, or some such rot. Always T.D., no matter where he
goes . . . But do let me make you some tea. We'll be closing
for the day soon and I'm just about caught up in all departments of my work."

"I'm afraid not. I really am in kind of a hurry, Mr. Hawkins. Please get word to T.D. and tell him to get off my ass."

"Oh? I'm afraid I don't, as they say, read you."

"Yes, you do. Ass is a simple Anglo-Saxon word with a
simple meaning. Tell him to call off his dogs and stop trailing
me around this country. Or I just might pack up and go
home."

There was a sharp rap on the door, followed by a few
moments of silence, then three short raps, a pause and two
more. Hawkins seemed a bit concerned, but quickly regained
his composure.

"I'm afraid we have some company. No need to worry, Mr.
Palma, not at all. It's Ernesto. You'll know him when you see
him." He walked to the door, slid back the double bolt, removed the chain and just before opening it asked innocently,
"And can we help you? State your business."

"Pepe sent me. He's with his Aunt Cintia."

Hawkins opened the door with no further hesitation and
admitted the same soldier whom Martin had met on the
bench and who a week before had visited him at Alicia's

home. So his meeting this soldier was, as he had assumed, no surprise rendezvous. He was being tailed and it was on orders from Rolando Duran, and probably he took *his* orders from the Anglo-Swiss Trading Company, which was directed by the CIA. But the question remained: Was Duran *also* a double agent for the Cuban intelligence apparatus? It was a basket of eels, no question. Why commission him and then have him trailed about in such a way as to endanger his life and limit his efficiency?

"Señor Palma, let me introduce Señor Ernesto Ordonez, one of our most trusted employees. We call him El Gato, the cat. He moves about so quietly on his little feline paws that no one ever seems to know that he is following them. Even in your case, you may not realize it but he's been with you practically since San Antonio. He *likes* you, Señor Palma. He says you are a great romantic."

Ernesto smiled through his thick mustache, revealing a mouth of gold. "*Buenos días,* Señor Palma. We are becoming good friends, no?"

"No is the right word. No. We are not good friends. And if you would enjoy a chance to become one, stop following me around. And tell your Señor Duran he may have helped me once but he doesn't own me. I want no more escorts, do you understand?"

"But, *señor,* be fair. I only take orders. I am not an important man."

"Well, the next time you receive such an order my advice to you is to ignore it."

"Mr. Palma is absolutely right, Ernesto. I'll wager that Señor Adolfo Maso wishes he had minded his own business instead of picking up Mr. Palma in that battered old truck of his." He stared Martin down with his glass-blue eyes. Martin could feel the air chill and see Reginald Hawkins transformed from a pleasant, easy-going British shopkeeper to the practiced agent. He knew the most opportune moment at which to reveal his knowledge of Maso's murder. This fellow was not going to be bullied.

"You're a man full of stories, Mr. Hawkins."

"Right you are, Señor Palma." Hawkins laughed. He'd decided to revert to his Colonel Blimp Englishman for the time being.

"I hope I've made my point."

"Oh, you have, and I shall certainly relay the information to T.D. He will understand your desire to go about alone, I'm sure. Meanwhile, let me show you something I'm sure you'll find most interesting."

He walked to the rear of the office and lifted a heavily bound accounting ledger from his desk. Just under it was a clear piece of plastic cut in the shape of a small screwdriver. Then, moving over to a small bookcase on the side wall, he removed one innocent-looking volume and uncovered a thin slot in the plaster wall behind. The plastic screwdriver was apparently electronically treated, because by bringing it close to the slot, he activated a circuit that caused the bookcase to swivel around and expose a small door. He motioned for Martin and Ernesto to follow him and almost immediately the bookcase slid back into position, hiding them from the view of anyone who might happen into the outer office.

"Here, Mr. Palma, I'd like to show you some interesting snapshots. You might even recognize this fellow here," he said, pointing.

The picture was obviously taken at the city morgue. A naked male body lay on a wheeled stretcher being pushed by an attendant into an examination room. The body lay face up and was clearly identifiable. It was Rolando Duran with a huge bloody scar cut across his neck and chest and several deep knife wounds in the cardiac region.

"You see, Mr. Palma, we too are professionals. We, too, were disturbed by Señor Duran's actions. Men who, shall we say, play both ends against the middle deserve their high pay—they are, after all, so short-lived. And if you are curious as to why Ernesto did not know of this and why he told you that Duran was visiting the Bureau of Health, the answer is that he did know. He was testing to see if you knew the facts too . . . And now it is time for me to close shop and not very wise for you to stay in this building too long. I shall certainly relay your wishes to T.D., if you are still certain that you must work alone."

Martin strained to hide his surprise at Duran's murder. "As I have said, I work best alone."

"As you desire," Hawkins said curtly. "You can leave by this rear door."

Chapter Eighteen

February Twelfth

Felipe Quevedo loved Paris almost as much as he did Havana. Her wide boulevards, her charming parks, her incredible and endless supply of restaurants all offering gourmet delights, her piquant, irresistible women, her wines—once he'd read in a poem that Paris was a woman with robins in her hair. Whatever, the man who could not find enchantment here was not insensitive, he was dead.

He found excuses for returning to Paris whenever he could. It pricked his conscience at times, but after all, Paris and France were always friendly to Cuba even in the earliest days of the Revolution. Parisian ballets had visited Havana when other countries were too concerned with cutting diplomatic ties. So, he reasoned, government travel allowances spent in Paris were certainly justified. And the fact that there was a variety of beautiful French women eager to help him spend those pesos in no way affected the ethics of the situation.

What did affect his ethics was the fact that he always came to Paris a few days before it was necessary and sought out female companionship, usually professional. A married man, he reasoned, had no time to search for women and there was always the threat of a serious romance to disturb one's equilibrium. The Castro regime had, immediately on taking power, ended the world's oldest profession. Prostitutes were driven from the streets, thrown into prison, outlawed, vilified. By the time Quevedo joined the team two years later, there were only a handful of houses of prostitution left on the island and most of these were in Havana's slums. These, too, were driven from the scene and a lot of old whores became factory workers and cane cutters. Quevedo heartily approved of this antiprostitution campaign, all the more so since it was backed by and run for the benefit of international crime syndicates . . . But in Paris, the same ground rules didn't apply. Feelings of guilt for his infidelity to a beautiful, faithful wife also traveled badly. They disappeared into nothingness once his plane was airborne.

He had been partying at his spacious suite at the hotel for two days when the message he was awaiting finally arrived. The name of the man who was traveling to meet him was Antonio Costa, a man bearing the credentials he had made an essential requirement if a meeting was to be held at all. Costa had lived in Cuba in the Batista era and was well known to all law-enforcement agencies. He was a subchieftain in the underworld family that had once ruled the island and was known for his efficiency, cruelty and complete devotion to the Mafia. Though he did not rank as high as Rocco Floriani and never would attain such status, he was definitely someone to be reckoned with. The fact that he himself was coming from Mexico to France to meet with Quevedo seemed reassuring. He was not above committing murder and would without remorse torture a terrorized creditor, but he would not likely swindle an entire government. For Costa, there were easier ways to get rich.

As soon as he received the message, Quevedo went into the bedroom and awakened his current companion, who was sleeping off a night of alcohol and sex. She protested mildly but he quieted her with the promise of a doubled fee if she was gone in fifteen minutes. She made it in thirteen and in gratitude he tripled his payment. Next, he made several telephone calls and ended by ringing the hotel's housekeeper. She promised faithfully to have his suite spotless within thirty minutes and she did not disappoint him. Quevedo had the reputation of being a most generous tipper, and maids, bellmen, housekeepers and waiters danced about him in devoted attendance.

Antonio Costa arrived at the hotel approximately one hour later, called Quevedo on the house phone as arranged and was immediately invited up. Elevator connections were near perfect and within three minutes he was knocking at Quevedo's door. He was admitted promptly.

"Are we alone?" he asked immediately.

"Of course," Quevedo answered. "Do you think I need my mother to help me negotiate?"

"It's not your mother I worry about. I don't like meeting with committees. Not when I don't bring my committee along with me. Mind if I check out the rooms?" He didn't wait for an answer. Reaching into a shoulder holster, he pulled out a forty-five and started a thorough check of the premises. He even looked under the bed, in the shower and into each closet. Quevedo walked with him.

"Don't forget under the rugs, Señor Costa. We Cubans have a new invention. It's called pistol-packing cockroaches."

"Very funny. Look, Quevedo, I'm fifty-three and I've been playing these games for thirty-four years. That's a long time at one job. And you know why I've lasted? Because I'm always careful. You want to be smart ass, be my guest. I'll light a candle for you at your funeral. *Capish?*"

"Be as careful as you wish. It's just a little funny when I've heard so many stories about what a tough guy you are to see you looking in toilets for surprises."

"Once I wasn't too careful and three guys jumped me, held

1 4 5

me upside down with my head in a crapper and flushed it four times 'till I almost drowned. I've been allergic to toilets ever since. Now let's cut the shit and get down to business." He didn't even smile when he said it.

"That's fine. That's why we're here. Sit down, I'll pour you a drink."

"Make it Scotch. And I still can't understand why we had to travel four thousand miles for a meeting that could have been held in Mexico City."

"Let's just say I'm allergic to tamales like you are to toilets . . . Okay, let's have the information."

"Just like that? You out of your mind? There's a million-dollar payment due before we even say what day it is. You know that. Raymondo told me he explained it in advance. You told him yes or I wouldn't be here. So let's see the dough first. Those planes fly west as well as east and I've got a reservation every hour just in case."

"You certainly are an impatient son of a bitch, if you don't mind the friendly criticism. I've got your money. We're going to count it together so there isn't any mixup."

"That's more like it. You know, you're making a hell of a deal. This guy is already in your country and he's got his heart set on chopping up your leader into meatballs. Once I count the money, I'll give you the dope on him and you can nail him quick, chop him up."

Quevedo walked over to a portable bar that filled one corner of the living room. Feeling under the counter top, he found a hidden button that he pressed, causing the front panels of the bar to swing wide open. There, concealed in a stack of whiskey bottles, was an old leather Gladstone bag that he lifted out and carried to a large desk on the other side of the room. Turning the bag over, he dumped out stack upon stack of bills, all in large denominations. Beckoning with his head to Costa, he said, "Here, a million dollars. Count them for yourself. You don't impress me as the trusting sort."

146

Costa moved to the table and started to count. He took out a leatherbound memo pad from his inner pocket, a sterling silver pencil from another, and kept a tab as he counted with the thoroughness of an accountant presiding at an annual audit for the Internal Revenue Service. The counting went on for at least fifteen minutes. At one point Costa thought he heard something suspicious, left the table, moved back into the bedroom to check it out again, ruffled the draperies, then finally returned to his counting.

It was another ten minutes before Costa was satisfied. "Okay," he said. "It's here. Now how do we get it deposited into the bank?"

"The money is here. How you get it into the bank is your problem."

"My problem is your problem. You know the deal. When the money is safe in the bank, then it's safe to give you the information. Until then, I'm a mummy."

Such colorful language, Quevedo thought. He actually *sounds* like a gangster. Better, though, not to be diverted by surface appearances. "You told me a few minutes ago that when you received the money you would tell me what I came here to learn. Now, I give you the money and you, as they say, stall on me. Suppose I put it in the bank for you, and then you give me some crazy story that doesn't hold up? Where am I then?"

"That's bullshit and you know it, Quevedo. My outfit never asks for more than a fair shake. That's all we need. Brains and guts take care of the rest. Now you get a guard, help me repack this dough, call an armored car and we'll go to the bank together. When I come out, then we'll come back here and I'll sing for you. Until then, no music. Make up your mind. I ain't got all week."

Once the money was out of the hotel room and in some locked vault to which he had no access, Quevedo realized, he would be completely at Costa's mercy. Any story the man

1 4 7

chose to tell would have to be acceptable. But Quevedo's ability to foresee developments such as this was precisely the asset that had catapulted him into his present position of power even though he had competitors in the Castro regime. He knew that Costa would not want to give him the balance of power by advance-telling his information while the money remained in Quevedo's hotel room. Señor Raymondo had explicitly mentioned this as one of the conditions of the deal. At the time Quevedo had purposely not focused on this aspect of the proposal because he feared that it would be a deal breaker. Instead, he chose to bide his time and make his stand once Costa was in his room and matters were thereby more susceptible to his control. On the same grounds, with *plausible* bravado and bluff, he felt he could bring the mobster around to his position, combined with the fact that once Costa had seen the money and handled it his natural greed could be expected to influence him toward an accommodation. He'd thought it through like planning a tournament chess match. Costa had used a standard opening and he was ready with his tactical reply.

"You're right, Costa. We don't have all week. So you indeed better think this through, and carefully. That forty-five you're carrying doesn't frighten me too much. Look here, I've got one, too," he said, taking out his own and pointing it at the Mafioso. "You want to see who shoots faster and quicker? A shoot-out, Yankee style? Well, go ahead, reach. I'll blow your arm off quicker than you can come in a whore."

Costa, surprised, stonewalled it. "You don't scare me, you want to shoot, shoot. You still don't find out who's gonna blast your fuckin' premier. I ain't exactly shittin' my pants, either."

But he was, and Quevedo knew it. "I don't really care one way or the other. You want to get out of this room alive, you do things my way from this point on. You and your kind bled my country white for over fifty years. I hate you and all you did and stand for. Normally I wouldn't even sit down and negotiate with you about who is next in the men's room, but you're *supposed* to have valuable information for us and my country doesn't go back on its word. You give me the information here and now and I give you the money. Maybe I'll go further if it sounds authentic. I'll send some of my men with you to see to it that you get to the bank safely. Which brings me to that point—my men are down the hall, in the elevators, and down on the street watching the windows in this suite. You wish proof, listen."

"Alfredo, can you hear me?" he asked, speaking into a small portable transmitter.

"Yes, sir. I hear you clear. I'm in the elevator."

"How about you, José?"

"Clear, sir. I'm just down the hall."

"And you, Roberto?"

"Five by five. I'm on the street."

"Stand by. Our guest seems intent on giving me trouble. You know the plan. If I don't wave my hand at the window in three minutes, come up here and break into this room. Just blast away as if you were quail hunting. Don't worry about me. I would welcome the chance to shoot it out with this filth." He turned off the transmitter, then said to Costa sarcastically, "You got the picture, Mr. American hotshot gangster? Three minutes. Talk, you get your money. We help you to the bank. Hold back, your family won't even know where to plant the flowers. You people enjoy floral arrangements, I understand. What about it?"

One of Costa's prime rules for survival was to know when he was playing the weaker hand. Little question now that he had played into a bad situation. He really should have known better. Raymondo's assurances that the Cuban government would be so grateful for the information had lured him into a false sense of security. So he'd fucked up. But like being dealt a weak poker hand, some played it better than others and he was also accustomed to making the most out of bad situations.

149

At first he'd thought that this Cuban son of a bitch was bluffing. But those walkie-talkies didn't lie, he did obviously have the place surrounded. Play it straight and get out alive. What the hell did he care about the crazy trying to bump off Castro? He'd give out the information he had and hope he could get the million bucks to the bank. If not, at least he could cooperate to the point of getting himself out alive. He'd never liked these fucking Frogs. Paris, who needed it?

"Okay, Quevedo. Maybe you got a point. You want the information, I want the money. I don't know what all the jawing's about. I tell you the story and you have your men help me to the bank. Okay?"

"What I said was if the information sounded authentic, you'd get the help. Now, let's get to it."

"Yeah . . . well, this is the story so far as we know. The CIA in Miami contacted one of our *capos* and asked for help to knock off your top guy. They've done it before. Hell, every school kid knows that. But this time they're in a rush to get the job done before that meeting coming up in Peru. They don't want Castro around when you guys make another pitch to get into the OAS. And they don't care what it costs to get the job done—"

"What did you do when they contacted you?"

"We made a deal. Two million dollars. Half of it up front. We found them a boy. And he's in Cuba right now."

"What's his name?"

"Martin. Used to be Martinez when he lived in Cuba, way back when he was younger."

"That narrows it down to about five thousand, maybe ten thousand families."

"Hey, I didn't pick his name. And I've got more for you. He's about forty, forty-five, thin, wiry, big with the muscles, an ex-jock. Also from what I hear a very pretty boy, silver hair, straight nose, a regular Valentino, if you know what I mean."

"I know. We read junk in Cuba too."

"He landed a couple of weeks ago. Came in somewhere on the northwest part of the island. Swam in at night."

"He must be the one who landed at La Esperanza . . . we got several reports about that—"

"Yeah, that's right. I remember them mentioning that name. Esperanza. Anyhow, he was born and raised in Cuba. He and his family had to run when you guys kicked out Batista. He was about twenty-five then and was already loaded from what I understand."

"Okay. So now we know he is a man about forty years old, very handsome, very rich. His name is or was Martinez, but he obviously isn't using that name this trip. He landed at La Esperanza and he is working for the CIA through your organization."

"That's the story."

"Well, you must know more than that for a million dollars . . ."

"What else do you want me to know?"

"Such as where he's headed, who he's working with, what his specific plans are, what name he's using, what business he was in when he lived in Cuba, what his family did—"

"Look, Quevedo, I'm not a fuckin' computer. I do know that the CIA offered him a lot of help but he didn't want any part of it. Seems he doesn't trust anybody. They did give him a list of contacts, some that we supplied to them, but there's no reason to believe he'll get in touch with any of them. He knows people there himself. Like I said, he lived there until he was twenty-five—"

"But can't you remember anything about his background that will help us find him . . . ?"

"Yeah . . . well"—it looked like he'd have to let it all out—"he was in the manufacturing and importing business. No, that's wrong, I mean when you send stuff out . . . exporting. Exporting business. Yeah, and I also remember he was a big-time athlete in college. Made the Olympic team or something like that. A swimmer, soccer player, basketball too. Regular all-American boy."

"Do you remember anything about his family, anything at all? Were they exporters and manufacturers too?"

"No. Wait a minute. I've got it. His old man used to work in the government. Yours. A real big wheel. He played some ball with my guys and they socked away a lot of dough together. That's how he got the money to run when Castro came in. The old man was a real big wheel."

"Anything else you might have *forgotten?*"

"Well, I remember they're saying he was a big war hero in Vietnam. Decorated for bravery, shit like that. But that was long after he left Cuba. Maybe you got a record of those guys, but that's all I know."

"Are you sure there's nothing else?"

"Shit, man, you've squeezed me dry as a cow's tit."

"Well, if that's really it"—he suspected it was—"there's no point in wasting more time. Still, I thought there'd be more for a million dollars. But a deal, as they say, is a deal. Here's your money and I'll get my men to escort you to the bank."

He got up and handed over the leather bag. At that moment there was a knock on the door and a voice from the hall. "Room service, monsieur."

Costa whirled around, pulled his gun from its shoulder holster, pointed it at the door. "What the hell is this?"

"For God's sake, Costa, you're too nervous to be a gangster. I ordered up some drinks to celebrate. Keep your gun pointed if it makes you feel better. I'll answer the door."

He walked to the door and, unlocking the latch, pulled it wide open. Sure enough, a waiter with a cart loaded with whiskey, ice and glasses was standing outside. A waiter understandably hesitant to enter when he saw the gun pointed in his direction.

"All right if I invite him in?" Quevedo asked, smiling.

"Okay," Costa said, "let him in." The waiter entered tentatively but gained some assurance when he saw Costa pocket the weapon. He rolled the cart to the center of the room, locked the wheels and spread the table wings to increase the service area. He was still so nervous that the glasses and bottles rattled like an old jalopy. The noise distracted Costa who himself appeared somewhat unnerved. Although his gun was back in its holster, he kept his eye on the waiter, still suspicious. And his concentration on the waiter was exactly what Quevedo had been counting on to give his man hiding in the bedroom, which he'd entered from an adjoining suite, an opportunity to enter swiftly now and club Costa into insensibility with one blow of a billyjack. Costa pitched forward on his face. Three more Cuban agents entered swiftly from the hall and injected him with a lethal poison that took effect in seconds. Costa, who had lived by the double-cross, died via the same route.

Quevedo hurriedly picked up the Gladstone and headed for the door. He congratulated his men on the good job. "Now dispose of the body and let's go home. We've got work to do." He opened the door and left.

But there was one more bit of business to be taken care of while he was still in Paris. A meeting with French intelligence officials had been scheduled before he'd left Havana. Present, also, were representatives of the French Foreign Office. There were international bridges to be established. The eye of Felipe Quevedo was always, consciously, trained toward the future.

Chapter Nineteen

February Fourteenth

Within twenty-four hours Felipe Quevedo was back in Havana and hard at work. He phoned Raymondo in Mexico City and thanked him for his assistance. Yes, he had met with Costa and had gained some valuable information. He had not learned all of the facts he needed but he felt reasonably certain that Costa's leads would be helpful. He had paid over the million dollars as directed but explained that Costa had changed the dice. He didn't want the money deposited in any bank but had insisted that he be escorted to the airport where he had boarded a plane for South Africa. That word, he believed, would surely be leaked to the Mafia, who would assume that they, too, had been double-crossed and that Costa was greedily keeping the money for himself. As the days lengthened into weeks and Costa failed to reappear, they would be convinced that he was a fugitive from his own people. Some would no doubt eventually suspect what had really happened but by that time they would be involved in other, more important matters, and he would be forgotten. Life among the soldiers of the underworld was, after all, not that precious.

Now the real challenge of tracking down the would-be assassin started in earnest. For Quevedo, such a task brought a new incentive to his existence. He was like a hunting dog whose instincts and senses were sharpened by the chase. His working day would be lengthened, his need for sleep lessened, even his intake of food would be reduced. All need for recreation, sexual fulfillment, rest and relaxation would be forgotten. He felt like the primeval hunter entering the jungle in search of prey. A very special prey.

He called together his most trusted people and filled them in on their assignments. No one but them was to learn a single fact regarding their search. If the assassin was well connected he would somehow receive word that he was being tracked and so be all the more cautious. They must move swiftly, silently, without mistakes. More than they could imagine or understand was at stake.

Knowledge that he alone controlled was a precious commodity for Quevedo. It gave him a feeling of unique power, and exalted him. He considered himself more than the ultimate civil servant. He had further dreams . . . Knowledge was power. And no man in the whole national administration, sometimes even including Fidel himself, had access to as much knowledge as Felipe Quevedo.

A starting point was governmental records of the closing days of the Batista regime. The popularity of the name "Martinez" was a problem, but by no means an insurmountable one. They were to check tax records, real-estate holdings, lists of civil-service workers, payroll reports—even the newspapers of the day and their morgues. In forty-eight hours they were to meet again with detailed reports and backgrounds on every Martinez of any note that they could uncover. They were to work night and day. All leaves were canceled.

After two days they reported back that there were literally

hundreds of Martinez families and many of the early records had yellowed with age or had been obliterated. The men who had first taken over the government had been long in patriotism but inexperienced and lacking in organizational talents and clerical skills. Reluctantly, Quevedo gave his team an additional two days to complete this initial assignment.

They met again and reported greater success. Now they had uncovered fifteen Martinez males who at one time or another had held positions of power in the national government. Three had died years ago, leaving no issue. That reduced their concentration to an even dozen. All twelve had fled from Cuba soon after the Castro takeover in early 1959 and thereby were subjects for suspicion. Dossiers had been kept on a number of these and newly computerized police files helped weed out others. From underground sources in Miami they'd learned that Garcia and Raul Martinez, brothers, had moved on to other cities after having annoyed their fellow countrymen because of their disillusionment with life in the States and had once applied for reentry to Cuba, which had been denied. That left ten. Mario Martinez had been an old friend of Quevedo's deputy chief and was beyond suspicion despite his political leanings.

Three of the remaining had been bachelors and two others had been blessed with daughters and no sons. So now the search was down to four.

One exile, Pablo Martinez, it had been reported, had become involved in left-wing causes, had migrated to Mexico and after five years had gained permission to return to Cuba. He had served a brief term as a political prisoner, had been completely reindoctrinated and was serving his country loyally, recently having been elected to the newly formed provincial assembly from his district. Not a likely prospect.

Another of the four, Gilberto Martinez, had risen to moderate heights in the Batista regime but had never played a more prominent role than that of assistant public works director, which hardly qualified him for inclusion on a list of "real big shots," which Costa had described.

That left only two. Alfonso Martinez, a physician of some note who had earned his medical degree in the United States and whose family was among the richest on the island, had been one of Batista's closest friends. He had held several jobs of cabinet rank, had risen to Surgeon General, and reportedly had fled the island in Batista's own private plane. His sympathies were well established. He had had three sons, two of whom headed for South America and the third for New York when the government fell. All of his sons had been students at the University of Havana.

The final name on the list—Juan Martinez—had been equally prominent and so was equally eligible. A traditional Cuban aristocrat, his was a family of wealthy landowners for centuries. He had gained prominence in a number of fields: A leading professor of economics, a University president, a dashing figure in society and politics, Minister of Finance under Batista, here, indeed, was that "real big shot" they might be seeking. He was reputed to have Mafia connections as well and had amassed a huge fortune through illegal dealings. More, he'd had a son, and an illustrious one at that. He, too, had gone to the University, where he had acquired considerable fame. It would seem that if the sons of Alfonso Martinez were innocent, Juan Martinez III, the heir of his famous father of the same name, might well be their man. The nose of Felipe Quevedo, Director of the Ministry of the Interior, Chief of Cuban Intelligence, itched deliciously. Game was in sight.

Now Quevedo dismissed his men and took over the duties of the search alone. He checked phone directories of the late Fifties and learned that the Juan Martinez family had lived at Miramar on the famous Fifth Avenue not far from the tunnel that emerges from under the Almendares River. Here were the apartments and townhouses of the richest of the rich. He drove to the neighborhood in the hope that someone would be left who might remember the Martinez clan. It would not be an easy task, because many of the larger homes had been converted into tenements for families of political prisoners who were undergoing rehabilitation. Others were divided up into workers' flats and their occupants had been residents of this neighborhood for only a few years. Some of the wealthy who had found a way to play the Castro game still lived in their old homes and these were the ones he sought out. A dogged, door-to-door investigation turned up nothing. Finally he came across an old man who had worked in the area as a handyman for many years. When the rich fled, he had exercised squatter's rights and moved his family into one of the poshest apartments. Now he was retired, lived on a government subsidy and in the area was considered a neighborhood "character."

Yes . . . he remembered the Martinez family clearly. He had never liked the old man, though he described the son as much more down-to-earth and easier to deal with. He remembered how Juan had been the University's outstanding soccer star. It wasn't clear in his mind how the younger Martinez had made his fortune, but he thought he had been the owner of a factory that made farm implements. He couldn't recall anything about him being in the export business, and probably wouldn't have understood it if he could, but he did know that both father and son made frequent trips—to the States, to England, France and Spain . . . Quevedo gave the old man five pesos and told him he might call on him again.

It was well past two o'clock in the afternoon and Quevedo had had no lunch. He considered stopping for food but the trail was too hot to leave for a moment. Instead, he bought a carton of pineapple juice from a street vendor and nibbled on a half-melted candy bar he found stashed in the glove compartment of his car. His next stop was the University.

He started in the athletic department but found no one

who was a holdover from the old days. Athletics, aside from group calisthenics, had been considered frivolous in the days immediately following the Revolution. All coaches and trainers had been dismissed and found employment in more necessary fields. A few stayed for a while as hygiene instructors but soon found this dull and moved on. It was only after the new government considered itself more secure that athletic competition became popular once again. By then there were new coaches, younger and more politically oriented. No one working in the department now had any recollection of a Juan Martinez though a few seemed to recall that someone by that name had once been the University's top administrative officer. Whether he had been a soccer and swimming star no one knew.

From the school's employment office Quevedo went through a list of everyone who had taught at the University for more than eighteen years, and found the list longer than he'd expected. He calculated that it would take two full days to interview each of the twenty-seven professors still active from the Batista days. He would accomplish this in twenty-four hours. Identifying himself to the Provost, he explained that he was working on a matter of top priority involving national security and demanded that all twenty-seven be directed to meet with him in consecutive half-hour intervals that would continue until two o'clock in the morning and resume at sunup. He loaded himself with Benzedrine, like a student preparing for final examinations, and stopped only for a fifteen-minute supper break and the calls of nature. By noon the next day he had spoken to all twenty-seven educators.

There was only one, Dr. Ernesto Cabrera, who remembered Juan Martinez III well. There were many, of course, who knew of him, his great athletic prowess, his superior scholastic achievements, but only Cabrera had known him intimately. Indeed, having taught him in several political science and economics courses, he offered the opinion that he

159

was the brightest student he had ever had the pleasure of tutoring. "But after all," he said, "with such a brilliant economist for a father, it was to be expected that he would excel." Cabrera had followed his career after he had left college as well. He had hoped young Martinez would decide to train for the legal profession but he was eager to start working and had resisted his urgings to continue his education in graduate school. Instead, he had gone into commerce. Cabrera confirmed that Martinez had enjoyed success in the manufacture of farm equipment. He also knew that this had led him into the exporting business, where once again he had experienced success. When the Martinez family had fled Cuba, Cabrera had lost all contact with them and had never heard their name mentioned again until this day when he was interviewed by Quevedo.

"And what happened to their home? To his business? Did no one remain to carry it on when he left?"

"No, not one member of the family remained," Cabrera answered. "The Martinez family, all of them, were named enemies of the state. All of their assets were appropriated by the government—liberated, as it is called."

"You do not think such action justified?"

"It was only a joke," Dr. Cabrera told him quietly, "only an old man's poor sense of humor."

"I would hope so. Some things one doesn't joke about."

Cabrera decided Quevedo was a humorless fanatic. He'd better watch his tongue.

"And did you know an Alfonso Martinez who was prominent about the same time?"

"Dr. Alfonso Martinez? Why, of course, who didn't know him? He was one of our country's most famous physicians. I believe he became Surgeon General in the old days."

"And did he have a family?"

"Oh, yes. Three of his sons came through the University. I believe I taught one of them. A fat, slovenly fellow and a very weak student. People used to tease him about his 'brother' Juan who got all of the brains and most of the muscles in the family while he inherited only the blubber. But, of course, it was only a joke. They were not related at all. I really can't tell you much about them except to suggest that over at the medical school you can talk to Dean Gutierrez. He will remember Dr. Alfonso Martinez quite well. Perhaps he can tell you more about his family."

Thanking the old professor and suggesting that he keep himself available for further questioning, Quevedo headed for the medical school. He was confident that he already had identified the rabbit he must track down, but thorough detective work required elimination of *all* possible alternatives. Gutierrez was out at a conference but Quevedo settled down to await his return. The previous days' lack of sleep caught up with him now, and he dozed in an easy chair outside the dean's office. A hesitant receptionist gently shook him awake. "Dr. Gutierrez will see you now." He awoke with a start, studied his watch and was amazed to realize he had slept for nearly two hours.

The old man was friendly and as cooperative as his memory would permit. Yes, he knew the Martinez family well. The old man had been arrogant but equally brilliant. The sons were all disappointments. He had learned through the grapevine that none had turned out well. The doctor's namesake, Alfonso, Jr., had gone to New York and had married a rich widow eighteen years his senior. He was reportedly living the life of a country gentleman. He hadn't heard anything about the other boys except that they had run off to South America, possibly to Ecuador. He hated to say it, but these were the type of exiles that Cuba needed more of in order to continue its remarkable progress. "I believe there is an old saying that goes, 'Good riddance to bad rubbish,' " he added.

"Is it possible that any of these men could have been athletic? Swimmers? Soccer stars?"

"You, my friend," laughed Gutierrez, "are barking up the wrong Martinez."

It seemed clear to Quevedo that any further time spent on the clan of Alfonso Martinez would be pure waste. Again he thanked the dean and took his leave. It was nearly six o'clock and he had been working steadily since early morning. But the surprise nap in the waiting room of Dr. Gutierrez was all the rest he needed now, and he plunged on with the search. Rushing back to the economics department, he caught up with Dr. Cabrera just as he was about to leave for home. After some insistent urging, the doctor agreed to join him for a glass of wine at a nearby café. Even though the professor had told all he remembered, experience had taught Quevedo that constant, even repetitive talk could sometimes uncover long-forgotten facts.

As Cabrera ordered a glass of white wine, Quevedo selected black coffee to keep himself stimulated. If he were fortunate enough to discover something new, he might find himself working into the late hours of the night. They sat at an outside table enjoying the cooling breezes of evening as the sun started its downward arc into its ocean bedroom. After a polite pause, Quevedo started his questioning once again.

"I am really fascinated by all you have told me about young Martinez—that is, Juan, your prize scholar. Did he make many friends while in your classes? Or was one so unusual too good for his fellow students?"

"Not at all. Not at all. He was very popular with his fellows. As a matter of fact, unless my old memory deceives me, I think he was elected president of the student body . . . no, no, now I remember . . . there were a number of students who asked him to run for the office but he just wasn't politically oriented. And the left-wingers resented his wealth and his father's position in the government. So he refused to run at all. I remember discussing this with him one afternoon when we met on the library steps."

"If he was as bright as you say, as athletic and as handsome, I'll bet he was a killer with the ladies."

"Well, of course, morals were much different in those days, you know. Generally, the young men couldn't visit the young ladies alone. Always the chaperones in the Spanish tradition. Personally, I think it mostly served as a strong factor in building large families. The young couples were so frustrated while courting that they never got out of bed the first years of their marriage."

"You may be right," Quevedo acknowledged lightly. "It's as good a theory as any . . . So, to the best of your recollection, Juan Martinez behaved much like all of his friends of the day, playing the field, taking out the girls and their mothers at the same time? Nobody special? No one girl you can remember who might hear from him from time to time even after he left?"

"I'm sure not. He did seem friendly for a while with a very bright Jewish girl who came here from New York to study and stayed for a long time. I really don't know much about her and I'd never remember her name. I only taught her for one semester in a single class."

"Are there records somewhere?"

"Records?"

"Yes, class records. Does the University keep students' attendance and grade records from years back? Is that possible?"

"Oh, yes, it's possible. I wouldn't know. But they probably could tell you over at the student matriculation center. Perhaps you could try there tomorrow morning."

"You've been a considerable help, Dr. Cabrera," Quevedo said, getting up and dropping a five-peso note on the table, "but I think I may try tonight."

Cabrera watched in amazement as Quevedo moved quickly down the street.

It took him a half-hour to find the students' records office after a late-working clerk in the matriculation center told him he had been misdirected. By the time he had puffed up the steps, the lights were out and the records office was closed for the night. It took him another hour to discover the name of the Dean of Admissions who was in charge of all record-keeping and another thirty minutes to reach him on the phone. Dean Escarcega did not enjoy being disturbed at home during the dinner hour, but a few sharp words from Quevedo convinced him he would be wise to cooperate with the Minister of the Interior. He was back at the office by eight-thirty.

To find the records of classes from prerevolutionary days was a most complicated but not impossible process. During the past five years computerized records had kept Cuban education at pace with the rest of the world and Escarcega could deliver even the remotest information about the University's student body in a matter of seconds. But in the late Fifties, this type of scientific advance was still in its early planning stages. Records were kept in old-fashioned looseleaf binders and stored in cardboard cartons lined with tinfoil to keep out dampness. An outmoded card-filing system served as an index to the storage cartons that had been placed in various storerooms spread throughout the entire campus.

"I can bring in some extra help tomorrow morning and we can speed up the job—"

"We'll do it ourselves. And we'll do it tonight," Quevedo told him.

By two o'clock in the morning, after thumbing through thousands of file cards, Escarcega finally found a reference to classes in basic economics taught by Dr. Ernesto Cabrera in the days just before the Castro takeover. He had given the same course for three years and then had moved on to more advanced classes as his own reputation spread. As bad luck would have it, the records for each of the three classes were stored in entirely different vaults in far-spread corners of the campus. Again, Escarcega asked for a recess until the morning when young assistants could help track down the information.

"Morning is now," Quevedo told him.

The sun was just nosing above the horizon when the last of the three vaults was reached. A half hour later Quevedo came across attendance records containing the name "Juan Martinez III." And six names lower on the list was an unmistakably Jewish female name—"Myra Rubin." Strange, but that name smelled familiar to his detective's nose. Thanking Escarcega sincerely, he dismissed him in time for breakfast. No need for him to write down the name—he would never forget it. Less need to seek his bed, because in such an agitated state he could never sleep. He could use a shower and a fresh shirt, though, and so he headed home. Within sixty minutes he was at it again. The trail was sizzling now, and he would not let it cool.

Although Quevedo prided himself on the accuracy of his own memory, he was forced to take a back seat in this area to his deputy Miguel Dávila. Of all the men he had ever come in contact with, none was a match for Dávila when it came to recall power. Once, in a mere exercise, Miguel had named every agent who had ever worked in the department and had topped this feat by giving the names of all of their wives and their hometowns. If the Department had been in any way involved in the history of Myra Rubin, it was Dávila who would remember. He called him at home and asked him to get to the office immediately.

It was an easy, near-automatic task for Dávila to give forth with a virtual barrage of facts about Myra. Actually, he had met her several times and been assigned briefly to work on her case. He had known her as one of the few foreigners, and probably the only United States citizen, who had openly taken up the Castro cause. She had worked with the power structure in the earliest days of the Revolution and had risen to a position of trust and influence. Later, he recalled, she had become disaffected with Cuban Communism and had fought to emigrate. Because of her knowledge of Cuban matters of state, the government had been reluctant to permit her to leave. It was during this period that he had been assigned to keep watch on her activities. He was certain that he could produce a complete dossier on Myra Rubin.

Exactly as Dávila had forecast, there was a thick folder substantiating all he had remembered. Since she was considered somewhat dangerous and certainly out of favor as far as the government was concerned, the records listed virtually none of her associates because all had shunned her in the final days. But there was one couple who'd remained loyal to her— Jorge and Alicia Ortiz, schoolteachers in the town of Guane. In fact, Myra had lived with them for a couple of months during her last days in Cuba. The records indicated that Jorge, a known opponent of the state, had died under mysterious circumstances several years ago, after Myra Rubin had left for Mexico City. One letter from Myra to Alicia mailed from Florida had been intercepted and examined. It expressed sorrow over Jorge's passing, so apparently word of his death had leaked to the States.

"Anything else?" Miguel asked his superior.

"Yes. Can you remember the name of the foreman on the night crew that built the Leaning Tower of Pisa?"

It was one of Quevedo's few attempts at humor.

"Sure, I remember. But why should I tell you? Then two of us will know."

They helped themselves to steaming cups of coffee. Quevedo dumped an ice cube in his. He couldn't waste time waiting for it to cool. There was work to be done in Guane and by speeding he could reach the town in two hours.

Chapter Twenty

February Seventeenth

As had been their custom all week, Martin and Alicia dined by candlelight. On several evenings following his grueling days of "peddling" in Havana, they had rushed off to bed before even finishing their meal. There was a shared sense of urgency in their love-making, a feeling that it was of limited, unknown term. But limited, as they both knew.

"You make love to me, dearest Carlos, as if you must use me all up by morning, like food that will spoil in the sun."

"You're right for the wrong reason. I figure that I've wasted too many years not knowing you. I want to make it up in a hurry. I really don't have time for a waiting game, which sounds corny, I know. They sang that in tribute to September."

"I'm familiar with the song. But that is a song for an old man. And you are young and handsome and smart—"

"Well, if I have to grow old, I want to do it this way. With you, naked in my arms. Now, please shut up and kiss me. Enough philosophy . . ."

On this night they chose to finish dinner and cap it with a delicate cognac he had purchased before boarding the bus to Guane. They sipped it while sitting on a small patio at the side of the house, enjoying a sky full of twinkling gems. The beauty of the moment created its poignancy, intensifying as it did the contrast with their job for the following day.

"I've been thinking," Martin said without introduction, "that you shouldn't go to the Isle of Pines with me tomorrow."

"Any why not? Don't tell me you've already found another woman in Havana?"

"Hardly. But I'm worried about that message Duran sent me before they caught up with him. Who knows how far he went? If he really had alerted the authorities and if he was right when he warned that we were being watched, it would be stupid of us to play into their hands by repeating trips together to the same place. The more variations we create, the more difficult it is for them. Besides, this is, after all, my job and I'm being paid well for it. You've paid your dues . . . your husband . . ."

"I'm not worried about 'paying dues,' as you put it. My *heart* is in this mission too."

"But until we're absolutely sure that Duran was lying for his own purposes when he sent us that message with the soldier last week, there is real danger. I can handle myself if it comes to that. I'm not sure I can protect us both. Maybe I'm being selfish, I don't know. I'd rather get over to the prison, speak to Pérez, and have you waiting here to hurry back to. I certainly can't think of a better incentive for making the trip there and back quickly."

"All right. I said I would help and not get in your way. If you really think it will be safer and easier alone, I won't argue—"

"I do. I'll be back tomorrow as early as I can make it and we'll have a real celebration."

"Bring back good news from the Isle of Pines and we'll have good reason for celebration. I promise you a feast, my darling."

"With you, my love, a hamburger would be Chateaubriand."

"Oh my God, listen to us."

They went quickly to bed, where there was no more need for talk.

He got up at dawn and boarded the earliest bus to the ferry. He was surprised to find a large crowd on the dock already awaiting the sailing of the first boat. Since families were restricted to weekend visiting, everyone wanted the longest possible time with loved ones. The trip across was calm and uneventful. There was no security check this time, and now he realized why Alicia had been alarmed by all the activity on their last trip. The contrast was obvious.

He walked from the dock to the prison as quickly as possible in order to avoid entanglement with the mob of visitors emerging from the ferry. The security procedures at the prison were identical to those of the week before, and he'd been seated for only a short time when he heard his name paged on the loudspeaker. He was admitted to the inner waiting room at once and after a short additional wait, Manuel Pérez entered the room and headed directly for his table. They shook hands formally and Pérez sat beside him, lighting a cigarette and offering him one as well, which he refused. They exchanged few words. Pérez seemed extremely agitated and hesitant to open their discussion. It was obvious that the thought of playing a part in Palma's game was almost too much for him to handle after years in a political prison. After nearly five minutes, Pérez got up and said, "Come, we'll walk on the athletic field again."

When they were reasonably isolated Pérez's whole manner

changed. "I've gotten the word to friends and there are several ready to help you."

"Several? How many people know I'm here?"

"It's a relative word. No one knows exactly who you are but there's a general awareness that CIA plots against Castro continue. I merely told my people that I had been contacted by someone who might need help in an emergency and they offered their help. In turn, they sent a warning to you."

Martin looked at him.

"Whether or not you are the only one in the field no one is in a position to say. But there's the general feeling that Cuban intelligence is very active and alert to a present danger. They've noticed that now whenever Fidel takes any kind of trip at all he is surrounded by security agents all of the way. Before he would just drop in, the way he did here at the prison last week, but only with his brother and a few friends. Once in a while there would be guards, but certainly not like last week here. It must mean that they suspect trouble and are trying their best to protect him. So you must be doubly cautious."

"There are no degrees of caution. Either you're careful or you lose your head."

"That sounds like a sensible policy. At any rate, I really haven't given you the important news. I contacted my Uncle Ramiro. You know about him, of course. He is still our Minister of Defense and as such sits on the Politburo. He is the senior field marshal of our armed forces. No man has won more medals for bravery, more military honors. I'm sure Fidel has no more real use for him—Uncle Ramiro is seventy-three now and the vogue is for young men. But Fidel recognizes his contribution, so he stays in office."

"How safe is it to confide in him if he still has his titles and sits in in the highest conferences—"

"Normally I would agree, but Uncle Ramiro is something very special, I assure you. He's lost his interest in power and

170

he personally doesn't go along with the new atheistic fashion—he's too strong in his Catholic upbringing for that. But he also won't take part in any plots against Fidel. That would be treacherous, disloyal. At the same time he won't go out of his way to *stop* such plots . . . he thinks that history will take care of Castro soon in any case, so why stand in its way? It may seem like convoluted thinking to you, but that's Uncle Ramiro, so why not take advantage of his willingness at least to be cooperative?"

It sounded to Martin as if Uncle Ramiro wanted it both ways, but he readily agreed that he should be taken advantage of. "And how will he help?"

"I'll tell you . . . please be patient . . . You must first know more about my uncle's views . . . Ever since the missile crisis of 1962 his confidence in our international policies has diminished. He thinks we are wrong in seeking Russia's help and relying on their friendship . . . they've certainly demonstrated their willingness to back down when it suits their convenience. He would like to see us move back into a friendship with the United States. If Fidel is, somehow, gone, it would be his intention to use his influence in seeking out that friendship and cutting Soviet ties. When you meet him, as you will, make certain you express views that are consistent with these ideas. Uncle Ramiro is no fool. He is a survivor. He will understand what your purpose is and why we have sent you to him. And I believe he will, in his fashion, help if he can . . ."

"That sounds fine. Forgive me for being impatient but how do I make contact with Marshal Pérez?"

"When you leave the Isle of Pines you must contact Señor Luis Fuentes, one of our most brilliant young lawyers. He is a rich charming bachelor and is considered by everyone to be most loyal to the government under which he has thrived. But his is an act. He despises Castro and works constantly for his overthrow. He's really the unofficial leader of our revolutionary underground. He lives in a fine house on the Avenida Latino America, not far from the Botanical Gardens. Come on, let's walk further away. Everyone here is suspicious."

They strolled around the athletic field and parade grounds for another five minutes or so, then rested on a deserted bench apart from the rest of the visitors.

"You were telling me about this Luis Fuentes," Martin said.

"Yes . . . You contact him at his home and use the password '*pez.*' We call ourselves 'the fishes,' for some forgotten reason. Anyhow, he will expect you and take you in. Then he will use his influence with my uncle, they are good friends, and get you a job as an assistant of some sort in my uncle's office. He will not, of course, reveal your assignment to my uncle, but Ramiro will assume that you are no friend of the government. From there on you must use your wits to get close to my uncle and gain his confidence. This way you should be able to meet some of the country's social and political leaders. There is no one in a position of power Uncle Ramiro doesn't have access to. But from there on, you will be on your own."

"It sounds very good . . . and my plan is to spread the word that I'm a free-lance journalist preparing a favorable biography of Fidel for worldwide distribution. Hopefully, his vanity should make him vulnerable, at least receptive . . ."

"It sounds all right. We will be praying for your success."

"It will all have to happen quickly. I've only two weeks left for this job."

"Then you'd better not waste any more time here. There are many people counting on you."

The two men rose and clasped hands solemnly. Martin's gratitude was expressed in silence. They said good-by, perhaps for the last time. Martin went back to the prison waiting room, checked out with the authorities and was on his way. He caught a return ferry almost immediately on reaching the dock, selected a quiet corner and planned for the days ahead. He felt no fear. The challenge was exhilarating. He had no intention of failing. And there was the open passion of Alicia Ortiz to strengthen him. When it was done, he would have to find a way to take her with him. He would insist on a divorce from Margaret, which she would probably give him with pleasure. Funny, he hadn't thought about her for weeks now. More than likely she'd told the children that he was a bum and deserted them. Well, on the face of it, he had. Margaret would never understand him risking his life to get rid of a dictator or to save his father. That took a little imagination, not exactly Margaret's strong suit. But why take it out on Margaret? She was exactly as he had married her and he got what he saw: a beautiful, fragile blonde, good blood lines, a wealthy family of in-laws with society connections, and not much brains. What was that old saying? Be careful what you ask for, you may get it . . .

The bus was waiting at the landside dock when the ferry moored. It was almost like the days in Miami when Armando Velez would be waiting for him with the limo whenever he landed at the airport. He wondered what had happened to Mandy since he'd disappeared. Well, that old son of a bitch would land on his feet no matter what the toss. No doubt he had a new position by now. No doubt he was just as lousy a driver and still lording it over his friends and neighbors.

Martin boarded the bus for the short ride to Guane. It was only one o'clock and he should be with Alicia in about thirty minutes. These good transportation connections gave him excellent vibrations. Even the midday heat wasn't too unbearable. He'd just relax and dream about the welcome that was waiting for him. He'd heard men say that most of the pleasure in love-making was in the anticipation. Bullshit! Dreaming was pleasant, doing was delicious.

Later, as he tried to reconstruct the events of the day, he was never really certain what had caused his first suspicions.

Was it the quiet of the marketplace on a beautiful Saturday afternoon when it should have been teeming with activity? Perhaps it was the contrast with the villages he had passed, all of which seemed to be staging concerts, fairs and various weekend celebrations. Guane was strangely silent. He noticed this from the window of the bus as it wound down the hill over which he'd first jettisoned Maso's truck. It was one of those subconscious checks that he had been accustomed to making in Vietnam. Whenever enemy troops were hiding in a town there was a strange, palpable silence instead of the normal hubbub of activity. This kind of calm was always a giveaway. He didn't like it. He'd have to make an immediate decision. He couldn't ask the driver to stop now even though he was the only passenger scheduled to disembark at Guane.

Moving up to the front of the vehicle he bent over the driver and, trying to sound casual, said, "I think I'll get off the other side of town. There's a back road closer to my house. It won't make any difference to you, will it?"

"No trouble," the driver answered. "Just tell me where to stop."

He returned to his seat and slumped low. Sure enough, he thought he spotted some cars parked near the bus stop, with men sitting in them, casually watching the road. Apparently they didn't notice him as the bus sped by without stopping. Once past the main intersection of the village, he moved forward again and told the driver, "Never mind stopping. I think I'll go on to Consolación del Sur."

"Just as you wish, señor. But that will cost you another two pesos, please."

He dropped the extra coins into the money box and again returned to his seat. It was an anxious forty-five minutes but if things were okay he could easily explain the situation to Alicia. Having gotten off at Consolación, he headed for a public phone by the side of the road and dialed Alicia's number. The phone rang without answer. Finally he heard a click. Alicia's voice.

1 7 4

"Hello," she said.

"Is Lolina there?"

"Who?"

"Lolina?"

"There is no Lolina here."

"She must be there. I left her there this morning."

"I am very sorry. There is no one here by that name. You must have a wrong number. Please do not bother me. . . ." She hung up.

It was enough. Alicia had obviously recognized his voice. The fact that she had broken off was her way of warning him. He must not even consider Alicia, he told himself. *Must not.* No doubt she was in the hands of government agents who would be furious that he'd escaped. He'd been foolish to allow himself to be vulnerable, to become emotionally attached in the midst of his mission. Well, his only chance now of saving her—or himself—was to avoid Guane and head immediately for Havana, contact Luis Fuentes, who might be in a position to help . . .

Buses were running regularly from Consolación del Sur to Havana; he had little trouble boarding the next one. Within two hours he was in the capital city climbing aboard another vehicle marked "Botanical Gardens." Though it was late in the afternoon there were still large crowds headed for the relaxation of a trip through these lovely walks lined with their rich wonders. Even the country people who had served the soil and been nurtured by it all of their lives were impressed by the Gardens' beauty. Martin found himself swallowed up by the crowds, and was grateful for the anonymity. Somehow, though, his thoughts were still with Alicia.

He found a public phone and, uncharacteristically, an up-to-date untorn telephone directory. There was a residential listing for attorney Luis Fuentes on the Avenida Latino America. He called the number and after about five rings a pleasant, not unfriendly male voice answered.

"Hello. This is the residence of Luis Fuentes."

"Señor Fuentes?"

"No. Señor is out for the afternoon. And who is calling, please?"

"He may or may not know my name. We are old friends. We used to fish together off Cienfuegos." The word fish was slightly emphasized. He hoped enough.

"And what is your name?"

"Carlos Palma. We have a mutual friend, Pepe. We live in San Pedro and I believe Señor Fuentes is familiar with Aunt Cintia."

"A moment, please. I think I hear Señor Fuentes coming in just now. Excuse me."

"This is Señor Fuentes. May I help, please?"

"This is Carlos Palma, you recall we once fished together. I'm in the neighborhood and need some legal advice, so . . . would be so kind as to permit me to visit your home? It is really quite urgent."

"You know where I live?"

"*Si*. I have the number. I can be there in a few minutes."

"Come over. I shall wait for you."

His ring was acknowledged promptly by an aide whose voice he recognized as belonging to the man who first had answered the phone. He was invited in immediately, as if identification was well established, indeed, as if he had been expected. The aide, who identified himself as Alfonzo Acebo, offered him coffee, which he was grateful for . . . he suddenly realized he hadn't eaten since leaving Alicia's early in the morning. They were soon joined by Luis Fuentes, a slim, foppish-looking man with a long oval face and deep-set gray eyes that gave him a look of age beyond his natural years. Fuentes was also tall and moved gracefully, as if trained in ballet earlier in his life. His appearance was soft and feminine, incongruous with the booming voice that resonated in Cuban courtrooms with such authority. It was as if a gazelle had swallowed a bull frog and taken over its voice.

"We've been expecting you, Señor Palma. You are welcome here."

"You're very kind, Señor Fuentes. I need help. Alicia Ortiz is in great danger . . . my fault, I'm afraid. And I'm also afraid I can't do much for her alone."

"The facts, please." Fuentes had abruptly become the professional lawyer.

Martin told him, including the abbreviated telephone call from Consolación del Sur.

Fuentes listened, nodded. "There is nothing you can do. Nothing we can do. Alicia is obviously in the hands of our intelligence machinery. They will torture her, if necessary, to learn about you. Any attempt to contact her is unwise for her as well as for you. You'll do best to wipe her from your mind—"

"Wipe her from my mind? That woman sacrificed herself for me. I have to try to help."

Fuentes got up, went over to the coffee table and helped himself to a cup, then turned and looked at Palma. "Señor Palma, let me be frank. Fidel Castro hid like an animal in the mountains of Oriente Province to overthrow the government of Batista. Anyone who opposed him once he gained power was killed, tortured, expelled. The man who would go against him, and have a chance of succeeding, needs to be equally cruel, determined. My cause is your mission. But I am no martyr, nor do I want to sacrifice myself, my career and my associates for the sake of your feelings—guilty or otherwise. They are your problem. Cope with them. Anyone caught is yesterday's news. You must forget Alicia Ortiz. Perhaps some miracle will save her, but it's not likely. I knew her husband and he paid the price of opposition. She understood the rules when she joined us, when she helped you. Either you accept them or I must ask you to leave immediately."

Martin knew the man spoke the truth. Besides, in a way he realized that to sacrifice himself in a predictably hopeless effort to rescue Alicia would betray what she'd been willing to risk her life for.

He told Fuentes he was ready to go forward and asked only for help to complete his mission. "Manuel has told me his plan and I assume you understand how and where I should go from here."

"Yes, the plan originated with me. I'm close to Ramiro Pérez, we understand each other. You will need new clothes and, forgive me, a haircut. You must present the appearance of a man of conventional attire and beliefs. Alfonzo will show you to your room and you are welcome to remain here as long as you want. I have some assorted clothing in the upstairs closets but if you need more, money is no problem and our shops remain open late today. A new wardrobe might be an asset. I have a dinner engagement this evening so Alfonzo will prepare food for you and we will talk again tomorrow. There's a garden party I've been invited to tomorrow afternoon and I have a feeling that the man we want you to meet may just be there. It would be the ideal time for introductions."

Next morning Martin got up early and bought the Sunday paper. Buried in the inner pages he found the item he more than anything wanted not to find. It was reported that a schoolteacher named Alicia Oritz had suffered a sudden, inexplicable mental breakdown, had run into the street waving a revolver, endangering the lives of her neighbors. Local police had been forced to shoot her. She had died en route to the hospital.

Chapter Twenty-One

February Nineteenth

Dressed appropriately, bathed and trimmed by a local barber, a refurbished Carlos Palma accompanied Luis Fuentes to his garden party that afternoon. It was hosted by Liliam Pazos, a Latin beauty who served as Castro's social directress. "We call her the 'Cuban Perle Mesta,'" Fuentes said, "but if I remember correctly, Mrs. Mesta was no beauty-contest winner and Liliam Pazos could be." Martin looked critically at the amply proportioned brunette in the décolleté dress and had to admit that Mrs. Mesta would have been no match.

"Come," Fuentes said, "you must start meeting people quickly."

They headed for the hostess who was smilingly greeting all her guests.

"Miss Pazos, I'd like you to meet my old friend, Carlos Palma. And he is old. See the gray at his temples?"

"I see them and I approve," Liliam answered, taking Martin's hand and squeezing it just a bit too intimately for a formal hostess greeting.

"Then I won't pull them out," he replied. "I hope you'll forgive me for inviting myself to your party. I dropped in on Luis and he insisted that there is always a shortage of eligible men. So put me out now or forever suffer the consequences."

"I'll bet there are lots of ladies who would enjoy such suffering," Liliam answered with a laugh. But she was already turning her attention to the next guest in line and busily flirting with him.

Liliam Pazos was a traitor to her class. Born to multimillionaire parents with vast holdings in cattle and oil fields in Argentina, she had come to Cuba as a young girl to visit family friends, had fallen in love with the island and decided to remain. Even though the government favored a redistribution of wealth and was a natural enemy of her own class, she found herself attracted to the fiery, dedicated revolutionaries who held power. Her striking looks were a passkey that unlocked social and economic barriers. Her aggressive personality carried her past even the most skeptical members of the power structure. Before long, her lovely face ornamented every major social function involving the upper echelons of the Castro regime, many of which she financed with her own funds. She was obviously the target of every male on the hunt and here, too, she knew when and how to submit. She was seen quite frequently in the company of Fidel himself, and it was an open secret that they were occasional lovers. In recent months there apparently had been a cooling between them because they were seldom seen together except in large crowds. Whether this was according to Liliam's desires or not no one was certain.

Fuentes led Martin to the bar and they both accepted long cool drinks to offset the afternoon sun. Martin looked back to the informal receiving line and focused is attention on Liliam Pazos. As striking as she was, she was no match for Alicia . . .

Fuentes noted the look. "I know this is difficult for you, but you must try to look as though you're enjoying it."

"I'll do my best," he said, and his face assumed a harlequin smile.

They moved about the garden, smiling and chatting with other guests, none of whom seemed to pay this Palma any special attention. A few of the unattached females noticed him, to be sure, and they took Luis aside to ask the usual question.

"Your friend is married?"

"Not necessarily."

"Like all men."

"Like all people," Luis corrected, and moved on.

About fifteen minutes later there was a noticeable stir in the crowd and Fuentes nudged Martin, inclining his head toward the entrance gate, where an important guest was arriving. It was an elderly gentleman in military attire who was pumping the hostess' hand and nodding warmly to all who were gathered around her. She took the old gentleman's arm and led him to the bar and refreshment table.

"Pérez?" Martin said.

"Yes," Fuentes answered. "We will meet him soon."

At an opportune moment Luis Fuentes led Martin over to Ramiro Pérez, standing alone for the moment, just having refilled his glass at the bar.

"Marshal Pérez, I have a friend here who would like to meet you," Fuentes opened.

"Well," the old general answered, "in the old days it was the girls who wanted to meet a soldier. But I guess we must grow accustomed to things changing."

"There are still plenty of girls here who are impressed by Ramiro Pérez, I'm sure of that. But men, too, admire heroes, and my friend here is no exception. May I present Señor Carlos Palma? He comes here from Santiago and will be my house guest for several days."

"I consider this a great honor, Marshal," Martin said, taking the old man's firm grip in his own.

"You are kind," Pérez answered. "Are you, too, an attorney like Señor Fuentes?"

"No, I'm afraid not."

"Actually," Fuentes broke in, "Señor Palma is highly educated and could have trained for the bar but elected not to. He does many things—commerce, journalism, government consulting. Many things. But his most notable talent is as a journalist, with particular emphasis on the historical meaning of current political events. You may recall that you and I have spoken several times about the importance of recording your recollections of the early days of the Revolution. No one has a greater grasp of the importance of those happenings than yourself, and, as you know, I feel strongly that it would truly be a shame if future students of our country's history were denied an opportunity to share your thoughts."

"Thank you, Señor Fuentes. Yes, of course, I recall that we've discussed this several times before. It's just that I never seem to have the time or the inspiration to put it all together. Like most military men, I've kept diaries and notes, but I'm hardly the literary type—"

"I doubt if the Bible was written by 'literary types,' Marshal Pérez, but its message has served as a guide to people for centuries—even those who may not believe in a deity." Fuentes's reference to the atheistic views of the day was not accidental.

"True. And modesty doesn't prevent me from saying that I would enjoy seeing my thoughts recorded—"

"Señor Palma would be the ideal man to help you accomplish this. The truth is he is looking for work in this area. Even temporary work, a few weeks or months perhaps, would be of great help. And I would consider it a personal favor as well, Marshal Pérez."

There was a meaningful, missed beat in their casual cocktail chatter, a brief silence that held its own significance for the

Marshal and Fuentes. Then Marshal Pérez spoke. "We in government are always short-handed these days. The pay isn't much, of course, but we can always use good minds and willing workers. When the Lord handed out talents, he offered my great, great grandfather a choice between broad shoulders and a facile mind. Apparently there was more need for broad shoulders at the time."

"From what I have read, your ancestors were amply endowed with both," Martin said, "and I'm grateful to you for the offer of a job. I'm sure I can be of some help with your writing and the money is really not that important. I'm living with Señor Fuentes for a few days but I'll move into my own quarters and as long as I have enough to sustain myself that will be fine."

"Good," Marshal Pérez said firmly. "We'll expect you tomorrow morning at the office to make arrangements."

"I'll be there. I'm sure the arrangements will be fine. Again, thank you, Marshal Pérez."

Later in the afternoon Martin was approached by the hostess, who, taking him by the arm, led him to an empty table away from the crowd.

"I must talk to the handsome man who is causing so many female tongues to wag," Liliam said.

"That's a good idea," Martin took it up, "and exactly where is he sitting?"

"Modest is charming too. He is sitting beside me and all of the eligible ladies would happily trade places with me. You must tell me all about yourself, Señor Palma."

"Must I?"

"Well, let's say because I'm intrigued enough to ask."

"I really don't know what to tell. I am an old friend of Señor Fuentes. We were at the University together many years ago. I live mostly in Santiago but I travel a good deal too. I've had a rather checkered career, I'm afraid, but essentially I make my living as a writer and journalist. I work for Reuters, the British press association, covering my native

Cuba and all of Latin America. Which, of course, is why I must travel. And I must say that our government has been most cooperative in giving me freedom to move abroad wherever my profession requires. Señor Fuentes tells me that you came here from Argentina. I've been there several times, but not for many years. Anything else you'd like to know?"

"Yes. A few vital statistics would be helpful."

"Statistics? Let's see, I'm six feet one; weight, one hundred seventy-five, size forty-two suit; a seven-and-one-eighth cap. I am forty-two years old. And you?"

"Ladies tell neither their age nor their dress size. And those were not exactly the statistics I was referring to."

"Oh? Well, I am an only son. I am once married and divorced. I have no children, no heirs."

"And how do you know Marshal Pérez . . . whom I saw you chatting with a while ago?"

"I met him at a garden party at the home of a beautiful lady, Liliam Pazos. Actually, as you probably know, he is an old friend of Luis Fuentes. Señor Fuentes had told me that the general was looking for someone to help him compile his memoirs. I happen to be between assignments for a few months and since I have a background in history from college days and am an experienced journalist, he suggested that I might be of help."

"Wonderful. Then we will have you with us for a while. I hope you and I can become good friends. Marshal Pérez is one of my favorites, you know. So I shall take the liberty of expecting a call from you soon. If not, I warn you that I will call you. Handsome, eligible men are in short supply in Havana. You'll be in great demand, I promise you!"

"I look forward. And I'll be the one to call, I promise you."

He started work the next day, reporting at nine o'clock sharp in Marshal Pérez's office, to discover that the old man had been at work for more than an hour. As a military man, he was accustomed to rising at dawn, reaching the office at eight or earlier, and completing his office work by noon. His whereabouts the rest of the day, he felt, was his own business and there was no one with sufficient authority to question him. He greeted Martin formally but in friendly fashion and invited him to join him in an early morning cigar. Cuban-grown and rolled cigars were a luxury that Martin had missed. They were one welcome advantage in his new life as Carlos Palma.

"I've gathered the preliminary work I've done on these memoirs we discussed with Señor Fuentes. It will take you a few days to go through it, I'm afraid. Forgive my poor spelling and penmanship. When you've had a chance to read it all and formulate some ideas, we'll get together again and make plans. Many of my assistants from the old days are still working in the government and they'll be happy to fill in my memory gaps. There's no hurry. Take your time and then come see me . . . By the way, you'll need some identification papers to get in and out of the building. Let me get my aide-de-camp," he said, pressing an intercom button.

Almost too swiftly the door swung open and Tomas Escalante entered. He was big, a rugged veteran of the battlefield, with a swarthy complexion dominated by a huge, ink-black mustache. He was distinctly business.

"Señor Palma will be working with us for a while, helping me compile my history of the movement. He'll need identification."

"We will want the usual Ministry of the Interior workup, no?"

"No, colonel, that will not be necessary. Señor Palma is well known to me, an old family friend. Just a pass, his photo, the usual preliminaries."

"It has been Señor Quevedo's orders, sir, that all new employees be interrogated before being given passes to these headquarters buildings. It would only be a matter of three or four hours, if you have no objections—"

"I have already said that I do object. I know all about

Quevedo's rules and regulations. If we had them before he joined the movement we might still be hiding out in the mountains. Next he'll be asking to cross-examine you, colonel."

"That, Marshal Pérez, is his privilege. I'm not arguing, sir, I'm just trying to comply with your wishes." But he actually did worry about the old man's "softness" and would have preferred the thorough Quevedo routine, even though there was no particular reason for him to suspect this dandified writer, at least not any more than he suspected any intellectual . . .

"He'll join you in the outer office in a moment. Just wait for him there, Colonel Escalante." Escalante saluted and left.

Turning to Martin, Marshal Pérez smiled. "Don't be upset by the 'army way' in this office, Señor Palma. Colonel Escalante is a good man, even if that Bulganin mustache is a bit foreign looking for my taste. So many of our most trusted officers think that they have to look and act Russian these days in order to make everyone confident that they are loyal. You understand . . . ?"

"I do, Marshal. It's the same all over the country, the young people think they aren't Cuban if they don't act Russian. It's a paradox." Martin remembered the instructions of Manuel Pérez on the Isle of Pines. Here was the perfect opportunity to let the Marshal know they shared certain areas of belief . . .

"Yes. I worry about it often. Let's suppose for some reason that we . . . change partners or go it alone one of these days. With all our young people acting Russian, forgetting their *own* rich heritage, we'll have to start educating our people all over again."

"Agreed. It is a problem. Friends, partners, aren't necessarily forever. Not much is. Anyone who reads history knows that." He'd said enough, he decided, for his purposes. He said good day and rejoined Escalante, who was waiting impatiently in the outer office. The colonel remained formal, but apparently was willing to go along with Pérez's orders although he clearly wasn't happy about it. He gave Palma a brief identification form, a badge to be carried with him at all times and instructions to attach a photograph of himself, which could be taken for him in these offices if he so desired. Martin thanked him and assured him he had plenty of pictures he could attach at home (he hardly wanted to risk the possibility that a negative might be filed for future reference).

Martin called Liliam Pazos the next afternoon and asked her to join him for dinner. She had a prior appointment but would reschedule it. She suggested that their first dinner be at her home; they could go out afterward to dance if the notion appealed. He explained that he would not be able to meet her until after eight o'clock since he was in the process of moving to the El Elegancia, a small but fashionable residential hotel near his office. "Perfect, time for a beauty nap," she explained. And, hating himself, he answered, "You really don't need it."

The evening was programmed: The table was laid with fine linen and china, the room was rich with the fragrance of gardenias, the burning tapers replaced the need for harsh electric lights. The help moved about silently, doing their jobs and saying discreet good-evenings at an early hour. Liliam looked festive in a white off-the-shoulder gown, and Martin knew, and she knew, from the outset that there would be no straying from her home that night.

They were in bed by ten o'clock. He tried to be responsive but it was impossible; it was a bad performance. He couldn't tell if Liliam was equally unmoved, because she too was an actor and spent much time expressing *amazement* that she had submitted to him so rapidly on their first appointment. She at least spared him fluttering eyes. He was tempted to say that he'd been the one to submit, not vice versa, and so forth, but he thought better of it. His reply that their getting together was "apparently meant to be" was bad enough. They made love again, a little more realistically than the first time, but still mostly going through the motions.

At her suggestion they dined again the following evening at the Habana Libre, once the plush Havana Hilton before all hotels were confiscated and nationalized, and Martin found it almost impossible to handle—this was where he and Alicia had planned to dine when he returned from the Isle of Pines . . .

"What's the trouble, *caro*, you seem upset. Is something wrong?"

"No, nothing, I'm just a little wound up from all the changes in my life these past few days. A new city, a new job, a new and wonderful lover. That's a good deal to absorb at one time—"

"True. But you will grow accustomed to it. And since we became friends so quickly, we should now feel like old friends." She reached across the table to squeeze his hand. "Just think how lucky we are. If Luis Fuentes had not known that Marshal Pérez needed a writer to help him, you would never have visited his home. And if I had not been having a garden party, and if Fuentes had not known that Marshal Pérez was also to be present, he might not have brought you along. You and I might never have met!"

"You're absolutely right . . . I'm a lucky ungrateful dog. And also, don't forget that if it hadn't been for our leader, you might not have wanted to move here from Argentina, and again history might have failed us . . . By the way, rumor has it that you and El Comandante are quite close . . ."

"I consider that a great honor," she replied (challenging? testing?).

He tried to recover quickly. "I understand completely, of course . . ." And then, allowing his attention to drift for the moment across the room, he received a shock. Facing him, seated at a table for two with another man, was Tad Duncan. Although Martin could see only the back of the second man's head, he quickly realized it was Reginald Hawkins, the man he'd met that day at the Anglo-Swiss Trading Company, the day he'd learned of Duran's death.

The obvious question was, what had brought Duncan to Cuba? Could his visit in some way be connected with Duran's murder? Probably not. The killing of a double agent was hardly a momentous happening in the world of espionage. Could it be a reaction to his own warning that he did not want to be trailed around Cuba like a fishing skiff towed by a yacht? Possible, but he clearly recalled having discussed this with Duncan when they first met in the States. Duncan had said he would not be tailed, but that he, himself, would decide if and when his own appearance in Havana was indicated.

Still, Duncan's appearance wasn't something he could dismiss. Here was, supposedly, a leader in the American intelligence apparatus, yet he boldly shows his face in Havana . . . There still was the possibility, Martin felt, that his mission was a setup, and he was a cat's paw, *against* the U.S. If he were captured and his target revealed, how would America alibi such an *obvious* attempt to assassinate a legitimate head of state? *Could* Duncan himself be a double agent? Unlikely, but possible . . . On the other hand, maybe Duncan's plan had called all along for his being kept under constant surveillance, regardless of their agreement. He could well be in Cuba merely to receive a first-hand report from Hawkins on their reactions to his activities to date . . .

Whatever, if this meant the start of a series of cat-and-mouse ploys with himself the mouse, to hell with it. If the CIA saw fit to follow him here on the job, so to speak, sure as hell they would follow him *out* of the country, and his life expectancy would be damned short. Duncan as employer *and* potential enemy was a no-win combination.

He had no doubt that Duncan had noticed him, assuming

of course that he had not followed him there in the first place. Nonetheless he decided to play it as if he hadn't been seen. He invited Liliam to dance and maneuvered her so that he kept his back to Duncan's table and stayed as far away on the dance floor as possible. At an early hour he suggested, meaningfully, that they return to her home and whether or not she particularly wanted another session in bed, she at least didn't argue, for which he was grateful. He signaled for the check, paid the bill and led Liliam out of the room, skirting the area where Hawkins and Duncan were seated.

In her car driving toward her elegant home, he worried if she was somehow suspicious.

"I didn't want to say anything," she told him, as though reading his thoughts, "but I'm glad that we left early. Last night, as you may remember"—and she smiled—"was a long one. I could use some rest . . ."

"Is that your way of telling me that I might not be invited in?"

"No, it's my way of saying that once you are invited in you're not going to stay until the sun rises. We'll save those sessions for the weekends, agreed?"

He wanted to say not only "agreed" but that he was relieved. What he did say was, "It sounds too much like a game plan for playing our football. When we're tired, we'll stop." He hoped he sounded more indignant than he felt.

Later that evening as he sat on her veranda drinking cognac and puffing a Cuban cigar, he felt that the time was right to risk bringing her into his plan more directly. "You've been so kind to me from the first moment we met that I hesitate to ask another favor . . . but I thought that since we share the same respect, and affection, for El Jefe that you might want to help. In addition to my work with Marshal Pérez, I'm in the midst of writing my own definitive biography of Fidel. I hope it will serve as an inspiration for young men all over the world. I want them to realize that no matter how mean their beginnings they can actually change history, *make* history, if they have the guts and the vision."

"What an exciting idea! I don't think there's ever been a friendly biography written and available outside Cuba about Fidel since he came to office—"

"There've been a few, but nothing complete, nothing inspirational. Too many start with the *Granma* landing. I want to go back, back to the days when he was a boy, when he was a student at the University and first felt the call. I've been picking the Marshal's recollections and other people's around the office. But I really need to get more intimate facts."

"But how can I help?"

"You know Fidel well. If you could manage to tell him about the project, I'm sure he would approve. Then all I need is a thirty-minute audience with the man himself. I could get the direct, straight answers to my questions, answers that no one else can possibly give accurately. History will be richer for that interview, if you can help out by asking him—"

"But of course I'll ask him. Except there will be a problem . . . I want you to know about it . . ."

"And that is?"

"And 'she' is," Liliam corrected. "Her name is Maria Díaz, Fidel's personal secretary—I guess that's the title for her. She was the first woman to join the movement. She actually fought with him and Raul in the Sierra Maestra. She worships the ground he walks on and he's as loyal to her for her support. At times she's been his mistress, but that's long over and, I'm sure, forgotten, at least by him. She's his housekeeper, his personal secretary, the female alter ego of Fidel Castro. And she hates and is deeply suspicious of any other woman he favors. You joked with me last night about my relationship with Fidel. As I told you, I'm not ashamed that he and I were once lovers. To the contrary. He is a god as far as I'm concerned. I would go back to him if he needed me. But Díaz, of course, hates me, just because Fidel once found me pleasing. She sniped away at both of us until any personal relationship became impossible. Now we see each other once in a while but it's on a quite formal basis. When I go to him with this request, and I shall, she will be very suspicious and will do all she can to defeat it. He may, in this instance, over-rule her, because he believes in his place in history. But it won't be easy. Maria Díaz will fight us."

"I've heard about her before. And I'm sorry if I was insensitive last night. But my schedule calls for the first draft to be finished by the end of this month. So I really must meet with Fidel as soon as possible."

"I do not make promises easily, Carlos. I will see him before the end of the week. And now that I know that we share a further admiration, I suggest you come over here and kiss me. I think it will be better than last night."

It was.

Chapter Twenty-Two

February Twenty-fourth

Three days later, by coded message, Tad Duncan received orders to return to Washington. In his eight years with the CIA he had received only one summons recalling him to headquarters, and that was on the occasion of the passing of the nation's chief executive. Such an order was nothing to take lightly.

He left Havana that same afternoon, boarding a flight for London. A United States Air Force superjet waited for him and, pausing only for tower clearance, headed back across the Atlantic. Benefiting by a five-hour time-zone advantage, he was back in the States before midnight. A helicopter stood by to take him to Langley.

Colonel Redfield, assigned as his escort, smiled as they two-stepped up to the main entrance. "We made it, Mr. Duncan. I promised I'd deliver you before the date changed and here we are."

"That's right, colonel. If I hadn't emptied my bladder in

Havana this morning, we'd have been late. So you have to give me some of the credit too."

"No question about it, sir. But we did bring an empty hot-water bottle along just in case. Frankly, I'm up for brigadier and I wasn't going to let anyone piss away my chance for promotion, no way."

"You fly-fly boys think of everything."

"We try to, sir. It's right down the hall and through the double doors." Both men had been waved by sentries after a nod of Redfield's head.

"I know this building pretty well, colonel. My pay checks are signed here."

The two men stared each other down. Apparently there was little affection lost between them.

"Look, Mr. Duncan, I didn't ask for this job and I didn't call you back from Havana. I had duty there myself in 1958 and it's a damn good life, or was . . . so don't take it out on me. She'll wait for you down there, whoever she is . . ."

"It's when I meet people like you, *colonel*, that I wonder what the hell I'm risking my life for in the first place. There's no 'she' waiting in Havana and since I've now arrived in one piece at my destination, I suggest you refuel your spaceship and take a flying fuck to the moon." He turned around then and disappeared behind the pair of heavy, oaken doors.

"Welcome home, Mr. Duncan. We missed you." It was Sally Marshall, the chief's private secretary. Tall, slim, chic, Sally at fifty-five had kept all of her appeal. She had served in the department for twenty-one years and risen from part-time typist to her present position. It was said that no key decision was made by the chief without first trying it out on her. Those on the departmental up-escalator had been permanently downed because they violated her standards of propriety. Despite her power, despite her dedication, despite all of the in-fighting that governmental jockeying involved, Sally Marshall had stayed a lady. She had gone quickly to the top of her profession on one asset alone: ability. She had been married only briefly during World War II—her husband, a West Pointer, had been killed at Salerno. She never remarried. She took the CIA for a lover and never regretted the choice.

"Truthfully, I can't say I missed you, Sally. I wasn't away long enough."

"True, Mr. Duncan." She never allowed herself the privilege or the familiarity of using first names. "But it's been a busy three days. The chief hasn't been home to change his shirt since Tuesday. Mrs. Barker trots over with his laundry and he sleeps right on that worn-out leather couch."

"Sounds like big doings. Is he in?"

"He's been waiting for you. I tried to convince him to go out for dinner but he'd have none of it. Inhaled some cold salad down at the cafeteria and then back to dispatches for dessert . . . I'll tell him you're here."

Marcus Oliver Barker looked no more like the Director of the Central Intelligence Agency than a duck-billed platypus resembles a giraffe. He was squat. He was paunchy. His wispy gray hair moved in all directions on the top of his balding pate like a herd of wild cattle in search of a leader. His vision was faulty and the thick lenses in his wire-framed glasses did nothing to add dignity to an already semicomic appearance. Though he loved an occasional round of golf, he was badly coordinated and the worst of duffers. His thin, piercing voice, far from conveying authority, crackled unpleasantly.

But Marcus Oliver Barker was smart. And those who made the error of judging this book by its cover were sure to end up in trouble. A Harvard Law School law-review editor, he had immediately on graduation found a position with the Department of Justice and moved upward with lightninglike speed. Five years later he switched departments and soon thereafter was tapped as Assistant Secretary of State for European Affairs. Whatever job he tackled was performed with speed and ability. It was obvious that the MOB—a sobriquet his initials virtually dictated—was on his way to the top. He had headed the CIA for the past ten years.

"Come in, come in, Tad," he squeaked, "don't stand there in the doorway forever. We'll have to charge you rent."

"You, I'll pay, chief." The two men exchanged warm hand-clasps. Barker's grip was amazingly strong despite his appearance.

"You wanted to see me, chief?" Duncan said as soon as he had slipped into a chair opposite Barker's desk. The MOB had a busy schedule. Even at midnight there was no time for small talk.

"Yes. Sorry to bring you back so abruptly. But we're running into trouble on the Hill."

"How?"

"We've got an internal leak. I have my suspicions, but I'm not ready to act yet. At any rate, every time we start moving in on a target—an *approved* target—the word somehow reaches the press. They've been pasting us left and right and eighteen ways to the ace."

"Well, chief, you've got broad shoulders. They've been giving you hell for years now and you just move right on over them—"

"It's different this time, Tad." Barker stopped to light his pipe, his only concession to stereotype. "They're gaining strength politically and they're hitting where it counts, with the appropriations people. I got a call from that ex-boy wonder out of the West, the rightly so-called Junior Senator. He was in this office yesterday telling me he'd gotten wind of three different plots to eliminate heads of foreign nations. I told him he was reading too many science-fiction magazines but he wouldn't quit. And he won't. We had quite a row."

"How did it come out?"

"A standoff. But he did say he had his sources and he was especially concerned with our relations with Cuba. How he

196

got wind of Shaving Mug I don't know, but he suggested he would be watching us. Suggested, hell. He said it. And he warned me, the righteous son of a bitch, that if we went ahead and touched that man, he'd see us kicked out of office."

"What's he so worked up about Cuba for? They sure as hell don't reciprocate."

"There's a whole group of them, the folks who're going to show us how to make friends with our enemies. What the hell do they care? They'll be out of office in six years and while they'll be cheering all of those Cuban dancers and athletes they've brought over here, we'll be facing the real music—of economic and military subversion of Latin America and Africa. They want to reopen diplomatic relations with gentle Fidel—the Latin lover. After all he's done to us around the world, and here too . . . He's up to his ass with Russia in Africa and we're sending senators to Havana like white doves. Worst of all, I'm convinced most of them are grandstanding to take advantage of the prevailing wisdom, and popular opinion, that we're all little Nixons, lying to and undermining the country. And, of course, we can't let them know who gives the orders around here. *They*, for Christ's sake, elected him."

"You weren't considering calling off Shaving Mug, were you, chief?"

"No, not calling off . . . cooling off. I was wondering if there was a way to hold off for about thirty days or so. Maybe all this bullshit will die down—"

"Chief . . . you told me March seventh was the deadline, which I assume somebody fairly important told you . . ."—Barker nodded—"and once Castro gets to Lima and they take him back in the OAS, we're in deep trouble. True, we're not exactly loved south of the border, but at least we're in decent control and respected. Once one note gets there, it's a whole different ball game. We just can't let that happen."

Barker swiveled around in his chair and pointed to a framed picture just above his desk. "You see that picture, Tad? That's me at my swearing-in ceremony. My dream that day was that in one year I'd build an organization so efficient and far-reaching that this country would never have to worry about surprise attack or *threat* of attack again. And I've done that. Now, ten years later, they're trying to destroy me and, more important, all those men and women who aren't afraid to put their lives on the line in service to this country . . . I'm not going to let them do that. Hell, last year some son of a bitch on the Senate Finance Committee tried to get me to agree—off the record, of course—to cut down my personnel by thirty percent. I said, 'Senator, they may be just statistics to you, but they're flesh and blood people to me. Why don't you do the same with your office staff?' He got the point but didn't think it was very funny."

"I'm sure. We cut back projects, we cut back jobs, it's the beginning of the end."

"Exactly. Now back to Shaving Mug. How's your man working out?"

"So far, five by five. He's moving up and looks confident. If we pull him, I'm not sure he'll go back. Or should."

"True . . . They can't trace him to us, you're sure of that?"

"Who's going to talk, chief? And he won't be around to tell the story . . . which, of course, is why I'm tailing him myself. To make sure of that."

Barker nodded. "All right. It's decided. Continue full speed ahead. By the time those senators get around to roasting our ass, they'll be running for reelection and I figure the public will be on our side—except for the cigar smokers. Okay, then, get your tail back to Havana."

Chapter Twenty-Three

February Eighteenth

The trap at Guane, in the home of Alicia Ortiz, had remained set, ready to be sprung all afternoon. By two o'clock, Felipe Quevedo was convinced that his man had escaped. It was at that hour that Alicia's torture began.

Quevedo insisted on tape recording every minute of it. Alicia was stripped before a group of five male agents. Electric wires were attached to her breasts, prods with electric connections were forced into her vagina and anus. Each time she refused to give information about the man she had been sheltering, currents were forced through her body. She was hung by her hands from an overhead water pipe and beaten with rubber truncheons on the back, sides and abdomen, with special concentration on the liver and kidneys. At one point water was forced down her throat with a one-inch hose until she nearly drowned. Artificial respiration was needed to revive her so that her treatment could continue. She refused to break.

When Martin had phoned from Consolación del Sur she

199

was cut down and guided to the phone with instructions that the slightest hint of warning would mean instant death. She thought that ironic, under the circumstances, but the will to live dies hard. By her voice and attitude, though, she felt, hoped, that she had given enough warning. She might still have screamed or said more, but she felt that such an overt confirmation that there was such a man as Carlos Palma working among them would be a critical error and destroy their group. Once she hung up they renewed their efforts. Now, believing they'd been deceived, they felt all the more resentful. Her agony lasted three more hours. She never spoke. They wrapped her body in a burlap sack, put it in the back of a police van and took it to an unmarked pauper's grave. The press release about her going berserk was Quevedo's contribution.

Quevedo moved his headquarters to Guane the next morning. Together with a few chosen assistants he cross-examined each local resident about the mystery man who had spent a week in their midst. He cajoled, threatened, bribed, used every psychological tool of his trade to learn any facts about the man named Juan Martinez, who he knew must be traveling under an assumed name on his mission to murder Fidel Castro.

Quevedo got little cooperation from the residents of Guane. Actually, there was not much they knew. Alicia and Carlos had remained aloof during most of his stay with her. On those few occasions when they faced neighbors, they had wisely chosen to use still another alias. Alicia had simply referred to him as her "friend, Gilberto." One neighbor insisted that she had called him "Humberto" and still another swore she heard him referred to as "Mauricio." No one had heard a last name. As for his physical description, there was an equal division of opinion. All mentioned that he usually wore a floppy straw hat that covered much of his face. Some said he was all gray, others insisted that he had simply a touch of white hair at the temples, while others were positive that his hair was coal black, his face unlined.

Quevedo returned to the University after two days of futile interrogation at Guane. Once again he canvassed all of the professors who had at one time known Juan Martinez but he learned little that he had not known previously. One professor actually produced a group picture of students celebrating a national holiday and insisted that Juan Martinez was among them. But the faces were so small that even enlargement with modern equipment gave little feature definition. Worse, the professor himself wasn't sure which man was Juan Martinez.

Quevedo became like a man obsessed. He could not sleep, he could not enjoy a meal, he could not face his wife or children without thinking about Juan Martinez and how he had succeeded in eluding him. His own special motives were all but lost in the frenzy of the challenge and his building frustration. He hallucinated at night, dreaming weird dreams of a man from outer space named Martinez who had landed on Cuba determined to wipe out every leader and torture him, Quevedo, to an excruciating death. Dark rings appeared under his eyes, he was short-tempered with his men. Felipe Quevedo was not trained for defeat.

The first small break in the case came—as they usually do—in an unpredictable way. There was a female agent of Mexican citizenship named Justina Ríos who spent some of her time in Cuba and traveled widely throughout Latin America. She sold her services to numerous countries for a price, usually a very high one. She was fearless, inventive and generally reliable. She would accept assignments on either side of a political fence, but once having committed herself to a mission, she could in no way be bought off by the opposition. She was treated with great respect in most intelligence circles because once she gave her word, it would not be broken, and the information she offered to sell was usually valid. Her only limitation was self-imposed; she would not work for the CIA, out of a long-standing bitterness against so-called Yankee imperialism. Justina Ríos was a woman of principle, even if selling information that often led to death was her business.

She called Miguel Dávila, Quevedo's assistant, from Mexico and told him she would be in Cuba the next morning. She said she had vital information that he would need. The price was high, one hundred thousand pesos. He offered to meet her at the airport but she refused, telling him she would see him at the Havana Grande hotel. Her arrival time was scheduled for 10:00 A.M.

They met as arranged and got right down to business in a hotel room he had reserved in advance. She demanded her money before talking and Dávila paid. Having pocketed her fee, she revealed her information. There was a high-ranking American foreign agent who had just arrived in Cuba and was setting a trap in Havana.

"But we've known that for weeks," Dávila said. "We've gotten warnings about that character and my boss has him identified. We'll have him any day now—"

"We are not talking about the same fellow," Justina Ríos said. "You mean the man brought in here by the CIA in their deal with the Mafia. Every agent in South America knows that story. They're even saying that your men eliminated the Mafia chieftain who brought you the tip."

"I don't know anything about that crazy story," Dávila lied. "But what do you mean, you're not talking about the same man?"

"I'm not. When I ask for one hundred thousand pesos, I've got something new to sell. You know that. Quevedo knows it too. I don't fuck with old news. The man I'm talking about is top-rank CIA. He's tall, blond, walks with a slight limp like a man favoring an old injury from athletics. He walks very straight, this fellow, could be an old military man. Oh, yes, I almost forgot: I understand he's going bald in front and likes to brush his hair down Hitler-style to try to hide it. He came to Cuba about three days ago. Flew in from Switzerland and booked at the El Esperante Hotel. He usually doesn't move around too much during the day, but generally eats out at night with a friend. Watch the hotel, you'll find him."

"And what's his connection with this other one?"

"That's your problem. You want me to do your work too? Okay, the price goes up. All I can tell you is that my man is not small time. I suggest you put someone on him, quickly . . ."

A watch was established at the El Esperante and by six o'clock that night the man with the limp was photographed with telescopic lenses that made each hair as legible as print on a billboard. Blown up on a screen before the entire staff, he was immediately identified as the local sales manager of the Anglo-Swiss Trading Company, a man known as Peter Roche. Miguel Dávila's elephantine memory recalled that at one time there had been some suspicion that Roche, who came and went from Havana at will, might be an American agent. Investigation, though, proved nothing. Actually, everyone swore that he was the most bitter anti-American in the entire foreign colony in Havana. On checking his dossier, Quevedo found that once again Dávila's recollections were correct. Not only was Roche established as anti-U.S. in his leanings, he had actually volunteered his services in an effort to bring them information from the countries in which he traveled that might help in Cuba's continuing conflict with its neighbor to the north. At one point he had warned them that Russia might not hold the line if its missiles were ever discovered on Cuban soil. Since it was not generally acknowledged that atomic warheads were being imported to Cuba, they could not deal with him. But later, when Russia backed off in the face of President Kennedy's threats, Roche had been proved correct. All of which, of course, did not prove that he couldn't have been recruited as an American agent *since* that time . . .

Justina Ríos's lead further fired up Quevedo's energies. An

educated, tested instinct told him there must be a connection between Peter Roche's sudden appearance in Havana—he normally traveled more than he was in his Havana office—and the illusive Juan Martinez. A check at immigration headquarters disclosed that Roche had not been in Havana for almost ninety days previously. Why did he now suddenly appear? Quevedo was convinced he could solve that mystery, and when he did, the trail would lead directly to Martinez.

Peter Roche, or at least the man who represented himself as Peter Roche, had now been identified. The challenge at this point was to keep him under surveillance and discover precisely what it was that he was about. Why had he returned to Havana and why had he chosen to live at the El Esperante and, apparently, remain distant from his place of employment? If he were a foreign agent the job of tailing him would have to be handled with the greatest finesse. Once he learned he was being followed, or even guessed that he was under suspicion, his whole course of action would be designed to mislead rather than enlighten those who watched him. It was a ticklish business. Quevedo felt that he and he alone would have to handle the assignment. It was part of the fever that had consumed him from the first moment he'd learned from Carmen Raymondo that Fidel's life was threatened by a foreign agent. To date he had come up with unsprung traps, but he felt that his luck was changing now. He turned the temporary control of the department over to Miguel Dávila and set himself up, with an adequate disguise, outside the El Esperante. He would function without food or rest if necessary but he would be a fly on Roche's ceiling, an omnipresence when Roche contacted—as he must—Juan Martinez. Roche, and Martinez, could wiggle. They would not escape.

And so it started. Tad Duncan, alias Peter Roche, knew almost at once that the man in the floppy Panama and dark glasses was not a tourist. Whoever he was, he had apparently seen too many Class B American movies. By his attempt at anonymity, Quevedo (no fool, certainly, but increasingly a victim of his obsession) had made himself a rather conspicuous target. Duncan decided that he would oblige him in his interest. He hired a car at the hotel desk and drove about town slowly enough for Quevedo to pick up his trail. He headed due east to Cárdenas, stopped for a few drinks at a neighborhood pub, then drove southeast to Cienfuegos. He took a walk by the sea, made several phone calls, all innocuous, then headed back to Havana and his hotel, with Quevedo trailing him all the way. Next he returned to the car, drove southwest to Pinar del Río, visited an old business friend, stopped at a roadside restaurant for dinner. Two hours later he emerged, drove four-and-a-half hours straight to Camagüey. Here he rented a hotel room for the night and retired. Setting his clock for five A.M., he rose early and headed almost due south to Santa Cruz del Sur. A weary Quevedo, fairly certain now, despite his obsession, that he was being taken, simply could not afford to let the trail—even an apparently diversionary one—cool off, and so he was forced to continue the pursuit. Roche headed next for Santiago de Cuba, where he lunched at a lovely terraced restaurant overlooking the sea. Quevedo meanwhile sat in his car, eating a stale ham sandwich. A seven-hour, pleasure-drive return to Havana did little to improve Quevedo's temper, which was reaching the explosion point. He accepted now the impossibility of conducting this entire investigation alone. If he were wrong and there were no connection between Peter Roche and the man known as Juan Martinez, he would be wasting many hours. As soon as he could find someone to relieve him in this phase of the job, he would do so.

Before looking for relief, he followed Roche into the lobby of the Habana Libre, saw him enter the Royal Palm lounge for a drink. It was especially dangerous to follow him into the bar—but Quevedo was now convinced that his man Roche knew he was being followed. What he didn't know was that his ultimate quarry was seated there at that minute awaiting the arrival of Liliam Pazos, with whom he was to dine. As soon as Martin saw Duncan (as he knew him) enter, he got to his feet, dropped five pesos on the bar, looked briefly at Duncan as their eyes met and, brushing past him, headed for the street. In so doing he nearly knocked down Quevedo, who was intently keeping his eye on Roche (as *he* knew him).

A Keystone Cops comedy, except here the subject was death.

Having phoned Liliam and informed her that he would not be able to meet her as planned but would contact her in about an hour, Martin headed for the Anglo-Swiss Trading Company offices. He was furious and had made up his mind to give Duncan a final warning. If they didn't stop tailing him, he was determined to give up the case and head back to the States. There, with his two hundred and fifty thousand dollars already banked safely away, he would make his new start in life all the same. Since the Mafia had already received much of its money, his father's position would also be greatly improved.

As he suspected, the lights in the Trading Company office were out and the door was locked and slide-bolted. He wrote out a note by the light of a streetlamp and slid it under the door: "Butchers need helpers. Barbers shave alone. Last warning."

But because of Roche's identification—which, of course, Martin knew nothing about—Quevedo had ordered one of his men to keep watch on the Anglo-Swiss offices. As soon as Martin left the note under the door, the agent, overlooking nothing . . . especially considering Quevedo's mood . . . picked up Martin's trail, radioing back to headquarters for someone to break into the Anglo-Swiss offices to find out the content of the note.

By now Quevedo had assigned one of his subordinates to

Roche, though he had little hope that Roche was much more than what Western detective-story writers called—he winced at the phrase—a "red herring." He had been gone from his office for almost thirty hours; he was badly in need of a shave and a shower; he was hungry.

At the Ministry headquarters he was surprised by two pieces of news waiting for him. The first: Octavio Orellano, the man he'd assigned to watch the Anglo-Swiss offices, had picked up the trail of another suspect who might well be involved . . . indeed, he even allowed himself to hope it might be Juan Martinez himself. The way his luck had been running these past few days, it was due for a change.

But then the second piece of news seemed even more promising. After constant investigation, one of the agents he'd left at Guane had turned up that a neighbor, who on first questioning swore he could add nothing of value to the search, now remembered seeing Alicia and her male companion heading for the ferry to the Isle of Pines early on a Saturday morning. He had been in the area to board a fishing boat for a Saturday-morning jaunt. Although he had not spoken to them, he was certain they were lined up with the families of the prisoners who were waiting to board the prison ferry.

On his own initiative, the agent had left Guane and taken the boat to the Isle of Pines, where he had carefully examined the visitation logs for the past several weeks. On the Saturday indicated, Alicia Ortiz had indeed visited the prison accompanied by a man named Carlos Palma. They had come to visit a prisoner named Manuel Pérez. And Carlos Palma had returned the following Saturday to visit Pérez once again. Which was the same day that they had taken care of Alicia Ortiz in her house . . . where she had received a suspicious phone call she'd hung up on . . .

Although prison documents weren't easily examined, the agent identified himself as a member of the Ministry of the

Interior and the administrative warden then turned over Manuel Pérez's records. The agent was interested to learn that Manuel Pérez was also the blood nephew of Ramiro Pérez, the nation's venerable Minister of Defense and a member of the Politburo. An ex-schoolteacher, Manuel had long been a leader in counterrevolutionary causes and, considered almost incorrigible, had been imprisoned at Isle of Pines for seven years. Recent reports, however, indicated a change in his attitude, and it was hoped that reintegration into society was possible after another three years. Before he attempted to interrogate him, the agent decided he would be well-advised to call the Ministry office and discuss the matter with his chief.

Quevedo had not been back twenty minutes when Santos Federico called from the Isle of Pines.

"Sir, I think I'm on to something important—"

"Well, what is it?"

"I've discovered that Alicia Ortiz and a male friend . . . a Carlos Palma . . . visited a prisoner here at the Isle of Pines named Manuel Pérez. He has a long history of counterrevolutionary activity. The male companion came back here the day we picked her up. And this Manuel Pérez is the nephew of Ramiro Pérez himself . . ."

This last was hardly news to Quevedo, but the possible connection between the man Palma and Alicia Ortiz and the Marshal's nephew was something else . . . "Stay where you are, Santos. I'll join you in a couple of hours. Talk to no one."

The spirit that had been drained from Quevedo during the previous thirty frustrating hours was revived, and the feeling of being duped, the stupidity of chasing one's tail all over the island, was suddenly forgotten. This time, he felt certain, he would not be denied.

But then, to dampen his enthusiasm, came a call from the homicide squad informing him that one of his agents, identified as Octavio Orellano, had been found murdered along the walks of the Cemetery de Colón not far from Calle Twelve. His body was still warm when discovered, but his throat had been cut from ear to ear. There was no evidence of a struggle.

Chapter Twenty-Four

February Twenty-Third

The news from the Isle of Pines, the break Quevedo had worked for so diligently these past weeks, demanded immediate attention. And word of the murder of an excellent agent like Octavio Orellano added impetus. Disdaining the hour-long auto trip and the slow prison ferry, Quevedo took his best men with him and commandeered a helicopter. He was at Santos Federico's side in less than forty-five minutes.

"Federico, has there been any contact with the prisoner that I don't know about?"

"None, sir. I follow instructions. You said 'talk to no one.' "

"Good. Have the warden set us up with a solitary cell and tell them to bring Pérez in there at once. You, myself, José and Marco are the only ones to be admitted."

"As you say. I'm sorry to hear about Octavio. He was a good man, we worked together for years."

"I know. Let's find who did it. We may learn about him right here, today."

Although prisoners undergoing rehabilitation at the Isle of

Pines were kept informed of current events, all news reports were carefully screened for national-security purposes. Quevedo was certain that there was no way for Manuel Pérez to have learned of Alicia Ortiz's death, unless underground sources had gotten to him in the last few days. Continuing to keep her death hidden was part of his plan for breaking Pérez.

"Señor Pérez, the Ministry of Interior is concerned about contacts between prisoners and those citizens whose loyalty may be subject to question. What do you know about Alicia Ortiz?"

Pérez strained to maintain outward composure. "I've known her for some years. We taught together. I was also acquainted with her husband before his death. I have no reason to believe that Alicia is in any way disloyal. She never joined her husband in any political activities. Why do you ask?"

"Why I ask is my business. Yours is to answer. No doubt you saw my assistants waiting outside the cell door. They can be called on to persuade people to tell the truth."

"Señor Quevedo, I have spent seven years of my life here, away from my family and those I love. I have been promised my freedom in three more years. The prison warden and information minister both say that I have been making good progress. With my freedom at last in sight, why should I lie?"

"I don't know the answer to that. You will have to tell me. But I do know that you are lying."

"About what?"

"About Alicia Ortiz. I spoke to her this morning and she admitted to me that she has been actively engaged in counter-revolutionary activities."

"I find that impossible to believe. But if it is true, why does that involve me? Alicia never spoke to me of such matters."

"Then why did she visit you so regularly?"

"Alicia is one of the kindest people I've ever known. For

years now she has been spending one Saturday nearly every month visiting friends who are not free to visit her. She also pays visits to sick friends at the hospital and volunteers her services to treat the aged. I never asked that she come to see me. She did it. And I was happy to have the company. Is that strange?"

"You make it sound very innocent. Does your uncle, the great Marshal Ramiro Pérez, visit you too?"

"I think you know that he and I do not see eye to eye. I have not seen or heard from Uncle Ramiro in five years or more."

"What about your new friend?"

"New friend?"

"Yes. Carlos Palma."

If Manuel had had any doubts about the seriousness of this interrogation, they were blown away by the last question, though it was not exactly unexpected. He had been preparing for it from the first question and had made up his mind to do his best to seem calm when it surfaced. How successful he was might well mean the difference between living and dying.

"I met this Palma for the first time . . . about two weeks ago when he came here with Alicia. I knew very little about him at the time. He said he was a writer, a journalist of some sort, I believe, very loyal to Cuba. Actually he's also apparently doing research on a biography of Fidel Castro."

"What do visits to the Isle of Pines have to do with a biography of Fidel?"

"Palma said he believed that the world doesn't really understand what a great man El Jefe is. He says all of the published interviews and biographies to date were written by Yankees or other unfriendly sources. He wants to show Fidel as a man of the people, with the call of God—"

"God?"

"I use 'God' only in its metaphysical sense. By the call of God I assume he means that Fidel was inspired to save our country—"

"But why did he come here to see you? Are you inspired by God too?"

"Hardly. He said he wants to show the world that even those who at one time opposed El Comandante now see their error. I am one of those, a kind of horrible example, I suppose. Palma said he wants everyone to know that even those who have been imprisoned here as long as I have can feel no resentment or recrimination. He thinks the world should be made aware of how well these institutions are run, not like in the Fascist countries where people are beaten and tortured." Pérez selected his last words carefully, and they were not lost on Quevedo.

"And so I'm to believe that a man you never knew before just happened to visit you with an old friend and selected you to tell the world how great a man Fidel Castro is."

"I'm sorry if you can't or won't believe me, sir. But it does make sense . . . Alicia Ortiz meets a man and he is writing a book about Fidel Castro. He wants to talk to someone who once was an enemy. She mentioned me, whom she visits, and they come here together. Those, sir, are the facts—"

"There are facts, and there is the truth. You are using facts to hide the truth. I would like to learn the truth from you the easy way. But if we must be brutal like our enemies, I suppose we must—"

"Señor Quevedo . . . you can force me to say anything you wish. But why? What have I done except cooperate? Why are you so determined to believe that I am making up stories?"

Quevedo changed his tone to one of confidence. "Look here, Manuel, we all understand that we must sometimes say things to protect old friends. After all, Alicia Ortiz is a beautiful lady and when she comes here with a lover who needs your help, well, sometimes one adjusts the truth just a bit. Now wouldn't you like to help your country? Wouldn't you like to show your gratitude to a government that has supported your family for seven years while you, a difficult fellow at times, you'll agree, have been reeducated in the ways of justice? As you say, the Fascists would have killed you and starved your family years ago. How about it?"

"Señor Quevedo. I am an educator, not a hero. I am not a particularly brave man. I know that you are intent on breaking me in one way or the other and frankly the prospect terrifies me. But I can't lie about my friends just to help you, or to save myself. What I have told you is the truth. You can believe it if you want to or you can convince yourself that I lie, I really can't change that. I owe no loyalties to Carlos Palma, a man I never met until a couple of weeks ago. I am not in love with Alicia Ortiz. Actually, as good as she has been to me, if I thought she was involved in anything against the interests of our country, I would turn against her too. I couldn't allow her to use me."

These were the words Quevedo was waiting for, which he felt would lead to Pérez's breakdown. Walking briskly to the entrance to the cell, he tapped and Santos answered by sliding back the face panel at the top of the door.

"Santos, bring Miss Ortiz into the next cell and start the interrogation. Keep the ventilation panels open. I want our friend here to learn just how loyal our beautiful schoolteacher and his friend really is."

"The whole treatment?"

"Sí. Strip her down. Use the water, the rubber hoses, the electric prods. Let that whore learn the price for betraying her country. And let this liar hear for himself about the writing of so-called biographies."

He turned back to Pérez and pointing to a stool next to the adjoining wall ordered, "You sit there." As Pérez turned to obey, Quevedo hit him a karate chop in the medulla area of his skull, which sent him into the wall. His glasses smashed as his face cracked against the unfinished stone surface. He crumpled to the floor, curled into a fetal position in an attempt to defend his vital organs. The sole of Quevedo's boot found its way through his defense, and his breath was driven from his body by a kick. As he wheezed, Quevedo took hold of him by both lapels and commenced banging his head against the wall. Blood came from his nose and mouth. With a remote hold on consciousness recording his pain, he felt another kick and heard the command, "On that stool." He half-crawled onto the three-legged perch and tried to get his breath. Satisfied that Pérez had absorbed enough punishment for the moment, Quevedo banged on the wall with a short club he had drawn from underneath his jacket. "All right. Begin."

Manuel could barely comprehend what was happening in the adjacent cell, but as consciousness returned he at least understood from the screams that Alicia was being subjected to outrageous punishment. What was especially terrible was that a muffled voice in the background, like a special-events director describing a public spectacle on television, gave minute descriptions of each new torture, even testifying to Alicia's changed physical condition as truncheons were applied to her ribs and electric prods were activated.

Amazingly, she failed to break. Time and again she refused to give them the information about Carlos Palma they demanded. For Pérez, in spite of the initial pain he'd experienced from Quevedo, Alicia's demonstration of courage in the next cell served to strengthen his resistance. To hell, literally, with Quevedo. He had new love for Alicia Ortiz, new hatred for the inhuman forces destroying her. The brainwashing used on him for seven long years was inadvertently obliterated by this demonstration. He felt a special pride that he had been a part of their prison system for seven years and was still his own man.

He could hear her cries growing weaker now and still, even in a whisper, she defied them. He heard the "announcer" ask if the "procedure" should continue since death was so near—and the muffled voice saying to continue until she talked.

Suddenly, Quevedo banged against the wall with his club.

"Enough . . . I'll tell you when to start again." A few more whimpers, then silence.

"Listen carefully, Pérez. Her life is completely in your hands. Give me information about Palma, we'll find him anyway, and I'll release her. I'm making you no promises about your own safety, but perhaps if we catch him quickly you won't have to face what she's going through. Help me and I'll let her live. And if your hero's conscience demands it, you can take all the beating you like. I'm an expert in this business. She can take maybe thirty minutes more, maybe less. She's already taken more than most men. A tough lady, your schoolteacher. You want it on your conscience that you could have saved her and didn't?"

It was an unexpected offer. From what he had heard, Pérez had little reason to doubt that Alicia would die if the beatings continued. He also knew that she had not given them the information they demanded. On the other hand, if he could give them some false leads, or even if he gave them part of what they wanted, he might save Alicia's life. It was worth a try. At least he could stall for a few minutes, perhaps give her time to recover . . .

"I'm not sure I understand your proposal."

"I think you do, but I'm glad to spell it out. Tell us where Palma is, what he plans next and we'll release Alicia Ortiz. Give us enough particulars and we'll release you too."

"No more years behind bars?"

"Right."

"And what proof do I have that you'll keep your word?"

"You don't. You'll have to gamble. If you don't, you'll never know the difference because you and she will both be dead."

At that moment there was a knock on the door and one of Quevedo's aides entered. He had a message that Miguel Dávila had called with a request that Quevedo return the call at once. Dávila had said it was most urgent. While the aide guarded Pérez, Quevedo found an official phone in the hall and reached Dávila. His news was startling. Working on his own, Dávila had speculated that perhaps the older Pérez, either by design or by naïvete, was playing a role in the assassination plot. He had contacted Ramiro Pérez's office and discovered that a Carlos Palma, a free-lance writer and journalist, had been added to the Marshal's staff that week. As a matter of fact, there was a chance that this Palma might be at a big anniversary celebration with Pérez that very evening, a party that Fidel Castro might well attend. Quevedo had heard enough. He assembled his men, alerted his helicopter pilot, and headed back to Havana.

Manuel Pérez was placed in solitary confinement for three months. When he emerged, pale and nearly broken, he was sentenced to life imprisonment for plotting the overthrow of the government. It was not until two years later that he learned he had been listening to a tape-recorded version of Alicia Ortiz's final ordeal.

Chapter Twenty-Five

February Twenty-Fourth

Martin had been aware that he was being watched while he wrote his warning to Duncan to leave him alone to complete his mission. For a moment he had considered bypassing the Anglo-Swiss Trading Company offices but once he had committed himself he'd decided to see it through. He had caught sight of Orellano off in the shadows and his main concern was whether there were any other agents in the stakeout team. He had moved away, ostensibly seeking light from the street-lamp, only because it gave him a better vantage point from which to observe his surroundings. The only consequence of that had been a false start by Orellano, whom he'd already pinpointed. Using an old infiltration technique he'd learned in the army, he turned around several times on various pretexts, always watchful for any motion on his perimeter, and finally concluded that Orellano was working alone. He hurried away, using the deserted walks of the cemetery as escape routes and drawing the trailing agent along. Hiding behind a large commemorative monument, he had come out suddenly and clubbed Orellano from the rear. A sharp hunting knife completed the job, and he disappeared as quickly as he had struck. Afraid that his clothing might be bloodstained, he hurried back to his hotel to change and shower. He thought that the CIA was getting more than it had bargained for.

He called Liliam as soon as he was dressed. She acted annoyed at first. "Am I supposed to spend all my time waiting for you to get ready to see me?"

"My dear, I'm a writer. I have to follow leads for new information when and where I find them. I met this man at a bar who knew Fidel as a boy. He was leaving for an eight-week trip abroad and would agree to talk to me only if I would go to the airport with him. I can't tell you how much I learned. I promise I'll make it up to you. Forgive?"

She did, and added, "The reason I was upset is that I have such terrific news for you and you wouldn't even stay on the phone long enough to hear me out."

"I'm all ears now."

"Do you know what day this is?"

"Friday?"

"Friday, February twenty-fourth."

"Proclamation of Baire Day. Of course . . ."

"Fidel calls it José Martí Day. He insists that Martí is the real father of Cuban independence and he always celebrates not only the twenty-sixth of July but February twenty-fourth as well. Government offices are giving parties all over Havana. I got in on one of the biggest by promising to pay for all the liquor. Not even the government turns down that kind of bargain these days."

"No more last-minute interviews, I promise."

"You still don't understand. The chances are very good that Fidel will be there too. I sent word through his social secretary that I have a very important matter to discuss with him. She indicated that she'll at least see to it that we get a few minutes alone sometime during the party. That will be my chance to speak to him about the interview. I'll try to sell him on the idea of giving your biography real authenticity by getting his own points of view across before you start actual writing. Now, are you proud of me?"

"And grateful . . . this is turning out to be quite a day for me. If we can wrap up that interview, I'll be on my way home." Martin could not resist the temptation of that one minor double entendre, which would escape her.

"If it works out, you'd better plan a stop at my home first. Your satisfaction may be your work . . . mine is my pleasure . . ."

"I'll make that stop whether I get the interview or not. I'll pick you up in half an hour."

The party at El Cocodrilo, Havana's newest and poshest private club, put Martin in mind of the gala days in pre-Revolution Cuba. The second-floor ballroom was bedecked with a thousand flowers intertwined around white wicker-based candelabra that lined the room. Streamers of blossoms reached from one end of the ceiling to the other. The walls were covered with elegant hangings, tastefully spotlighted by moving beams of light. Four open bars served champagne, cognac and the finest whiskey. At one end of the room, on a decorated bandstand, a small band beat out a constant stream of Latin American tunes. They were spelled by a *rock* combo—extraordinary—that apparently had not heard that Castro and Uncle Sam were barely on speaking terms. Finally, at the other end of the ballroom, a thirty-five-piece orchestra, lush with fiddles and strings, offered interludes of danceable waltzes and fox-trots for those who had not entered the rock age. The women wore long dresses, which flowed in the tropic night like petals in the breeze. Most of the men wore dinner jackets though some, like Martin, were in dark suits. And everywhere there were large pictures of José Martí, whose birthday was being celebrated. There was even a likeness of Martí carved from a huge block of ice. It was a night of gala splendor, the perfect night, Martin thought, to complete his assignment. And he had better work quickly. Dispatching that agent might have been necessary, but it also left a fresh and bloody trail.

Liliam Pazos was radiant in her exquisite pale-green gown. Even Martin had difficulty keeping his eyes off her.

"You look gorgeous, darling. No wonder Fidel is willing to grant you a few words. I have a feeling that once he gets a look at you in this outfit he's going to insist on reviving old times. I may be looking for a new lady before the night is over—"

She shut him up by taking him onto the dance floor, but she was obviously pleased. Dancing with Liliam Pazos was like trying to complete a sentence in the presence of a non-stop talker. She seemed to know everybody and kept stopping to chat or nodding a hello in the middle of a beat.

"You like to dance?" he said.

"You're just jealous of my popularity. Uh uh. I spoke too soon."

"How's that?"

"There's Maria Díaz. Looks like she just swallowed a porcupine. I wouldn't turn my back on her if the lights go out. She's radiating hate to me from way across the dance floor."

"I can't believe it. Must be in your head."

"If she had her way it would be in my back. Come along. We have to talk to her sooner or later. Might as well get it over with now." And she steered him off the floor and over to a small group of men and women seated at what was obviously the number-one ringside table.

Even from a thirty-yard distance, Martin could feel Maria Díaz's hostility, as Liliam had said. She was a small, dark-complexioned woman, almost masculine in appearance. She would have looked more appropriately dressed in green fatigues than in the boxy, ill-fitting gown that seemed unnatural on her wiry body. Her forehead was lined. She was obviously a serious-minded woman, uneasy with the frivolities of dancing and partying. She realized that Liliam Pazos and her escort were headed in her direction but did little to encourage the meeting. She actually creased her forehead more intently as they approached.

"Maria," Liliam opened pleasantly, "how lovely you look. I don't ever remember seeing you in an evening gown before."

"There's a good reason for that," Maria answered. "I don't remember ever wearing one before. I doubt if I'll ever wear one again. I feel silly as hell in this getup. It's like Mardi Gras time."

"I think it's kind of fun to dress up once in a while."

"Then you do it," Maria snapped back. "No wonder the men sneer at us and think of us as the weaker sex when we parade around in this kind of fluff—"

"I'd like you to meet Señor Carlos Palma. Carlos, this is Maria Díaz, El Comandante's right arm."

"I'm happy to finally meet you. Anyone who knows anything about our country's recent history has nothing but the highest regard for Maria Díaz."

"That sort of makes me a legend in my time, doesn't it?" she said sarcastically.

"You're too young to be a legend. But I'll wager you will be one day—an inspiration to all Cuban women."

"Señor Palma," she said, "I think you should know that I suffer from severe allergies, the most serious of which is an allergy to bullshit."

For a brief moment he had thought he had seen her softening a bit but apparently his association with Liliam Pazos was not the best calling card. Which was exactly what Liliam had predicted. The heavy silence, punctuated only by the rhythms of the band, was finally broken by Maria.

"Are you new in Havana, Señor Palma?"

"In a way, yes. I make my original home in Santiago de

Cuba. I'm a writer and journalist and have had the good fortune to be able to travel abroad to gather my background material. But I'm always happiest when I come home to Cuba. As a famous English poet once asked, "What do they know of England who only England know?"

"Yes," she said, cutting him off abruptly, "I'm quite familiar with that verse. And what are you doing now that you are back home?"

"I'm fortunate enough to be working in the offices of Field Marshal Pérez."

"You are a military expert too?"

"Not at all," he answered pleasantly. "I am a writer, as I said. I had some time off between assignments and heard that Marshal Pérez was gathering his memoirs for a definitive history of the military forces in Cuba since the days of the *Granma* landing. I offered my assistance and, fortunately for me, he accepted. I'm not sure I'll be able to complete the job before I leave, but I'll do my best."

"And your family? Do they still live in Oriente Province?"

"Actually I have no family. I have been divorced for many years and my parents are gone. A few cousins here and there scattered throughout the country—"

"Well," Liliam broke in, "I think you make a fine addition to Havana. And now, I think we should finish our dance. We hope to see you later, Maria."

"Perhaps. Who can tell?" And she turned abruptly back to the other members of her party.

The evening progressed uneventfully. There were toasts to José Martí, huzzahs for the modern protector of Cuban independence, Fidel Castro. There was also a constant ebb and flow of the audience. There were many Martí celebrations going on throughout the island and it was a measure of status to travel from one party to the next.

As the hour grew later, Martin began to wonder if indeed the country's chief would make an appearance. He stationed himself whenever possible close to the entrance doors and examined each newcomer. His greatest shock came when two couples entered arm in arm, singing the Cuban national anthem at the top of their lungs, apparently none the worse for a full evening of drinking the grape, and Martin immediately recognized one of the men, even before they were fully inside the ballroom, as Duncan. This time their eyes met directly, if briefly. Neither acknowledged the other but it seemed obvious to Martin that a confrontation was coming. Duncan lurched forward, dragging his three friends with him and approached Martin. Pulling out a bottle of champagne he'd concealed under his dinner jacket, he held it aloft and shouted, "Sir, join me in toasting the two greatest men in Cuban history, 'Martí and Castro'!" Surprised by the intimate contact, Martin responded weakly, "To Martí and Castro. I salute them both." Then, turning to Liliam, who was standing by his side, "I share their sentiments but I wish they came from a little less liquid source."

Laughing, Liliam said, "Don't be a sobersides. Tonight's the night to get drunk. By the way, that fellow looks familiar to me . . . oh, yes . . . his name is Peter Roche, he's a Swiss executive with some sort of business interests in Havana. Been around for years. Some people think he's more Cuban than most Cubans."

Martin nodded, holding his tongue and his breath. He was damned upset to see Duncan. The CIA man might not have received word yet of the note he'd left at the Anglo-Swiss offices earlier that evening, but there had to have been some note taken of Octavio Orellano's death, and as a foreign agent Duncan must have sources to keep him briefed on any such developments in the Cuban intelligence apparatus. It would be natural for the Havana police to start an immediate investigation throughout the neighborhood, and since the Interior Ministry knew where Orellano had been assigned, they would reasonably start by questioning the owners of all shops in the area as well as occupants of the Anglo-Swiss offices, and even though it was a holiday they would then interrogate people in their homes.

If not for the possibility that Numero Uno would show at the party, Martin would have departed at once. From the beginning of his mission, he'd understood that the less he had to do with his employers the greater his own chances for survival. And so far he had been right. *Their* one contact, Rolando Duran, had very probably been a counter-agent. It was Alicia Ortiz, a friend of Myra Rubin, who had not only led him to the highest connection but had been willing to sacrifice her own life—he pushed the memory of her from his mind . . . rage would dilute logic, and it was a matter of logic that once he'd performed his mission he would be more than expendable, he would be dangerous to U.S. intelligence sources. Obviously he must avoid all contacts with them wherever possible.

Duncan and his lady of the evening danced by, somewhat less exuberant now, and again their eyes met. With a slight head signal Duncan indicated that he wanted to meet with Martin somewhere outside the ballroom. He inclined his head toward the restroom area the next time he danced by and there was a look of insistence in his eye. Apparently he was growing annoyed by Martin's refusal to make verbal contact. But again Martin looked right through him as if the signal were meant for somebody else. Duncan was about to force the issue with a direct approach when, suddenly, all three orchestras appeared on the bandstands and together blared out a combined trumpet and drum tattoo, followed by the solemn notes of the national anthem, "The Hymn of Bayamo," sung by a man with a resonant bass baritone. As he sang, "March to the battle, people of Bayamo," the audience joined in, and when they sang, "to live in chains is to die, to die for one's country is to live," tears were in many eyes. Then there was a moment of silence. Up the stairs and through the entrance arch, at the most dramatic moment, a group of men dressed in green fatigues made their appearance.

And there he was, Fidel Castro himself.

As if to tease the men about him, who were consciously underdressed, he wore an uncharacteristic handsome dress uniform and tie, perhaps out of respect to Cuba's greatest writer, thinker and father image—José Martí. Or out of one-upmanship, or both. Whatever, this sort of quixotic whimsy was a constant problem for those whose job it was to protect him. If he'd been in battle greens, and they likewise, even a sniper with a telescopic lens might be confused trying to pick him off from a distance. Now that he was dressed like a dandy, he was dangerously conspicuous for security purposes.

Fidel and his party headed now for the main bandstand while the assembled crowd enthusiastically chanted his name as he reached for the microphone, stepped up on the stage and held his hand high for silence. The audience fell under his spell.

In his customary soft but high-pitched voice, Fidel first asked for a glass of wine that was immediately fetched. Then, holding it high, he said, "To José Martí and to all patriots! To Cuba, and the People's Revolution!"

For five minutes the revelers cheered and shouted, sang and yelled patriotic slogans while Fidel continued smiling. Then, at precisely the correct moment, his sense of the dramatic near-impeccable, he again raised his hand.

"I bid you greetings. As you know, I usually like to keep my speeches very short"—pause, waiting for the laughter to subside—"and don't laugh. Only last week at the Plaza de la Revolución I limited my remarks to three hours and forty-five minutes. I must be growing old."

Again laughter, mixed with "Not you, you will live forever!"

"Tonight, I will only tell you what you already know. We are young. We are strong. We will, with the people's strength, our greatest weapon, prevail over our enemies. José Martí, whose birthday we celebrate today, always said that a man could be judged not only by the company he kept, but also by the enemies he made. The more important the man, the more important his enemies. Judged by this standard, we are very important indeed."

Martin was standing not fifteen feet from the podium. Here was the man he had come to kill. And he could have done the job then and there, except with the security agents sitting at the edge of the stage it would also be an act of suicide. He wanted to live to enjoy the fruits of his labor. He still needed that private interview.

As Fidel's speech droned on, the early charismatic spell wore thin. Martin had read and heard the same words spoken in dozens of places. Politicians were politicians, generals were generals. Long-winded leaders of men were long-winded leaders of men. Even Fidel Castro.

The dancers were beginning to shift positions now. The high voice continued its harangue, winding circuitously over the same ground, but for most of them Fidel could do no wrong. Especially since he'd chosen to honor this particular gathering for his major speech of the evening. Elsewhere he would lead a brief toast. But finally, after a full hour, he was obviously winding down. In closing he asked again for a full glass of wine and offered a toast: "To this active participation of the Cuban people, without whose involvement our Revolution is nothing. To the people! To the Revolution! To Cuba!" And then he was finished and the cheering started again.

Stepping down from the podium, he looked around the room. He smiled broadly, then, having spotted Maria Díaz and her party, headed in that direction. Liliam immediately took Martin by the hand and, moving swiftly in a flanking maneuver, reached the Díaz table before Fidel and his security guards had joined them. Maria was by no means unaware of Liliam's move and frowned in clear disapproval. As Fidel reached the group, Liliam moved to his side and spoke first.

"A magnificent speech, Fidel. We thank you once again for your inspiration."

"Thank you, Liliam. Are you sure you stayed awake?" He smiled when he said it.

At that moment the orchestra started up with a Latin medley that they knew would please Fidel, who immediately asked Liliam to join him on the dance floor. It was virtually a solo performance . . . no one had the nerve to join in while Fidel was on the floor. A graceful athlete, he moved with great skill for a big man and Liliam followed him fluidly as he led her in a rhumba, a fox-trot and, finally, a sweeping tango. The crowd loved it, applauding loudly as they finished. Liliam was speaking animatedly as they headed back to Maria's table, and then, approaching Martin directly, she made the introductions before Castro had a chance even to greet Maria.

"Fidel, this is the friend I have been telling you about. May I present Carlos Palma?"

Fidel looked closely at this Palma . . . perhaps remembering him, Martin worried, from their recent brief encounter at the Isle of Pines prison.

"Liliam tells me that you are writing a book about me," Castro said. ". . . Haven't we met some place before, Señor Palma?"

"El Comandante, I have never had the honor. I've been told my face is a common one. With all those you have met, perhaps I remind you of someone else—"

"Perhaps. But your face is far from common. Liliam has good taste. She always did," he added, and laughed.

"Thank you. You're very kind. I did want to speak to you about the work because only you can fill in gaps that will be vital for accurate historical perspective. If you could possibly find time, no more than thirty minutes, I'm sure we could get at the missing information—"

"Please, Fidel," Liliam said, taking his hand, "I too would

2 2 8

be grateful. And you must consider your place in history. It's important to you, and to Cuba as well."

Her old influence was working.

"Well, thirty minutes means two hours," he said, laughing. "Just like my ten-minute speeches. But I agree. Since you say time is important and since I myself am planning to be away from Havana for at least three weeks, we'd better try to do it soon. Perhaps some time in the next few days."

"That," said Martin, "would be perfect. Any time. Any place. I'll be there night or day."

"I grant interviews only at night. Day is for working."

As he moved away quickly to greet Maria Díaz, an aide took Fidel by the elbow and led him a few paces away from the group. Handing him a dispatch, the aide stood by watching solemnly as Fidel read its contents, his expression darkening. He said a few abrupt words to the aide, motioned to his entourage, whirled around and headed for the main door without pausing to say a word of goodnight to those around him. All pleasure had drained from his face, and his abrupt departure threw a pall over the crowd that resisted the orchestra's resumption.

Martin of course couldn't be certain what the note said, but he suspected it conveyed some word of a threat to Castro's safety. How else to explain his hurried departure in the midst of a gala celebration? Martin also realized that, in some way, the message could well involve him, though not under his present identity. Not yet. It was best that he leave too. He'd make the necessary explanations to Liliam later.

Noticing a side entrance to his left, he headed for the door, which turned out to be the gateway to a fire escape. He rushed down the steps and headed into the night.

Chapter Twenty-Six

February Twenty-Fourth

In the excitement over the upcoming meeting with Fidel Castro and arranging for his crucial private face-to-face, Martin had briefly forgotten about Duncan. But Duncan had not forgotten Martin. The rest of his party—all CIA—had been assigned to watch Martin's every move. Duncan could not believe that Martin would be crazy enough to attempt a martyr's killing, which it would surely be in the presence of so many witnesses and security police, but years in his business had taught him never to rule out anything. He too had been watching Martin closely throughout the evening, especially while Castro was droning on.

He had been impressed by Martin's success in talking to Castro alone, but although he'd once studied lipreading he still couldn't make out the contents of their conversation from so great a distance. One of his party tried to brush by as if by accident, but security guards huddled about Castro. When he saw Fidel suddenly go serious and hurriedly leave the room, he assumed that something considered a threat to Castro's safety had come to their attention. Like Martin, he was fairly sure that there could be no other explanation for such an abrupt departure. He also saw Martin move toward the fire escape and decided he'd better keep him in sight. He immediately went out after him.

It was a bad move for both of them. Quevedo's agents had all entrances and exits to the building well covered. They both were immediately taken into custody by heavily armed guards who gagged them. They were pushed into waiting limousines, clubbed insensible and pushed to the rear floors. Both were then injected with heavy doses of sodium pentothal, which assured them a long, chemically induced nap. The limos, meanwhile, led by police motorcycle escorts, headed off into the outskirts of Havana. There Duncan and Martin were pulled from the cars and thrown into the back of an armored truck that took them south by east to a secured country estate, one of the few remaining vestiges of the Batista days, now used as a confinement area for important political prisoners. Each was put in a separate wing, confined behind locked doors with a twenty-four-hour guard. Martin was chained by the ankle to a heavy iron ring welded into the floor, with just enough leeway to reach a chamber pot in one corner.

Duncan was the first to regain consciousness. He woke with a splitting headache, sore in every muscle, yet so far as he could tell, without serious physical injury. He retched on an empty stomach but spit up only a spoonful of bile. He gradually became aware that he was not alone. Seated comfortably across the room in a leather armchair was a man who peered at him intently. He turned to face him but the man calmly lighted a cigarette and made no move in his direction. As he got to his feet, the man spoke.

"Come, Señor Duncan, no need for karate. We see no need for physical violence. Come have a seat over here where we can talk without raising our voices." He pointed to a similar chair just opposite where he sat.

Duncan, clearer now and beginning to reconstruct what had happened to him as he had left the dance, did as asked. "How long have I been out?"

"Fourteen hours. Your friend, I assume Señor Palma is acquainted with you, is still sleeping. My congratulations. My men gave you enough to keep most out for much longer. You have a strong system."

"And who are you?"

"Felipe Quevedo. Minister of the Interior. Chief of Cuban intelligence. No doubt you know of me."

"No doubt. And you have heard of me."

"Yes, but you are brighter than we are. For so many years we knew you only as Peter Roche of the Anglo-Swiss Trading Company. And we were naïve enough—or desperate enough for Western friends—to believe your often-expressed anti-Yankee sentiments. You took advantage of our vulnerability, which only makes me respect you more, my friend. I do not expect you to apologize for our stupidity—"

"To make a plausible mistake is not stupid"—Duncan figured, in these circumstances, flattery couldn't hurt him—"but to repeat it, that is inexcusable."

"Agreed. I also want to congratulate you on your record. Not many men with military backgrounds transfer so easily to our line of work. Usually the G-2 colonel is heavy-handed and unimaginative. But my sources tell me you were very shrewd as head of undercover operations in South America. When the FBI and the CIA both use the same man one can be certain that he comes with good credentials. I must admit that I envy you your West Point training. You see, I am mostly self-educated so I tend to be envious of those with formal schooling . . . Cigarette?"

"Thank you. I can't understand what I've done to deserve this celebrity treatment, but I appreciate it all the same.

What, by the way, are your plans for me? If you don't mind a direct question."

"Not at all. You deceived me as Peter Roche all these years, you're entitled to that. I assume that Palma is your man of the moment. Actually, we've long since been tipped off that he is here for yet another of your tries at our leader—"

"Well," Duncan broke in, "I must say, you worked it neat with your triple-cross in Paris. One can appreciate that. Not only did those greedy bastards get paid a king's ransom, they tried to double their commission by double-crossing their own man."

"They have one god—money. I learned that many years ago. I never work with them. But with your man in place, why are *you* here now?"

"When you let loose a wolf to kill a fox who's killing the chickens, you should be ready to take care of the wolf when the job is done."

Quevedo smiled. "You don't trust Señor Palma to stay silent. Or not to attempt blackmail, which could embarrass you. After all, you can't afford to let the world know you're still at this same old game in spite of all the newspaper exposés and noble speeches. As one professional to another, I assure you I would have done the same. An agent whose tongue wags is more dangerous than the enemy. Basic. But wouldn't it have been better to hire another agent to do the follow-up job for you? You're not in a very good position to help your country now. Or to complete your assignment."

"True. But who knew Cuba as well as I? Who could get in and out of Havana without raising suspicion as easily as I? And finally, if I had hired another agent to take care of Señor Palma, would I not need another one to eliminate him? And so on?"

Quevedo laughed. "You are absolutely correct."

"We agree on so many things it's too bad we couldn't work together. We'd be better partners than enemies."

233

Quevedo looked intently at him. "An interesting notion
. . . perhaps even a possibility . . ."

"Forget it. I don't intend to hire on as a double—"

"That is not what I had in mind. Actually—and this may as-
tonish you—I think our work may serve each other's needs."

"Please explain, Señor Quevedo . . ." Though he was already beginning to have an idea what was being suggested.

"Why do you think I am here, alone with you, smoking cig-
arettes, chatting as if we were old friends? At this moment I
should be orchestrating a procedure of torture, complete with
rubber hoses and demands for information. I suspect it occurs
to you that there is something I want that a beating won't accomplish . . ."

"Frankly, that thought has occurred to me, but it has also
occurred that it's not unusual to set up a prisoner. Whatever,
I prefer this to electric prods up my tail."

"Reasonable. So now, we get to facts. I am a gambler,
Señor Duncan. I have always been a gambler. I gambled in
Paris with the Mafia. And right now I'm inclined to gamble
that by working with you, riding your horse, I can achieve my
goal more quickly. You have, in fact, inadvertently given me a
most unexpected, so to speak, career opportunity."

"And exactly what is that goal?"

"The Premiership of Cuba. You see, Señor, though I am
paid to protect our leader, that does not mean that I love him.
I did once. When I first joined our party I was, how do you
say it, 'gung ho.' It was all new then and I was very idealistic.
I believed in all they told me and I was hurt, very hurt, that
they treated me like an outsider because I was two years late
in joining the Movement. Was it my fault that I was too
young to fight in 1957 and 1958? Eventually, of course, I was
accepted and rose steadily and finally Fidel offered me Minister of Interior. I was delighted. My life's ambition seemed fulfilled—"

"I can understand, your reputation is international, that

should be very satisfying . . ." Duncan decided it was time to lie well.

"It was for a while. Then I started seeing things happening in the government I was serving, disturbing things that made me wonder if I was not stupid to be risking my life. You'll recall that when Stalin died there was a tremendous backlash against him, and what they termed his 'cult of personality.' We're seeing the same power struggle now in Red China. Here, too, I assure you that powerful enemies have been building, good men who resent the Castro personality clique. The movement is young yet, but the men behind it are dedicated and determined to steer this country back to a sane course where ideas, not men, will control decision-making. I am young, Señor Duncan, only forty-one, and if I were patient, chances are some day the men around Fidel Castro would turn to me for leadership. But I don't wish to wait to see my country destroyed by its crazy marriage to a Russian bear that makes friends of convenience, for as long as convenience serves. We don't easily forget the missiles . . . When we are no longer of use, Russia will leave us like a whore at the church. *That* is why I talk to you, and offer a deal that can bring us both what we want by the same act."

Duncan looked at him, shaking his head. "All very interesting, and even attractive. Except I must say I'm at a loss to understand"—he wasn't entirely, but felt it politic to let Quevedo tell him how brilliant he was—"why you haven't simply let our man complete his assignment, and me do what I would after. Why the great effort to find out who he was, to confirm his assignment . . . the trip to Paris, as you say, was a gamble, though one that paid off . . ."

Quevedo welcomed the opportunity to state what already seemed rather obvious to Duncan. "Señor Duncan, finding the assassin doesn't necessarily mean stopping him. It was necessary to control him, and then to let his employers—the estimable CIA, in this instance you—know that it was I who had done them a service. However successful I might be in running my country's affairs after Castro, I am not such a fool as to think what you have planned for him could not also be planned for me, and that sooner or later you would succeed. And I think there would be little problem about your people exposing me. After all, to do that would be to expose themselves as well . . ."

"You've worked it out really quite well," Duncan said. "So far, that is. Where do *we* go from here?" Duncan could hardly believe his good fortune, although he had heard rumors of Quevedo's ambitions, his anti-Russian sentiments.

"It's simple. You have planted a man here to kill Fidel. Next, you plan to kill this man. First, I help him do his job. Then I help you do yours. And I help you escape. Next, my people declare me the most logical man to assume power. And since we are already organizing for that end, no one will be in a good position to stop us. Like all beautiful things, it is very simple."

"It is. But between simple plans and accomplished results . . . well, we have a good deal of planning to do, you and I . . ."

"Of course. We must examine each other's plans and make adjustments where necessary. But let's start with a few basics. No one is to know anything about our relationship. Even my own men will believe I am releasing you, when we agree that it is wise, for *our* purposes and not for your benefit. Second, Carlos Palma must continue to think of us as blood enemies. Should he learn we are working together he would trust neither of us, possibly change his own operation plans. We both need to be credible in his eyes . . . too bad for him, he will require appropriately credible mistreatment by my people . . . He could be extremely dangerous to both of us. Finally, we must move quickly. The longer this cake bakes, the more likely it is to fall. Do you agree?"

2 3 6

"I agree completely."

"Good. I will contact you within the next twelve hours."

He got up and the two faced each other. No further words were necessary.

Chapter Twenty-Seven

February Twenty-Fifth—Five A.M.

Martin regained consciousness about two hours later. He found himself lying on a bare wooden floor, tethered like an elephant at the zoo. A heavy-link chain bound by a spring lock to his right ankle was connected to a stout iron ring fastened in the floor. He calculated the diameter of his circle of confinement to be about fifteen feet. A chamber pot set up in one corner of the room was the only object within his reach. There were three large floor-to-ceiling windows in the room, all beyond his reach and heavily barred. A stout oak door was reenforced with a steel fascia, its hinges inaccessible from inside. He checked the shackles on both ends of the chain; only a blowtorch could possibly break them.

Like the leaves of an artichoke, the clouds of darkness peeled gradually from his brain. He clearly recalled being taken by Cuban agents and dumped into a limousine. But from the moment he was rapped on the head there was an almost complete loss of memory. Somehow, though, he seemed able to re-create being transferred to another vehicle in the darkness—but he remembered nothing of the injection of sodium pentothal or being shackled to the floor in this room. It was his first experience that required escape; he'd never been a prisoner before.

He was covered with sweat and the lump on his head throbbed. His whole body seemed sore, as if he had been banged and kicked. He examined himself as well as he could and discovered a few discolorations where he ached the most. There were no apparent cuts. He sat up and by pulling on the chain was able to stand. In one direction, opposite the windows, he was able to reach the wall. He turned around and slid into a sitting position, using the partition for support. He was terribly thirsty. He crawled to the chamber pot and urinated, then went back to his sitting position by the wall, and waited. Judging from the position of the sun, which he could barely see through the barred windows, it was early morning. The room temperature must have been in the high eighties. He pulled off his shirt and felt some relief. He realized then that his suit jacket was missing, as was his wallet and everything else he'd carried in his trouser pockets.

He calculated that at least two more hours passed before he heard footsteps in the area outside. By this time the sun was higher and the room even hotter. His thirst had gotten worse and, despite his discomfort, he was beginning to feel the first pains of hunger. He thought of the famous tale of the man chained to the wall and bricked up in the wine cellar to face a slow, agonizing death. He also recalled the tortures inflicted on those unlucky enough to have been taken prisoner in Vietnam, and by comparison fear of starvation seemed the less terrifying.

He heard the door rattle and visualized heavy iron bars being slid from their moorings on the outside of his prison door. Two uniformed guards entered but neither said a word to him. One picked up the chamber pot and dumped its contents into a large container he was carrying. The other placed a small tray in front of him. It contained a banana, a single slice of pineapple and a small tumbler of warm water. As he reached for the glass, the guard kicked his hand, overturning the glass and knocking the strip of pineapple onto the dusty floor. "Next time watch your manners," he said, and the two men turned and left, bolting and barring the door behind them.

He grabbed for the overturned glass and was able to lick up a few droplets of water that still clung to its sides. The pineapple also helped a bit in slaking his thirst. In his situation the dirt on the floor seemed unimportant. He peeled the banana and gulped it down. Then he returned to his post, and again he waited.

When the sun had set completely a small lamp on the other side of the room was activated, apparently by an external timing device. Its bulb couldn't have been stronger than twenty watts. The guards came and went every four hours. They never spoke. His rations were the same. After a midnight visit by the guards he forced himself to try to sleep . . . if escape were ever possible he'd need whatever strength he could get . . . He created mental challenges to preserve his sanity. He was amazed, for example, how he could reconstruct statistics from annual financial statements of United Ventures, Ltd., statements he hadn't read in four years. He avoided thinking about his family. Once in a special class for infiltrators in Vietnam he had been instructed in ways to survive while an enemy captive. As best he could he re-created the teachings of those classes that he'd then considered academic and now promised himself that he would follow them. Among those teachings had been a warning to avoid subjects that might bring on feelings of high emotion, such as guilt. And then in spite of himself he started to think of Alicia Ortiz, and immediately forced her from his mind. He switched to an image of Billie Lane and wondered who was servicing her now. For the first time in many weeks he thought that he would like to survive to give her one last go-round. She had been great in the sack.

The guards came and went like windup dolls, but none would speak, even when he tried to taunt them into conversation. The one who had kicked him on that first visit glowered at him but there was no more physical abuse. It was solitary confinement with silent sentries. Once he asked for fresh underwear—he was beginning to offend himself—but there was no response. Fifteen minutes later the door opened a crack and a lacy brassiere was tossed across the floor. He found himself still able to laugh.

He tried to keep track of time and dates but like a shipwrecked sailor he soon lost count. He worried about his physical condition—without exercise he could feel his muscles stiffening up. He started a regimen of calisthenics in spite of the heat. Goddamn it, he wanted to be ready.

On the fourth . . . or fifth . . . day there was a crack of light. The guards who had been visiting him from the first had remained the same. There were four distinct teams, each apparently working a six-hour shift. He began to recognize them and assign them names. Then—he was sure he hadn't imagined it—one of the guards repeated on consecutive shifts. The man came back eight hours later and changed the chamber pot without a partner and not according to the usual schedule. As he left he looked at Martin steadily, and nodded. He didn't say a word. Martin nodded back. The man left. What the hell? The man was back at the prescribed time on the next shift. When his partner turned toward the window, he nodded again and held up both thumbs. Martin reassured himself that he was not hallucinating. It was certainly reason for hope in an otherwise dismal swamp.

Eight hours later—Martin thought it must be around four A.M.—the guard returned once again with a different partner. How he was managing to switch from team to team was amazing. Perhaps, Martin thought, these fellows are allowed to work different shifts for their personal convenience. It was the only explanation he could allow himself. Again, as the partner turned toward the wall, the now friendly guard nodded to Martin and seemed to be alerting him to a new development. Martin got up and leaned against the wall, ready to move fast if there was need for help. Suddenly the man he was now beginning to build his faith on pulled out a gun and pushed it into his partner's back.

"Sorry, Eduardo," he said, "but we are on different teams. I want you to live. So cooperate."

"You son of a bitch," the other guard said, "so this is why you've had all these personal emergencies that made us change shifts. If I ever get out of this you'll answer to me—"

"You'll get out of this if you do as I say. If you don't . . ."

In a matter of minutes the guard was stripped, gagged, bound and shackled in Martin's place. A pass key unlocked the ring around Martin's ankle.

Just before leaving the room, the friendly guard said, "I almost forgot. Manuel Pérez sends his regards." Then, signaling silently for Martin to follow, he led the way into the hall, meticulously rebarred and secured the door.

With Martin trailing, they headed to the end of the hall, and the guard pointed upward. Silently mounting the stairs, he led back toward the other side of the house and came to a large standing portrait of José Martí. He pushed this aside, motioning for Martin to help him, then reached for a small button in the middle of the wall panel. The light was dim, and at first he had trouble finding it. When he did he pushed the button and the wall panel parted. The procedure was reversed and they found themselves closeted in a small glass-encased chamber that served as a crow's nest from which the entire countryside could be observed. On the floor of the observation cubicle there was a coiled rope ladder. The guard now pushed aside one of the glass panels, hooked the ends of the ladder to two bent iron hooks, which jutted from beneath the glass windows, and indicated that this was their escape route.

"I go first," he said, and was out the window, scampering nimbly down the ladder. When he was about ten feet from the ground, Martin followed and in no more than thirty seconds they were both on the ground, running full speed toward a Jaguar sedan parked by the side of the road. The guard, who now identified himself as Rosario Bonilla, got behind the wheel, Martin slipped in beside him and they were off in a burst of screeching rubber. In his most active imaginings, Martin could hardly have anticipated this sort of efficiency from the underground: a chained animal one minute, freed the next and speeding down the road in a luxury sedan. It was, he thought, almost too good to be true. He had better watch his angel carefully. And he'd start by asking a few questions.

"Hey, you saved my life. How . . . ?"

"Is nothing. I work for the underground for years. Pérez sends me word that you need help, I make the arrangements."

"Some timing . . ."

"We have connections in the Ministry of the Interior. They send word to Pérez. He send word back to me. You see?"

Martin didn't like the way the man used Pérez's name so freely . . . "How many days have I been here?"

"Five. Maybe six. We get word about you the day after they arrested you . . ."

A danger signal was flashing. Bonilla didn't seem to know *where* he'd been taken. He decided to go along, and find out what he could. "We're heading back to Havana? Any special reason?"

"No. I just assumed that was where you wanted to go. That's where your . . . mission is, right?"

Again a warning flashed. This fellow seemed to know too much and too little. Certainly Pérez would not have revealed the nature of his mission, or even that he was on a particular assignment. If not Pérez, then the information had to come from the government itself. And that meant that regardless of his pretense, Bonilla had some very special information.

"And how many kilometers to Havana from here, Rosario?"

"Fifteen, maybe thirteen. We'll be back in less than a half hour. No traffic this time of morning but we don't want to stir up the police by speeding."

"Tell me, Rosario, what do you think of CORU?"

"Coru? Who is he?"

"It, not 'he.' Coordination of United Revolutionary Organizations. It's the umbrella agency in the U.S. that specializes in anti-Castro activities. Didn't you know that . . . ?"

"Oh, of course . . . CORU . . . for a moment I thought you were talking about Amadeo Coru, a friend of mine in the underground. We never acknowledge knowing each other. For obvious reasons."

A good try, Martin thought, but not good enough. He would have to deal with Rosario Bonilla. Soon. For a while they rode along in silence while Martin tried to think about his next move.

"Rosario," Martin said. "I see by the road signs we are coming close to Havana. Where do we go from here?"

"That is up to you. To confer with your friends? You'll need them to help you . . ."

. . . "help *you*," and not "help *us*" seemed damning. More so was Bonilla suggesting he contact "friends"—it seemed he'd been told to try to find out Palma's accomplices. Which he ought to know if he were legitimate . . . Bonilla might have been helping, but he was no friend, however unsubtle he was. The time to act was now.

"Hey, I need to urinate," Martin said. "Pull over there by that field. Nobody will see me in the dark."

"Sure, but better hurry. They've probably found the guard at the mansion now and they'll be on our trail."

At first Martin had thought that he would have to kill Bonilla, but after some thought he decided more bloodshed was unnecessary, and if unnecessary, then unwise . . . If indeed Bonilla was a phony, and it seemed he was, the *fact* remained that, for whatever reason, he had helped Martin escape a trap and was now taking him back to the area where his mission had to be performed. He also hardly had a monopoly on knowledge about Carlos Palma's existence, his appearance . . . even his objective? That was now information shared, in some degree at least, by Cuban intelligence. *Why* they'd decided to set him free, and why they'd allow him to return to the area where Castro was located was still in doubt, even though it seemed likely it was to watch him as he betrayed his associates. But, if they knew his mission, wasn't that damned risky . . . ? Well, Martin told himself, he *still* might succeed if he were daring and ingenious enough. First, he needed to get away from them for a few hours to set his own trap. And for that he needed to dump Rosario Bonilla and keep him out of the picture for at least several hours.

Bonilla had by now pulled the car over into the field as Martin had asked, and Martin moved into the underbrush and started to relieve himself. A few moments later he zipped up and rushed off into the woods. After waiting a reasonable time, Rosario . . . a perfect "guard" for Quevedo's and Duncan's purpose . . . called to Palma several times, received no answer. He got out of the car. His bosses would not appreciate this. Returning to the car, he picked up a flashlight and entered the underbrush. He flashed the light about, saw nothing. Meanwhile, keeping his voice friendly, he kept repeating, "Señor Palma, I am your friend. You will be caught here. Let me help you." The last time he repeated the phrase, he was flying tackled from the rear by an agile Martin who had circled back and had been following him step by step. It was a relatively easy job, practiced in Vietnam many times. Grabbing Rosario by the collar he held him to the ground.

"Bonilla, you are a lousy actor. I know they told you to see where and to whom I led you. I can easily kill you but I won't unless necessary. Do you want to live, Rosario?"

"*Si*, señor. I am a family man," he responded reasonably.

"Turn over on your stomach. And don't fight me."

Frightened to death, Rosario Bonilla lay down like a lamb while Martin stripped off his clothes and removed his weapons, a .38 Special service revolver, a sharpened stiletto and a pair of handcuffs, the last of which he used to attach Bonilla to a small sapling. He buried the revolver and stiletto several feet away, at first tempted to keep them but quickly realizing how incriminating they could be. Having gagged Bonilla with his own socks, he returned to the car and found a length of rope in the trunk. He returned and forced the by-now paralyzed agent onto the ground, face downward, tied his ankles, spread eagle fashion to two other outlying trees. As final precaution he took an old blanket he'd found in the car and covered his body with it, throwing limbs of trees and large piles of leaves on top of them. If Bonilla escaped from this setup, Martin thought, they should change his name to Harry Houdini.

He picked up the flashlight, clicked it off and returned to the car. He took over the wheel and headed into Havana. At the first deserted public phone he got out and rang the Luis Fuentes home. It was just getting light now and he would have to work quickly. It took a long time for the phone to be answered but finally he recognized the voice of Alfonzo Acebo, Fuentes's aide.

"This is fish-face, is he there?"

"No, sorry, he's trying a very important murder case in your home city of Santiago de Cuba. He'll be there all week. . . . we hear you have been busy . . ."

"Yes. Bad news spreads quickly . . . How can I talk to my lawyer when he is away? I must have advice at once."

"I am trained in the law too. Come right away. Do not ring. The door will be open."

"I have a car I want to sell very quickly. How can I manage this?"

"It is an official make . . . ?"

"Exactly."

"There is a police depot just three blocks north of here on San Lazaro, near the Havana Central Hospital. Drive it there and leave it with the others. It will fit in nicely."

Hot coffee and sweet rolls were waiting for him in Luis Fuentes's home. Best of all, Alfonzo had drawn a hot bath. He'd not had a body cleansing now in six days. When he emerged and wrapped himself in one of Fuentes's robes he lighted a Havana and considered the luxurious prospect of a nap.

"Señor, it is not for me to advise beyond dumping police cars, but you do look exhausted. Four hours of sleep will do you much good."

"Eight hours would be better, but I'm afraid I'm what is known in the business as a hot property, and unless I move quickly I will be cold as hell . . ." He smiled at his own badly mixed metaphors. "I'll sleep for one hour, that's all I need, all I can afford. At nine o'clock you must wake me and help me."

Exactly one hour later Alfonzo moved into the bedroom that had been assigned to Martin and found him so deep in sleep that he decided not to awaken him, despite Martin's order. He waited another hour and returned to find him still sleeping but this time he decided that he would have to awaken him.

"You really needed the rest, señor, but I tried to follow your instructions. Forgive me, but I, too, fell asleep . . . You have been asleep for two hours—"

"Never mind, but next time let me make the decision."

"As you say, señor. Incidentally, Señor Fuentes called while you were sleeping. He was pleased that you are here and again offers the services of this household. The story of your capture is known by CORU workers in Havana but no one yet knows that you are free. What happened to your accomplice? Did he escape too?"

"Accomplice? I have none. I don't know what you're talking about."

"The question is Señor Fuentes's, not mine. The story out is that the night you were taken at the celebration they also arrested a tall blond American who'd been representing himself for years as a man named Peter Roche from the Anglo-Swiss Trading Company. Señor Fuentes naturally assumed that you were working with him—"

"No, I'm alone. I don't know any Peter Roche . . ." He did, of course, know Duncan, and realized for the first time that he hadn't thought what might have happened to him. Martin hoped he'd been less "fortunate" and was still out of circulation . . . "Is that clock accurate, Alfonzo?"

"*Si*, señor. It is just nine o'clock.

"Now, I have to get to work. Your nearest phone is . . . ?"

". . . in the library, right down the hall. I'll be downstairs if you need me."

He called Liliam Pazos, concocting four different stories as the phone rang. She answered with the warmth of an arctic blizzard. He wasn't surprised. Well, to business. "Darling, I'm so glad you are home, I was traveling, just got back to Havana and hated the prospect of finding you out—"

"Sudden travel seems to be your specialty. Such as the other night when you were inexplicably attracted to the back stairs and left me alone at the party . . . You know, Carlos, you are a very handsome man. But don't believe you are the *only* stud in Havana. And the others are polite. Do I make myself at all clear?"

"Liliam, I'd be disappointed in you if you weren't angry with me . . . but there's an explanation, I assure you—" Martin was relieved for another reason that she was angry *and* talking to him . . . It meant that the story about his disappearance had not spread beyond intelligence circles. Otherwise Liliam Pazos would surely have known he'd been arrested and would have avoided even talking to him.

"My excuse," he said, "is the truth. I lied to you about my job with Marshal Pérez—"

"I assume that you lied about a number of things as well—"

"Liliam, give me a chance"—what a possessive prima donna . . . Cuban, American, they were sisters under the skin—"I'll give you the straight story and then you can decide if you want to see me again. Fair enough?"

The arctic winds were, perhaps, beginning to abate. "All right, let me hear. What *is* your job with Pérez?"

"Actually I'm serving him as an intelligence liaison aide. He needs help in keeping the military informed of developments in the civilian departments of government."

"And he has no intelligence aides of his own? That sounds preposterous—"

"Of course he does. But everybody knows them. They've been with him for years. He wanted someone new, someone with a fresh approach, someone the civilian heads won't be so likely to have in their pocket. So he put out that story about writing a history of the department and gave me the job—"

"Are you telling me that that whole story about you writing a biography of Fidel is also bullshit? You let me use my influence to get you a personal interview when you knew the basis for it was fictitious?"

"Hold on, Liliam. Of course that part of the story is completely true. I've been working on this biography for over three years. I am a writer, and I *do* need that interview."

"Well . . . *perhaps* I understand the Pérez business, but you still haven't explained why you ran off the night of the Martí party."

"I'm surprised at you, Liliam. Don't you know why Fidel left so quickly?"

249

"No, I don't. He seemed furious but he didn't call me to apologize, any more than you did."

"I thought everybody knew by now. There was an uprising against the government out in Oriente Province. Not major, of course, but upsetting to Castro. It's not too unusual, though. Some army colonel gets bypassed for promotion to general and, being human, starts some agitating against the government. This particular guy was apparently crazy to start with but he did succeed in lining up a platoon. They had their own gripes, the usual soldiers' complaints about pay, food, time off. And, apparently, they had contacted the Americans at Guantánamo, and *that* was what really infuriated Fidel—"

"I didn't hear a word about it—"

"Of course not. Why should Castro help a story circulate that troops are mutinying? Hell, every newspaper in the United States would play it up bigger than the missile crisis."

"And what did all of this have to do with you?"

"Marshal Pérez had had warnings about this crazy colonel and his threatened mutiny earlier in the afternoon. As Minister of Defense he was directly responsible. He'd told me that if anything like this happened I was to report to his office at once. When Fidel rushed off, and I later learned that he'd gone to the scene to direct operations, I had to go to work. Which, my love, is why I've been so long in getting back to you."

"And don't people make phone calls from Oriente Province?"

"Not if they're working on secret government matters. Marshal Pérez put an immediate news blackout into effect and ordered his staff to remain silent. I got back exactly one hour ago, ate, bathed and here I am."

Silence, and then Liliam Pazos began to laugh. It was a good sound. It had to mean a breakthrough in the icy perimeter.

"What's funny?" he asked.

"I was just thinking. The story is logical, I must admit. But even if it weren't true, it would take a writer to work up an alibi that involved. The only thing you left out was a bomb scare."

"I am a writer, Liliam, and I like to think I do have an imagination. But what I told you is gospel. Please believe me. And please be available for tonight."

"Well, as usual, you're in luck. I do happen to be free. And . . . I got a call from my friend in Fidel's office yesterday afternoon. Fidel is now back in town and apparently in need of some relaxation. He's visiting his good friend Rafael Escoto at his home in Miramar. They will be playing dominoes all night tonight. Fidel is crazy about the game. When he starts, he sometimes plays for three days in a row, don't ask me why, although he does tend to make a marathon out of most things . . . Anyhow, my friend said tonight might be the perfect time to try and get you your interview. Fidel may take several breaks in his game and he *might* just agree to go into another room and talk. At any rate he'll be there most of the night and I'm a good friend of Escoto's. As a matter of fact, he's in my debt . . . We can drop in, or, if you'd rather, I'll call my friend first and get us an invitation. That way we shouldn't have trouble with the security men."

"I'd like that much better . . . I hope I'm not being too particular, but I really would rather meet with him in his offices rather than at a party. Somehow, the whole atmosphere might be wrong and—"

"Fidel has no offices as such. One day he works from one suite, the next he may be across town in another building. But I suppose that it would be better at one of his places where he could check dates and places and that sort of thing."

"Exactly. You've done so much for me, Liliam, I'll be genuinely grateful if you can arrange this. Let him or his assistant know that I'll meet El Comandante at his office at any time, night or day, at his convenience, of course. I said it once before but maybe your reminding him . . ."

"I'll try . . . and, Carlos . . ."

"Yes?"

"You really are a son of a bitch. I'll pick you up this evening. I'm getting hungry. Ciao."

"Let me pick you up in a cab. If we want a car we can always come back and get yours."

He remembered at the last instant that she thought he was still at the El Elegancia. His much touted imagination was not up to explaining his new quarters at Señor Luis Fuentes's home.

Chapter Twenty-Eight

March Second

Liliam had managed the invitation as she'd promised, and it was after dinner, near eleven o'clock, when they drove to the Escoto home in her car. Martin could *feel* the pressure rising. There were still too many unknowns. He was particularly concerned over the whereabouts of Duncan, and the reason he'd been released by Cuban authorities . . . well, be careful, but don't look a gift horse in the mouth forever.

Security at the Escoto home was surprisingly light. He'd expected to see a whole convoy of official vehicles lining the street but there were only a few in evidence. After they had identified themselves to security agents, they were admitted and Rafael Escoto greeted them pleasantly. A noisy game of dominoes was in progress. Liliam knew many of the players, who looked up and waved. Sitting to one side and holding a drink in her hand was Maria Díaz. She nodded but immediately turned her attention back to the game without attempting conversation. Fidel Castro was nowhere to be seen.

After helping themselves to drinks, Martin and Liliam approached Rafael, who was also a spectator. Drawing him aside, Liliam asked, "And where is El Comandante? I thought he wouldn't miss this game for all the coffee in Cuba."

"He was here. He received an unexpected call and had to go off to his office. By the way," he said, turning to Martin, "you are the man who has requested the interview, correct?"

"Yes. I don't like to bother him when he finds time to play, but he said he is planning to leave the country soon and he has indicated that he might find time to favor me with a half hour."

"He left a message for you. He said to tell you that he will be busy for about an hour or so. But if you have the patience to wait for him at his offices, he'll try to see you later tonight. He's working at El Templete in the Old Havana section. There are some municipal problems that involve him and he'll be there until he goes home. I doubt if he'll get back here tonight, but with Fidel one can never tell. He once showed up at five in the morning and demanded a game."

"It's very nice of him to bother to send me a message," Martin said. "I'll go there at once."

Everything was working out so smoothly, too smoothly? But if Castro were suspicious, would he open himself up to such incredible personal danger? Not likely. But why wouldn't Castro know he was suspected, had in fact been arrested and then released to be put under surveillance? . . . Unless he, Martin, had been overthinking the whole situation. Clumsy as his "escape" had been, suppose it had not been set up by Cuban intelligence but by a legitimate underground agent . . . or suppose it had been set up by someone else . . . by the target himself? . . . Castro was known for his flamboyant bravado . . . But here he was, doing it again, thinking things into the ground . . . There was *no* way to be sure without following through. If he were being set up, could he possibly not test it . . . ? That was the risk. For such a job, could he have expected it to be any less . . . ?

Liliam offered to accompany him to Castro's office, but she didn't seem too eager to do so. She believed Castro still found her attractive, he was human, and he might possibly resent her association with another man . . . at least when confronted with it. She'd served her function to both men in setting up the interview. Surely they could handle their own business.

"Do you need me to go with you?" she asked tentatively.

"I'd love you to, but it doesn't really make much sense. He may not see me for hours. When he does I'll have to be alone with him . . ."

"I think you're right. Shall I drive you to El Templete?"

"Actually I'd appreciate your lending me your car. I'll drop you off at your home and then go to his office. That way I won't need to bother with getting a cab when I'm finished. I'll call you tomorrow and arrange to drop off the car. And tomorrow night . . . we will really celebrate!"

"I will, this last time, take you at your word. And of course you may have the car. I still think you are a son of a bitch, which it seems is my taste in men . . ."

He was greeted at El Templete and led to a spacious waiting room, supplied with cigars and reading matter. Within the office he could hear Castro's high-pitched voice talking, arguing with aides from time to time, but it was impossible to make out any of the words. Occasionally a secretary or a guard would enter the waiting room, but no one engaged him in any conversation. They would nod pleasantly, then go about their business. He became aware that he had not been checked for weapons and began to wish for Bonilla's gun and stiletto. Maybe he'd been too cautious . . .

Waiting, his mind, in spite of himself, drifted to the relative ease with which he'd reached the very offices where Castro conducted business without even the formality of a security check. He reviewed the key actors in his life over the past weeks . . . Myra Rubin, the lovely Alicia Ortiz, Manuel Pérez, who'd spent seven years of his life in captivity, who could hardly be attracted to those who'd imprisoned him. And Luis Fuentes, and Marshal Ramiro Pérez . . . Nothing that Fuentes or Ramiro Pérez had said or done could reasonably cause the slightest suspicion in him. And aside from logic, his own instincts . . . and he trusted them, they'd proved out in the past . . . told him that he had not been double-crossed by those people who'd offered their help—

His thoughts were interrupted by the sudden appearance of an armed guard who nodded his greeting but said nothing. He carried a carbine slung across his shoulder. He was a huge fellow, enormous shoulders, swarthy complexion, bearded like El Jefe. Clearly no man to meet on a jungle path or on a moonless night. Why he'd suddenly entered the office, Martin had, of course, no idea. He looked at Martin, paced up and down a few times—almost, Martin thought, as though he were walking sentry duty—then settled into a straight-backed chair across the room, directly opposite Martin. He placed the carbine on a magazine table to his right, made no effort to pick up any reading material. He sat, and he stared.

Martin decided to try small talk. "Tough working all night, yes?"

"It's my job."

"Every night?"

"Most."

"I used to work at night when I was younger. I was a clerk for the postal department. My uncle got me the job during vacations from school. They made all the young guys work at night and all the regulars got the easy assignments during the day. I hated it."

"I like my job." He said no more and made it clear he didn't want to hear more. He just sat upright and stared.

It was not easy to ignore such a presence, and to help himself Martin tried to recapture his train of thought . . . which now led to the CIA itself, except it was hardly likely that they would double-cross him before he managed to accomplish his mission, or failed in the attempt. Then, of course, it was a different story. Which brought him to Duncan. Duncan would be a threat afterward . . . but suppose he were a double agent, working for Castro too . . . possible . . . ?

He suddenly became aware that the guard was standing, towering over him. He'd moved so quietly Martin hadn't heard him get up from his chair across the room.

"You got a match?"

"Sorry. But I believe there're some over on that desk," Martin said, pointing across the room.

"Thank you."

He could not be sure, but it seemed to him that the soldier almost backed over to the desk, never taking his eye from him. No friend. Well, if no security measures had been taken to screen him, wasn't it at least reasonable that an armed guard should be outside the Premier's office? Now it was instinct again . . . and it told him that this was no mere palace guard.

Martin tried to bring himself out of it. He didn't like what was happening to him . . . to bring off what lay before him he would need the same steel nerves that had served him well during past crises. Before he'd always been capable of thinking through each situation, even as it was developing around him, and no tension had ever disrupted his effectiveness. But now he could feel himself beginning to sweat. Not just the normal sticky film that coats one's body when the temperature rises or when physical activity opens the pores. It was *mental* perspiration that began to frazzle him.

He sat there for an hour. Two. Three. At least the tension served to keep his nerves on edge and thereby fight off weariness. He could still hear Castro's voice from inside but apparently he continued to be busy with matters of state. At one point a male secretary came out to inform him that he had not been forgotten, Premier Castro was sorry that his work was taking him so long, but he definitely would see him that night.

The secretary walked around the room, almost as if conducting a tour of examination, smiling affably at Martin as he made a pretense of fussily checking items on some of the unoccupied desks. This whole show seemed a bit much. After all, Carlos Palma was only a journalist, not that important. Besides, Fidel Castro was famous for keeping the whole world waiting beyond the exasperation point. Why so polite? And the secretary's fussing . . . it was almost as if Castro were waiting for something to happen before admitting him for the interview. Whatever that might be, he would just have to handle it when, and if, it occurred. The tension continued to build. He could feel pain from the pressure on his eardrums as the office clocks ticked away. The secretary smiled and returned to the inner office. The guard continued to sit there.

At four o'clock, the outer door to the waiting room opened and a lean, handsome, intense-looking man in civilian clothing entered. He smiled at Martin and walked over to the guard, who was seated opposite him and had lifted his carbine.

Addressing himself to the soldier, he said, "You may leave now. Just stand by at the main door."

"I have orders to remain here—"

"You question my authority? You know who I am, I am not accustomed to insubordination. Now get out!"

The big man rose sheepishly, slung the carbine back over his shoulder and retreated from a losing fight, moving out the door. The newcomer watched him depart, took a deep breath, as if to regain his composure, then turning to Martin, smiled and said, "Sorry, señor. He's a loyal fellow, but not so bright, I'm afraid"—and he pointed to his head. "Let me introduce myself," he added, drawing up a chair and seating himself close to and facing Martin. "My name is Suarez. Marcello Suarez."

His correct name was Felipe Quevedo.

Martin was not certain whether or not he'd just witnessed a scene played for his benefit. Whatever, he took an immediate dislike to the stranger. He had a near-photographic memory for faces, though not necessarily for names or numbers, and he was certain that this man was somehow, somewhere known to him. At least he'd seen his face before . . . Before he'd left the States, Duncan had supplied him with a thick morgue of pictures of leaders of present-day Cuba and those involved in national security he might possibly come up against. He'd studied the pictures for many hours while in Philadelphia and, as directed, had burned them when he was finished with them. The man he now faced had been among them, he was sure, and he was almost as sure that he was a high-ranking security officer.

"I'm glad to know you, Señor Suarez. My name is Carlos Palma," he said, extending his hand.

"Yes, I know," Quevedo said. "Premier Castro had told us about you. He is interested in giving you the information you need so that his life may, finally, be reported accurately. He apologizes for keeping you waiting so long, but he is a busy man."

"I know that. I'm flattered that people here should be so concerned with my convenience. After all, the Premier has matters of state that claim his first attention."

"Right. And how understanding of you . . . Señor Palma? Is that correct? Carlos Palma?"

"*Si*, Señor Florez, the name is Palma."

"Suarez," Quevedo corrected, "Marcello Suarez. I am chief of security here at El Templete. You understand this interview is only a formality. Your credentials are excellent . . . why, one word from Liliam Pazos alone is nearly enough to get you an ambassadorship in Cuba," he said, either in obvious good humor or unexpected criticism of his leader.

"Well, I must say I'd find it hard to say no to that lady too," Martin replied.

"I agree . . . Well, there are a few basic questions that

have been raised by my men and I hope you won't be offended if I turn to you for answers."

"Not at all." Was it coming now? He'd almost convinced himself that the worry about his fortuituous escape was groundless . . . how else would he have gotten so far . . . But now—

"I was certain you would not mind . . . By the way, we have dispensed with the usual searching of guests and similar unpleasant, and in your case unnecessary, formalities. You are, of course, unarmed?"

"With a pen and a pencil only. The writer's weapons."

Quevedo nodded, smiling. "Of course, which is why we have dispensed with the usual personal search. We are interested, however"—he needed to be decently credible as an intelligence officer, Quevedo reminded himself—"in who commissioned this biography and where it will be distributed."

Martin wondered at the man's extraordinary pleasantness—at *everybody's* extraordinary pleasantness. "Actually I'm doing the work on speculation. My publishers in Spain and Italy have promised me an advance payment if I present a good first draft. Then they plan to distribute the book throughout the world, including the United States . . . They feel it can be very popular . . ."

"I'm sure they're right. And will the Premier have a chance to examine what you write before it is printed?"

"No mention has been made of that, but, of course, I'd be honored. The purpose of this interview is to ensure the highest level of accuracy. I have no fears about the Premier's finding objection in anything I'll write. It will, of course, be favorable."

"Of course. But the Premier will nonetheless have final review. A few more questions, if you don't mind."

"Not at all."

"Are you familiar with a man named Peter Roche?"

Martin was startled. "I don't believe so . . . Why do you ask?"

"There is a foreigner—he's of Swiss citizenship—named Roche who frequently is in our city. He's an executive with the Anglo-Swiss Trading Company here in Havana. Some of our people have begun to suspect him . . . we wondered if by chance you knew anything about him" . . . Quevedo was beginning to enjoy himself, playing it straight with this mouse who would do his work for him . . . "He seems to favor several aliases. Sometimes 'Dunlop,' sometimes 'Davis,' sometimes 'Duncan' . . . Do any of these names sound familiar?"

And now, as he talked, it also occurred to Quevedo that he had better be convincing in his role for another reason . . . that even though he was confident Duncan was willing to work with him, there was the possibility that *he* was the subject of a frameup, with Duncan serving as a counter-agent charged with getting evidence of disloyalty that could hang Quevedo. Not so farfetched. More than one at the CIA, indeed, in his own apparatus, had gone such a route. He might be in a setup, no matter how outlandish that might seem at first glance. Castro had at times demonstrated just such near-paranoid characteristics and was not above staging an elaborate plot to test the loyalty of the men surrounding him.

"Señor Suarez," Martin replied cautiously, "as a journalist I've traveled all over the world several times, following stories wherever they led me. The names you mention are common Anglo-Saxon names and I suppose at one time or another I have met more than one 'Davis' or 'Dunlop' or 'Duncan.' I think the best answer I can give you is that I know of nobody with one of those names in Havana."

"I see. You would, of course, recognize the names if you had had any recent contact with them."

"Of course."

"And if I were to say that your interview would be cancelled if I had evidence that you were lying to me, you would still answer in the negative?"

Martin had no alternative. "I would, Señor Suarez. I do not lie."

"Good. That settles the matter. I'll report to El Jefe everything that you have told me and I'm sure he'll be pleased. He'll be seeing you in a few minutes now. Please be ready." The two men smiled at each other.

It seemed impossible, but in spite of all the risks, the suspicions, here he was, finally about to be face to face with his quarry. Alone. He felt an elation beyond description. He would not allow further doubts or fears. Instinct told him Suarez wasn't to be trusted, but his questions seemed in order and . . . *enough.* He would worry about Suarez afterward. . . .

Quevedo was equally tense, and exhilarated. After years of longing for real power, the moment was approaching. Palma would kill Fidel Castro, whose own well-known childish bravado would work against him. Afterward, as the assassin tried to escape, he would kill Palma. And in having personally destroyed the man who had taken the life of Cuba's beloved benefactor, he would be rewarded as a hero, and drafted to lead his country in Fidel's tradition. As for Duncan, he would deal with him in his own way and in his own time. He looked forward to it. He'd not forget Duncan making a damn fool of him—

The door to Castro's office opened and the smiling secretary came out. He walked directly over to Suarez. Warmly, and with a show of affection, he took him by the arm and led him into the inner office. The door closed behind them. After a brief pause, loud voices were heard inside. Martin strained to hear what was happening but could not decipher the muffled speech. He decided that it was probably a joyous meeting to two old comrades. Castro was not exactly known for restraint.

Five minutes later the door to Castro's office opened again, and there the bearded leader stood, bracketed by two huge bodyguards. Expecting to be in Castro's presence alone, Martin was somewhat disconcerted but fought to disguise his feeling.

"Come in, Señor Palma," Castro said matter-of-factly with neither warmth nor hostility. "I hope you will forgive the long delay."

"I understand, sir, that you have other concerns besides this interview."

"True. I hope you will not object to a personal search." They were in the office now and the door had been abruptly shut behind them by one of the guards. "It is a rule for my protection that I do not support. But even I must not interfere with certain rules."

It took only a few seconds, and Martin was now grateful for his caution about the weapons, and curious about Suarez's indulgence.

Castro smiled. "Well, I may still be in danger . . . you know the old saying, 'The pen is mightier than the sword.' But we, of course, have nothing to fear from *your* writing, correct, Mr. Palma?"

"Correct."

"All right," Castro said, turning to the two guards, "you may leave us now."

They were alone. The moment had arrived. Martin had no gun. No knive. But he did have a specially designed silken thread with the tensile strength of steel attached to the inner left sleeve of his jacket. Fidel Castro would not be the first man he had killed by strangulation with a garotte in hand-to-hand combat. Death via this ancient weapon, he knew from experience, took a little longer, but it was silent, less bloody and appropriate for the circumstances, as he'd long ago anticipated.

Castro wedged his large frame behind his desk and directed

his interviewer to be seated in front of him. "So, Señor Palma, it has been a long and trying day for me but I am at your disposal."

Reclining behind his heavy mahogany desk, he kept his hands behind his head and swiveled from side to side, keeping his eyes on his interviewer at all times. Then, suddenly and unexpectedly, showing amazing agility for a large man, he leaped from his chair, moved in front of the desk and crossed the room toward Martin's chair. Moving a small side-chair into position, he sat down again close to him. In one sense that would make an assassin's task easier; in another, he was so close to his target that he was cramped and limited. It was a case of nearer being farther.

"Señor Palma, if you wish something fresh in your writing, let us open by speaking of loyalty. You consider it a treasured character trait?"

"Why, yes, of course."

"There are some who would disagree, Señor Palma. In fact, some say the trouble with my government is that I have placed in positions of power too many who are loyal to me and my ideals and too few who are smart. The younger generation does not appreciate the value of loyalty. They think at times I am a fool, keeping with me many who are virtually illiterate but who have a feel for this Revolution, a *sense* of it, and what it truly means."

"The young will grow older and then they will learn, sir. I agree with you. Loyalty is a rare attribute these days." A strange subject, Martin thought, for Castro to put to an interviewer.

"Good. We are starting on a sound footing. And what do you think of treachery?"

"What is there to think about it?"

"Do you think it exists in Cuba?"

It was almost as if Martin were the subject and Castro was conducting the interview. "Really, El Comandante, I would have no way of knowing that. It seems to me that our people are loyal and happy under your leadership. But how would I know about treachery? Traitors would hardly tell me of their plans."

"True. But you are a reporter. I am told that you are very intelligent. What instinct does not teach us, knowledge should. You've been observing our government for some time now. You should have a good sense about the possibility of disloyal citizens plotting against me."

"I can only speak for myself, sir. Your government is fair. Our people seem content—"

"I hope you do not mind my turning this interview around, as it were. I'm always with my own staff and I like to get an outsider's view when I can."

"Not at all," Martin said, feeling increasingly uneasy.

"Now, if loyalty is a treasured asset in the heart of a follower, what is a leader to do when he discovers that someone close to him is indeed a traitor? Should he be shot? Should he be tortured? Should he be placed in prison for years to teach him and other would-be traitors a lesson?"

"I really have no experience in such matters. How can I tell Fidel Castro what to do with his enemies?"

"Well, let us look at it another way. A man who rules a country in today's world of violence is a constant target for every psychopath who travels the road. In my case the danger is even greater because of our 'good neighbor' to the north. Do you know, can you imagine, what the United States government would give someone who could succeed in killing me? Do you know how often they try? Month after month we uncover their plots. They really are quite foolish, Señor Palma. They do not understand that even if they were to succeed—believe me, even if they were to succeed, I tell you what I have built will continue, will endure. The Revolution is now, the Revolution will survive with or without Fidel. *That* is what you must say in your book."

"They are powerful words, El Jefe. I will remember them."

"Good. And now, a final question. If I were to discover, for example, that you, Señor Palma, were not really a writer at all but rather, say, a hired assassin working for a capitalistic country, what would I best do with you?"

Castro's whole body tensed as he seemed to challenge Martin to make his move.

This, Martin knew, truly was the moment. No alternative to action now. He reached inside his jacket sleeve and—incredibly, theatrically, from behind the lush velour curtain that draped the rear wall of the office, a man emerged, literally waving a sawed-off shotgun and shouting, "Thus dies Cuba's traitor!" and fired off an entire round into Castro's chest. Castro fell forward, blood coming from multiple gaping wounds in his chest. The noise was deafening. The man momentarily pointed his gun at Martin, apparently decided that another killing was superfluous, turned around toward the curtain he'd emerged from and made his escape.

Martin's mission was completed, however unexpectedly. He was no safer, though, since he'd be certain to be considered an accomplice. He immediately ran in the direction of the killer, some twenty steps behind. He followed him on a circuitous route that led down a fire escape and out into the night. He ran to Liliam Pazos's car, sped off in the direction of José Martí International Airport, a route he'd carefully precharted. No time now to dwell on the bizarre ending to his mission. Time only to concentrate on getting away.

He reached the airport in twenty minutes, surprised that he was not, so far as he could tell, being chased. Apparently the police-security people were too intent on capturing the real killer, who had so unexpectedly usurped his mission. At the airport he parked the car by the side of the road and hurried to the Cubana Airlines counter, which was just setting up for the morning's activities. He asked to see Señor

2 6 6

Bonfiglia. It was important. Bonfiglia was already on the job and came out to meet him at the passenger counter.

"Shaving Mug."

"You are The Barber?"

Martin nodded.

"Our first flight for Mexico City leaves in fifteen minutes. Gate Twelve. Go aboard, please. This pass will admit you," Bonfiglia said, handing him a ticket.

As he was boarding, Martin scribbled a note for delivery by Bonfiglia to Duncan's headquarters: "Haircut finished. Barber retired."

In less than five minutes Martin was seated aboard, strapped in for takeoff. At least the escape plan had worked so far.

Al El Templete, a very alive and delighted Fidel Castro was breakfasting with his aides. He had quickly showered to wash away the red dye he'd activated, which looked so much like blood he almost wondered for a moment if those had indeed been blanks in the "assassin's" shotgun. A good, if somewhat flamboyant, job, was his critique. Still, the man was the leading star of the Cuban National Theatre, and Fidel had promised him a surprise, real-life role when . . . if . . . the occasion should ever arrive. All in all, a bravura performance.

And Castro himself hadn't done such a bad job of acting either, if he did say so himself. At the insistence of his aides, who were worried that his prank—a wild one, this time— would turn into a real tragedy, he had carefully rehearsed the entire charade: practiced falling, pulling on the cord that released the bloodlike dye contained in a rubber bladder secreted under his shirt, and gasping like a properly dying man as life appeared to be pouring from his chest. It was also at their insistence that Martin had been searched once inside

Fidel's office. They pointed out that a frustrated would-be assassin with a weapon might just take pride in shooting, stabbing or whatever his target to take credit for the killing of Fidel Castro. One shouldn't underestimate the fanaticism of anyone who would take on such an assignment.

Fidel now offered a toast to the assembled aides: "Friends, I give you the CIA. May we all live to enjoy close-up photographs of their faces when they learn the news of my death, and resurrection."

But Castro's mood was not altogether as it seemed.

He had come to know about the threat of death from the days of the very first landing of the *Granma* at Oriente Province. So many CIA plots against his life had failed that he now tended to look on them almost as he would a game of chess. He had a conviction that he would not, could not, be killed until his work was completed. Which, of course, made him vulnerable, as a few of his aides sometimes tried to point out.

What he could not accept, however, with such equanimity was the conviction that those around him were not always loyal. His questions to Martin at the opening of the interview were not idle. When Felipe Quevedo had entered Castro's inner office, just before Martin himself had been admitted, he had been arrested by armed guards, stripped of his weapon and manacled. For months, warned by Maria Díaz, Castro had been aware of Quevedo's jealousy, his opposition to Cuba's Russian alliance, his private ambitions for power. He hadn't been removed from office, but he had been under constant surveillance. His actions had been monitored, reported. When he moved in to take charge of the arrest of Duncan and Palma, Díaz, on Fidel's authority, had ordered the rooms where the prisoners were to be kept wired with recording equipment. Quevedo's conversation with Duncan became a matter of record. Any last doubts Castro may have held about Quevedo's loyalty were now gone. As usual, Maria Díaz had been accurate in her assessment of people. As a dangerous enemy of the State, Quevedo had been taken off to solitary confinement. He would be tried, and convicted, on charges of treason by the highest court.

Martin, of course, had misunderstood the meaning of Castro's questions to him, assuming they'd been meant for him. And at this moment his thoughts were concentrated only on escape. The airplane's motors were roaring now as the plane prepared to move down the runway into position for takeoff.

Chapter Twenty-Nine

March Third

Three minutes after takeoff from José Martí International Airport, the DC-9 with seventy-three persons aboard exploded in midflight. Among the dead were fifty-seven Cuban nationals.

The charred remains of the recovered bodies were laid out at the Havana morgue. Records there indicated that a man who identified himself as Pietro Hostos had sought and received permission to examine the remains, explaining that his brother was missing and he was certain that he had planned to be aboard the flight. After carefully examining the remains of all male victims and searching through their pockets for possible clues to identification, he said, with rather subdued enthusiasm, that he had apparently erred, that his brother was not among the victims. Thanking the medical examiners, he left.

Routine check of airline records did reveal that the original manifest indicated that there had been seventy-four, not seventy-three, passengers aboard at the time of takeoff. After all bodies were identified by next of kin, it was established that the missing passenger had been issued fraudulent papers and was listed as "C. Marco, resident, Porto Alegre, Brazil." No one at Cubana Airlines had any knowledge of his true identity or how he had managed to get aboard without a regularly issued ticket and proper immigration or foreign-passenger clearance.

Ministry of the Interior deputies, shaken by the Quevedo scandal, began an immediate investigation. They arrested Señor Bonfiglia and held him for questioning. They discovered that there was no record of a Pietro Hostos living at the address he had listed when seeking permission to examine the bodies. They also located an eyewitness who definitely recalled seeing a man rush aboard the aircraft just five minutes before takeoff.

Chapter Thirty

March Tenth

One week after the air disaster, having just returned from the meeting of the Organization of American States at Lima, Peru, Fidel Castro renounced the 1973 agreement between the United States and Cuba, which had been successful in virtually eliminating commercial airline hijacking in the Western Hemisphere. His action was not unexpected. For days the government-controlled press in Cuba had repeatedly accused the CIA of being directly involved in the crash in which seventy-three persons were killed. It was an issue energetically debated on the floor of the OAS conference.

At a mass funeral in memory of the deceased, Fidel Castro charged that during the 1960s alone there were twenty-four CIA-sponsored assassination attempts against his life. A number of these had been confirmed by the United States Senate.

"We suspect that the United States government has not renounced such practices," he said.

The CIA refused to dignify the accusation with comment.

Chapter Thirty-One

March Third

The ease with which, as "C. Marco," he'd escaped Cuban police authorities and managed to board an international flight troubled John Martin as soon as he slipped into his seat and strapped himself in for takeoff. The same sort of nagging thoughts that had troubled him at El Templete waiting for the Castro interview returned. It just had been too easy. If the chief executive of any nation were assassinated, at least all road, rail and air transportation would immediately have been suspended. Especially in the case of flights to foreign destinations. And road blocks would have been set up immediately to prevent the assassin's escape. But he had had a clear passage to the airport.

And what about Señor Bonfiglia? Even though he obviously was in the employ of the CIA, would he have been so easily able to slip a last-minute passenger aboard? Perhaps. But if by chance he were a double agent, would it not be extremely easy for him to wire ahead, notifying a contact that Martin was scheduled to arrive at Mexico City on the current flight?

Martin suddenly was certain that the CIA itself would be waiting. After all, from the beginning he'd seen clearly that once having accomplished his assignment he'd be a marked man. No government intelligence apparatus could afford the exposure of being responsible for assassination plots. What had been rumored in the United States press for months now would become established fact. The CIA knew nothing of the real assassin, he was convinced. They would assume it was he, their man, who'd done the job. He would be a walking time bomb that had to be defused—eliminated. He'd recognized that and said as much in his first meeting with Tad Duncan. Duncan had made no attempt to deny it, just tried to ignore it, as though too farfetched to be considered. But it wasn't farfetched. It was, he was convinced, a certainty. He had to get off at once.

Unstrapping himself, he hurried forward, explaining to the startled head flight attendant that he had mislaid valuable government papers and had to rush back to his hotel. Over her protests that the landing stairway was in the process of being backed away from the aircraft, he insisted that he would protest all the way to El Comandante if she did not go along with his wishes. Wanting to avoid an ugly scene, she tapped on the window for the ground crew's attention, had them reconnect the stairs and considered herself lucky to be rid of this crazy passenger.

The plane was in the air by the time Martin had completed the hundred-yard walk back to the terminal.

Needing a few moments to collect his thoughts, he moved to the visitors' observation platform and lit a cigarette. He could still see the aircraft he had just left gracefully completing a long gentle sweep west–northwest as it found its course and headed for Mexico City. He heard and saw the explosion that ripped the plane into pieces, and followed in horror as the flaming wreckage slowly, crazily fell earthward. Whatever doubts he had then about his fear of his employer were gone.

2 7 4

The CIA would work toward his own elimination with the same doggedness that it had sought the death of Castro. He'd managed to save his life. For now.

What about the future?

The CIA had provided him with a half-dozen different aliases and papers to support each identity. He had kept these intact throughout his month on the island. He would have preferred changing aliases now, but realized that the boarding pass issued by Bonfiglia to "C. Marco" was probably his best bet. Pushing past a crowd of weeping relatives of the DC-9's victims, he moved to the Air Cubana ticket counter, where a few clerks were wandering about in a state of shock. Martin decided on an aggressive course.

"Look here, miss, I'm as sorry as you are about this awful tragedy, but life goes on. I was supposed to be on that flight and I just missed it by five minutes. Maybe God was being good to me, who knows? Anyhow, here's my boarding pass and I have to be on the next plane. I see you have a flight for Merida in a half hour. I can get a flight to Mexico City from there. Please revalidate my ticket and boarding pass. And please hurry. I have to make a few more calls."

Fighting back tears, the clerk quickly determined that there was room on the Merida flight. The boarding pass he held out to her was a little unorthodox but at such a time, who cared about bureaucratic nonsense? . . . She restamped his papers, changing the flight time and destination, and passed them back across the counter. Mumbling his thanks, Martin put them into his pocket and headed for the bank of public telephones. They were booth-enclosed, giving him camouflage and at the same time enabling him to keep the entire terminal floor under surveillance. By opening the folding door a crack, he gained ventilation and was able to follow all of the public-address announcements being made.

Pretending to be engaged in a series of personal calls, Martin stayed in the phone booth until the flight to Merida was called. The terminal was swarming with uniformed police, soldiers, plainclothesmen and airport officials, but all seemed too involved in the grim work of recovering bodies and questioning employees of Air Cubana to concern themselves with other outgoing flights. There was the usual security check as he entered the loading area but since he was unarmed and carried identification as "C. Marco, Brazilian tourist," he had no trouble boarding.

The plane took off without incident and, completely drained, Martin slept during most of the flight to Merida, where he had little trouble booking a flight to Mexico City. He was on the ground for only forty-five minutes. He landed at his destination some two hours later. Mexican newspapers were already carrying incomplete stories of the air tragedy at Havana. One ridiculous report said that Fidel Castro had personally inspected the wreckage and was making charges of foreign involvement, especially the United States. Maybe Fidel was immortal after all. Obviously, Martin decided, it was a fiction put out by the Cuban government, picked up unquestioningly by some journalists. Why not? It was plausible. How should anybody know this soon about Castro's death? . . . but sooner or later the news would have to get out.

Chapter Thirty-Two

March Fourth

Martin spent most of the next several days in a third-class hotel reading all the news dispatches he could find in the local and Cuban papers. From these, along with radio reports, he became convinced that *somehow* he had been taken in, that, by God, Fidel Castro was indeed actually alive. There were now radiophotos of El Comandante at the scene of the disaster and there were taped speeches of his attacks on the CIA, which, he assured the world, had been responsible for bombing the aircraft. One of the stories said that a CIA plot to assassinate the Cuban leader had been frustrated within one hour of the air disaster. There was a direct quotation:

> "Sometimes we choose to play along with these murderous Yankee spies, but they can hardly fool us. The world knows these bumbling assassins for what they are . . ."

Which was no help to Martin. Duncan *and* the Mafia would be even more anxious to get rid of him, a failed assassin.

To them, he was not only a threat but an incompetent as well. A double qualification for death.

Like every other Cuban who'd lived in Miami, Martin was well aware of the black market in fraudulent documents centered in Mexico. For a few hundred dollars one could purchase false birth certificates, social security cards, alien resident identifications and similar bogus records. After an hour spent in a rundown bar he made contact with a counterfeiter who supplied him with a whole new identity. He realized the danger of attempting to cross the border into the United States using the documents he had been given by Duncan at the start. No doubt the border was being scrutinized by intelligence agents, hoping that he would make just such a mistake.

Now, with his new alias, he was Alejandro Cordenza of Newark, New Jersey. He flew to New Orleans and then boarded a direct flight to Philadelphia. Local newspapers carried detailed reports of Castro's arrival in Lima and quoted his opening speech before a plenary session of the Organization of American States. It was now a foregone conclusion that Cuba would be readmitted to that family of nations. Latin America had even more reason to stand against the common enemy from the north.

Though he'd never given Duncan specifics about his residency on the University campus, he knew there would be little trouble tracing him. He realized, by hindsight, that it had been unwise to reveal where he would go for physical reconditioning, but at the time it had seemed an innocent enough bit of information. In any case, he had no choice but to head there, since the bulk of the advance payment money was still deposited in the vault he had rented in the small branch bank on the campus near the hotel.

Arriving in Philadelphia after banking hours, he took a cab to the same hotel he'd stayed in a month earlier, a month that now seemed a century. To his surprise, and displeasure, the desk clerk recognized him.

"Mr. Martinez. Nice to have you back."

"I'll only be staying overnight this time, Charley, but it's nice to see you too. You've got a good memory for names."

The desk clerk smiled. "Sometimes it pays off."

"I'm sure . . . by the way, was there a lady here asking for me?"

"I shouldn't tell you . . . but what the hell, you're a nice guy . . . Yeah, somebody was here asking about you, but not a lady. A man. Sorry about that. He was kind of middle aged, okay dressed. Had a Latin name like yours. I think he said it was Castillo, or something like that. He said he was on your tail, that you were a deadbeat and had loused up his kid sister. I figured he was bullshit, knowing you, but I took his money. He said I should call him if you showed." He handed Martin a pink phone slip with a local number.

"Thanks, Charley. I appreciate this. And you're right . . . he's bullshit."

"No problem. You've had dinner yet? I can make a reservation for you if you want."

"Thanks, no. I've eaten. I'll just sack out and get some sleep. See you in the morning."

He spent a sleepless night sitting up in an easy chair, his face to the door, which he had barricaded with a dresser and a desk. He was at the bank at nine the next morning, got to his vault and found the money and a gun he had put there. By ten-thirty he had boarded a flight to Cleveland, where he took on the less conspicuous name of Paul Crater.

That night, in a shadowed entryway, he committed his first of three holdups. In each case he demanded only wallets, ignoring all jewelry and cash. He needed drivers' licenses, social security cards, credit cards and voting registrations, to help him change identity. The next day he moved on to Chicago, where he repeated his selective crime wave. Since he was careful never to harm any of his victims, he felt reasonably confident that the police wouldn't bother to investigate his bloodless crimes.

By the time he reached Los Angeles he'd become a catalogue of aliases. He would look for employment in some inconspicuous white-collar job. Although he had a large amount of money at his disposal, he realized that conspicuous consumption was out of the question. He'd begun this looking for a fresh start, a new life . . . no strings, no trouble. He'd ended it as a modern Flying Dutchman, condemned by what he'd not done to wander and live in the shadows . . .

He hoped his father, and Uncle, were satisfied.